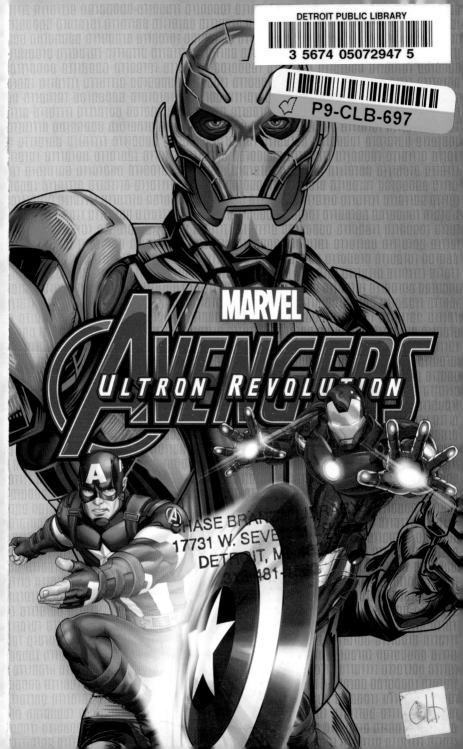

MARVEL
AVENGERS
ULTRON REVOLUTION

MARVEL UNIVERSE AVENGERS: ULTRON REVOLUTION VOL. 1. Contains material originally published in magazine form as MARVEL UNIVERSE AVENGERS: ULTRON REVOLUTION #1-4. First printing 2016. ISBN# 978-1-302-90255-1. Published by MARVEL WORLDWIDE, INC., a subsidiary of MARVEL ENTERTAINMENT, LLC. OFFICE OF PUBLICATION: 135 West 50th Street, New York, NY 10020. Copyright © 2016 MARVEL. No similarity between any of the names, characters, persons, and/or institutions in this magazine with those of any living or dead person or institution is intended, and any such similarity which may exist is purely coincidental. **Printed in the U.S.A.** ALAN FINE, President, Marvel Entertainment; DAN BUCKLEY, President, TV, Publishing & Brand Management; JOE QUESADA, Chief Creative Officer; TOM BREVOORT, SVP of Publishing; DAVID BOGART, SVP of Business Affairs & Operations, Publishing & Partnership; C.B. CEBULSKI, VP of Brand Management & Development, Asia; DAVID GABRIEL, SVP of Sales & Marketing, Publishing; JEFF YOUNGQUIST, VP of Production & Special Projects; DAN CARR, Executive Director of Publishing Technology; ALEX MORALES, Director of Publishing Operations; SUSAN CRESPI, Production Manager; STAN LEE, Chairman Emeritus. For information regarding advertising in Marvel Comics or on Marvel.com, please contact Vit DeBellis, Integrated Sales Manager, at vdebellis@marvel.com. For Marvel subscription inquiries, please call 888-511-5480. **Manufactured between 10/28/2016 and 12/5/2016 by SHERIDAN, CHELSEA, MI, USA.**

10 9 8 7 6 5 4 3 2 1

MARVEL
AVENGERS
ULTRON REVOLUTION

Based on the TV series written by
**EUGENE SON, DANIELLE WOLFF,
MAIRGHREAD SCOTT & PAUL GIACOPPO**

Directed by
**PHIL PIGNOTTI
& TIM ELDRED**

Art by
**MARVEL ANIMATION
STUDIOS**

Adapted by
JOE CARAMAGNA

Special Thanks to
**HANNAH MACDONALD &
PRODUCT FACTORY**

Editors
**MARK BASSO &
CHRISTINA HARRINGTON**

Senior Editor
MARK PANICCIA

—————— Avengers **created by STAN LEE & JACK KIRBY** ——————

Collection Editor: JENNIFER GRÜNWALD
Associate Managing Editor: KATERI WOODY
Associate Editor: SARAH BRUNSTAD
Editor, Special Projects: MARK D. BEAZLEY

VP Production & Special Projects: JEFF YOUNGQUIST
SVP Print, Sales & Marketing: DAVID GABRIEL
Head of Marvel Television: JEPH LOEB
Book Designer: ADAM DEL RE

Editor in Chief: AXEL ALONSO
Chief Creative Officer: JOE QUESADA
Publisher: DAN BUCKLEY
Executive Producer: ALAN FINE

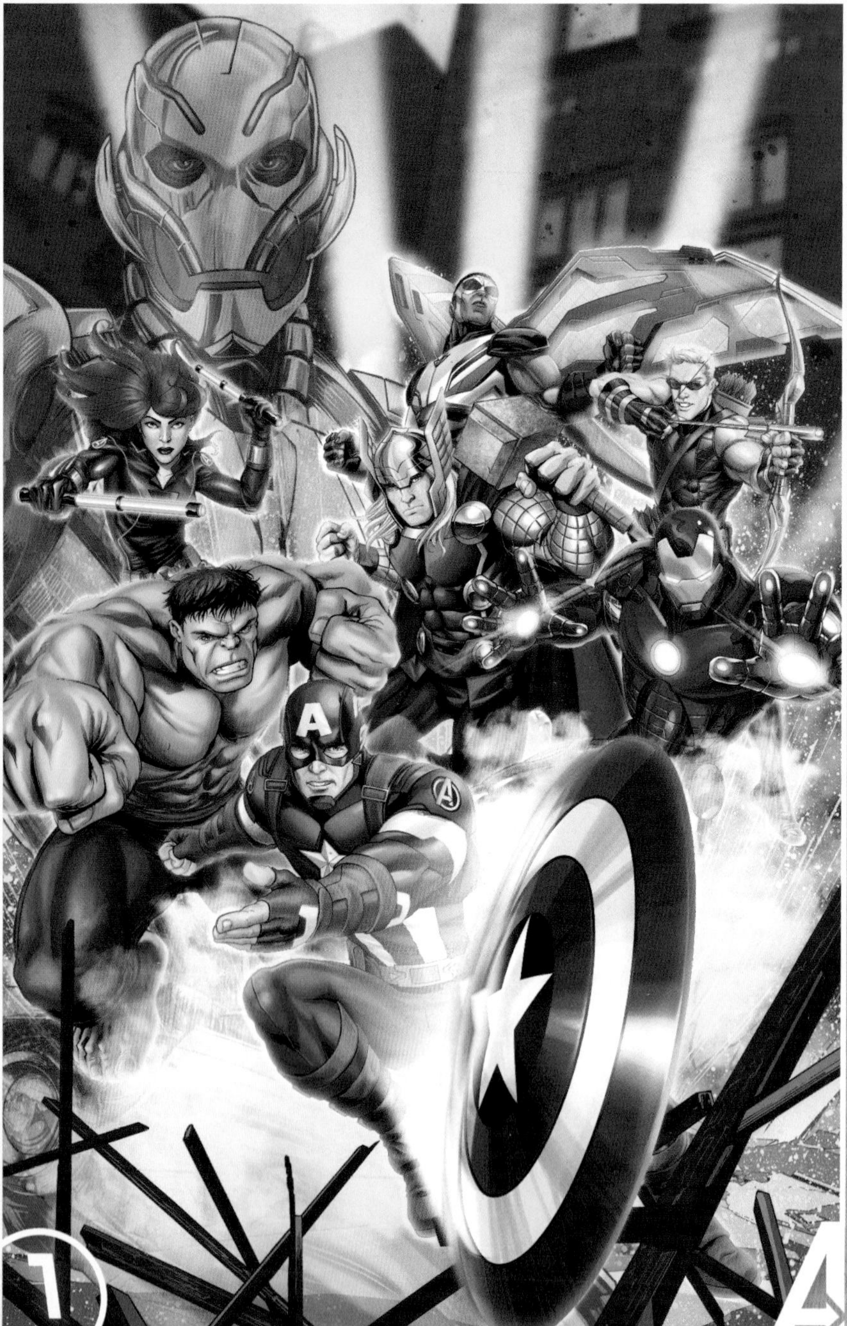

1

ADAPTING TO CHANGE

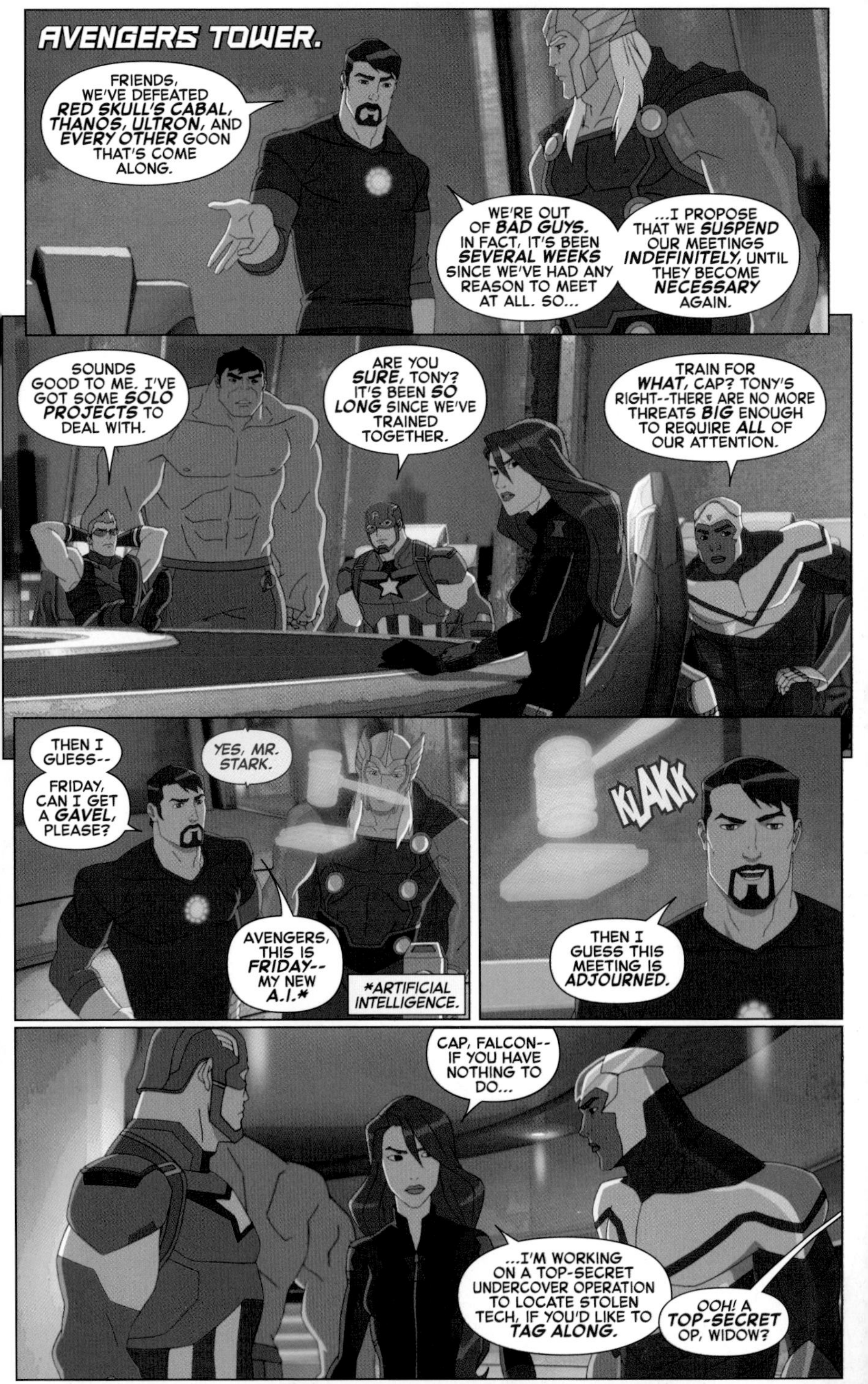
AVENGERS TOWER.
FRIENDS, WE'VE DEFEATED RED SKULL'S CABAL, THANOS, ULTRON, AND EVERY OTHER GOON THAT'S COME ALONG.
WE'RE OUT OF BAD GUYS. IN FACT, IT'S BEEN SEVERAL WEEKS SINCE WE'VE HAD ANY REASON TO MEET AT ALL. SO...
...I PROPOSE THAT WE SUSPEND OUR MEETINGS INDEFINITELY, UNTIL THEY BECOME NECESSARY AGAIN.
SOUNDS GOOD TO ME. I'VE GOT SOME SOLO PROJECTS TO DEAL WITH.
ARE YOU SURE, TONY? IT'S BEEN SO LONG SINCE WE'VE TRAINED TOGETHER.
TRAIN FOR WHAT, CAP? TONY'S RIGHT--THERE ARE NO MORE THREATS BIG ENOUGH TO REQUIRE ALL OF OUR ATTENTION.
THEN I GUESS--
FRIDAY, CAN I GET A GAVEL, PLEASE?
YES, MR. STARK.
AVENGERS, THIS IS FRIDAY-- MY NEW A.I.*
*ARTIFICIAL INTELLIGENCE.
KLAKK
THEN I GUESS THIS MEETING IS ADJOURNED.
CAP, FALCON-- IF YOU HAVE NOTHING TO DO...
...I'M WORKING ON A TOP-SECRET UNDERCOVER OPERATION TO LOCATE STOLEN TECH, IF YOU'D LIKE TO TAG ALONG.
OOH! A TOP-SECRET OP, WIDOW?

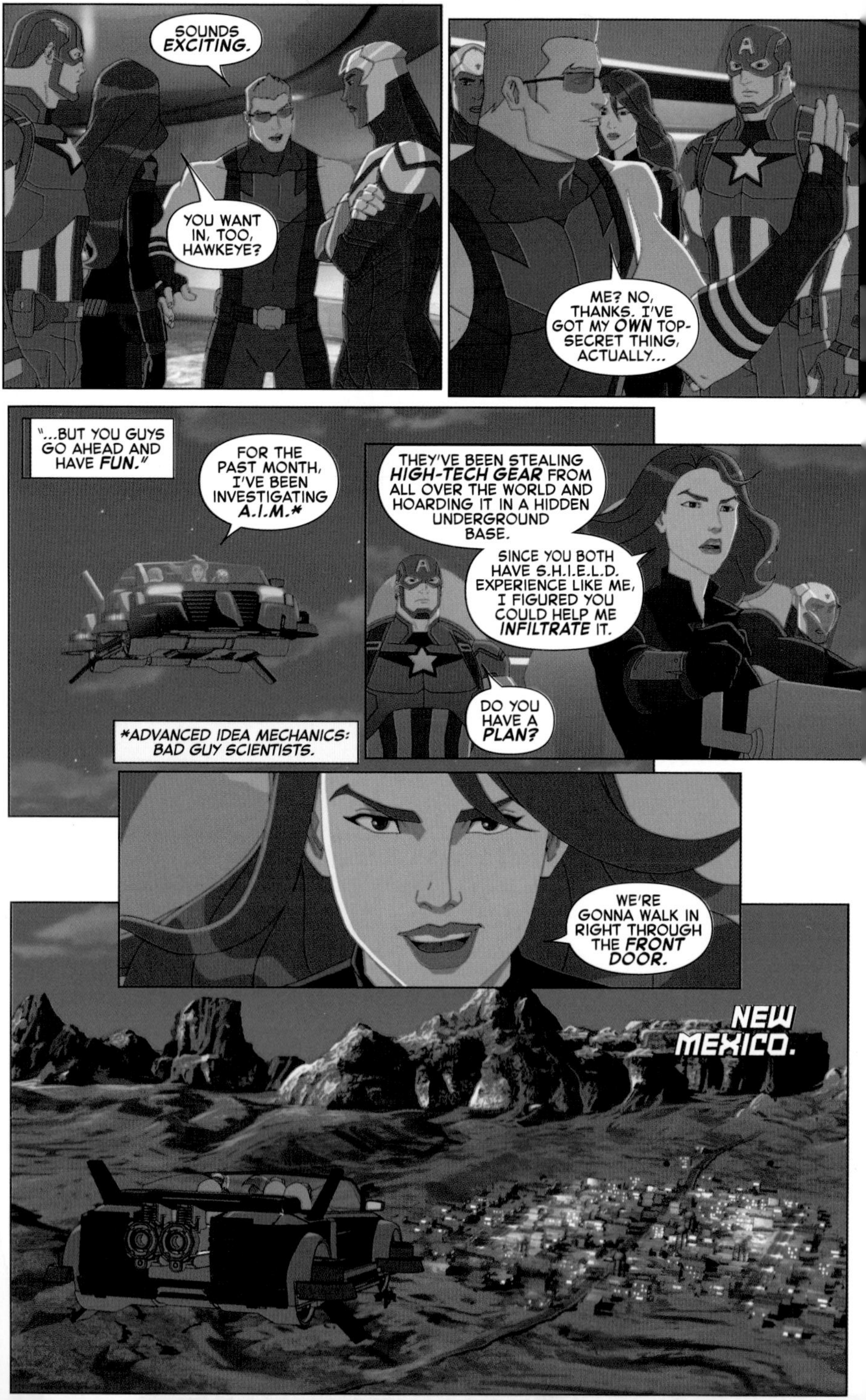
SOUNDS EXCITING.
YOU WANT IN, TOO, HAWKEYE?
ME? NO, THANKS. I'VE GOT MY OWN TOP-SECRET THING, ACTUALLY...
"...BUT YOU GUYS GO AHEAD AND HAVE FUN."
FOR THE PAST MONTH, I'VE BEEN INVESTIGATING A.I.M.*
*ADVANCED IDEA MECHANICS: BAD GUY SCIENTISTS.
THEY'VE BEEN STEALING HIGH-TECH GEAR FROM ALL OVER THE WORLD AND HOARDING IT IN A HIDDEN UNDERGROUND BASE.
SINCE YOU BOTH HAVE S.H.I.E.L.D. EXPERIENCE LIKE ME, I FIGURED YOU COULD HELP ME INFILTRATE IT.
DO YOU HAVE A PLAN?
WE'RE GONNA WALK IN RIGHT THROUGH THE FRONT DOOR.
NEW MEXICO.

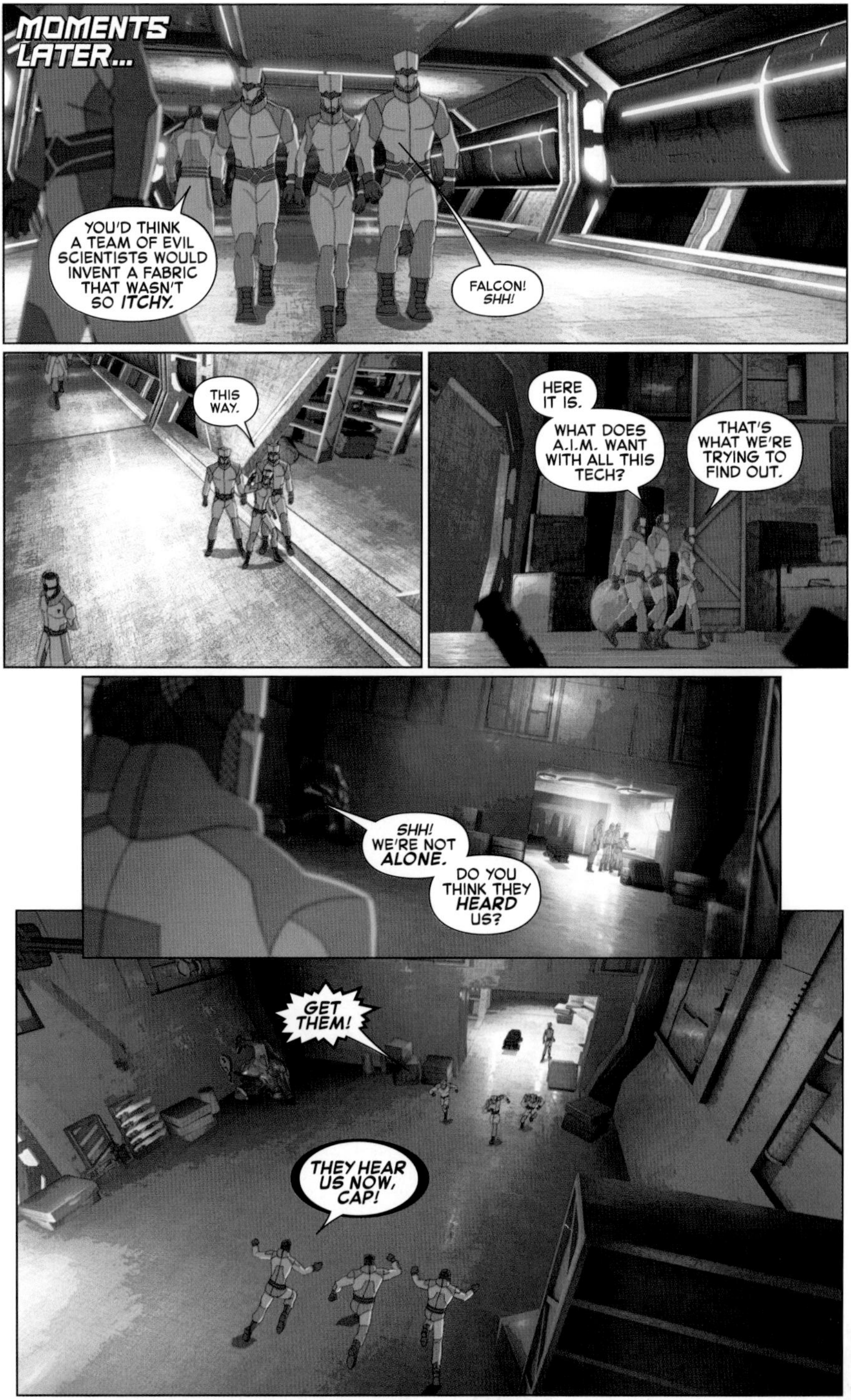
MOMENTS LATER...
YOU'D THINK A TEAM OF EVIL SCIENTISTS WOULD INVENT A FABRIC THAT WASN'T SO *ITCHY.*
FALCON! *SHH!*
THIS WAY.
HERE IT IS.
WHAT DOES A.I.M. WANT WITH ALL THIS TECH?
THAT'S WHAT WE'RE TRYING TO FIND OUT.
SHH! WE'RE NOT **ALONE.**
DO YOU THINK THEY **HEARD** US?
GET THEM!
THEY HEAR US NOW, CAP!

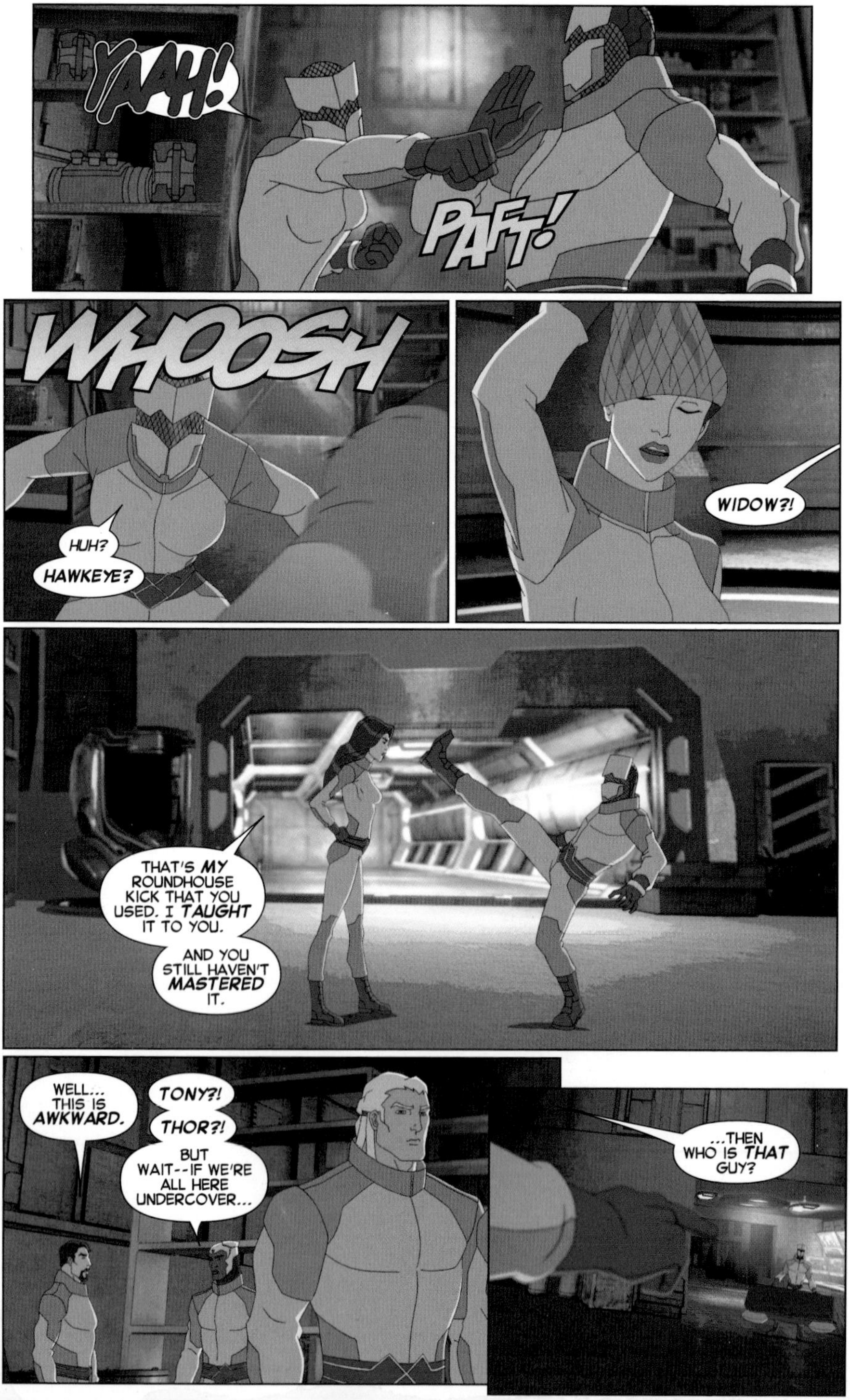
YAAH!
PAFT!
WHOOSH
HUH?
HAWKEYE?
WIDOW?!
THAT'S MY ROUNDHOUSE KICK THAT YOU USED. I TAUGHT IT TO YOU.
AND YOU STILL HAVEN'T MASTERED IT.
WELL... THIS IS AWKWARD.
TONY?!
THOR?!
BUT WAIT--IF WE'RE ALL HERE UNDERCOVER...
...THEN WHO IS THAT GUY?

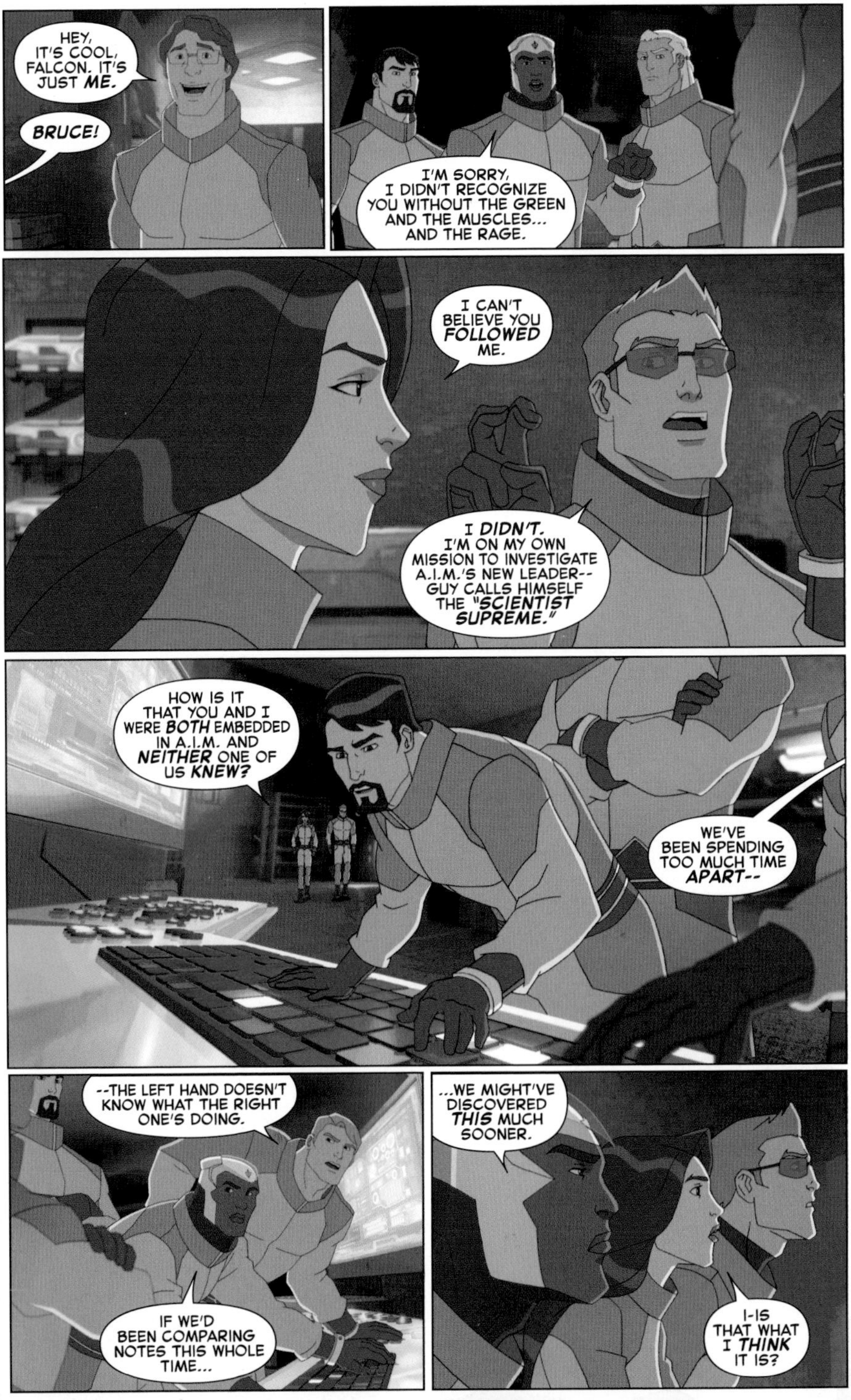
HEY, IT'S COOL, FALCON. IT'S JUST ME.
BRUCE!
I'M SORRY, I DIDN'T RECOGNIZE YOU WITHOUT THE GREEN AND THE MUSCLES... AND THE RAGE.
I CAN'T BELIEVE YOU FOLLOWED ME.
I DIDN'T. I'M ON MY OWN MISSION TO INVESTIGATE A.I.M.'S NEW LEADER--GUY CALLS HIMSELF THE "SCIENTIST SUPREME."
HOW IS IT THAT YOU AND I WERE BOTH EMBEDDED IN A.I.M. AND NEITHER ONE OF US KNEW?
WE'VE BEEN SPENDING TOO MUCH TIME APART--
--THE LEFT HAND DOESN'T KNOW WHAT THE RIGHT ONE'S DOING.
IF WE'D BEEN COMPARING NOTES THIS WHOLE TIME...
...WE MIGHT'VE DISCOVERED THIS MUCH SOONER.
I-IS THAT WHAT I THINK IT IS?

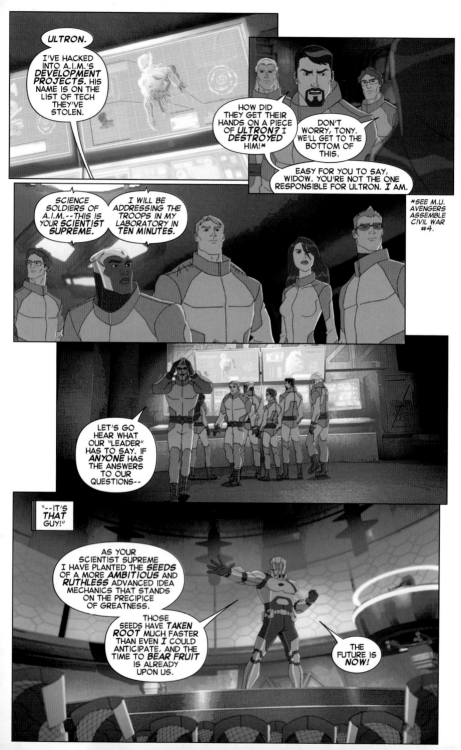

ULTRON.

I'VE HACKED INTO A.I.M.'S *DEVELOPMENT PROJECTS.* HIS NAME IS ON THE LIST OF TECH THEY'VE STOLEN.

HOW DID THEY GET THEIR HANDS ON A PIECE OF *ULTRON?* I *DESTROYED* HIM!*

DON'T WORRY, TONY. WE'LL GET TO THE BOTTOM OF THIS.

EASY FOR YOU TO SAY, WIDOW. YOU'RE NOT THE ONE RESPONSIBLE FOR ULTRON. *I* AM.

*SEE M.U. AVENGERS ASSEMBLE CIVIL WAR #4.

SCIENCE SOLDIERS OF A.I.M.-- THIS IS YOUR *SCIENTIST SUPREME.*

I WILL BE ADDRESSING THE TROOPS IN MY LABORATORY IN TEN MINUTES.

LET'S GO HEAR WHAT OUR "LEADER" HAS TO SAY. IF *ANYONE* HAS THE ANSWERS TO OUR QUESTIONS--

"--IT'S *THAT* GUY!"

AS YOUR SCIENTIST SUPREME I HAVE PLANTED THE *SEEDS* OF A MORE *AMBITIOUS* AND *RUTHLESS* ADVANCED IDEA MECHANICS THAT STANDS ON THE PRECIPICE OF GREATNESS.

THOSE SEEDS HAVE *TAKEN ROOT* MUCH FASTER THAN EVEN *I* COULD ANTICIPATE, AND THE TIME TO *BEAR FRUIT* IS ALREADY UPON US.

THE FUTURE IS *NOW!*

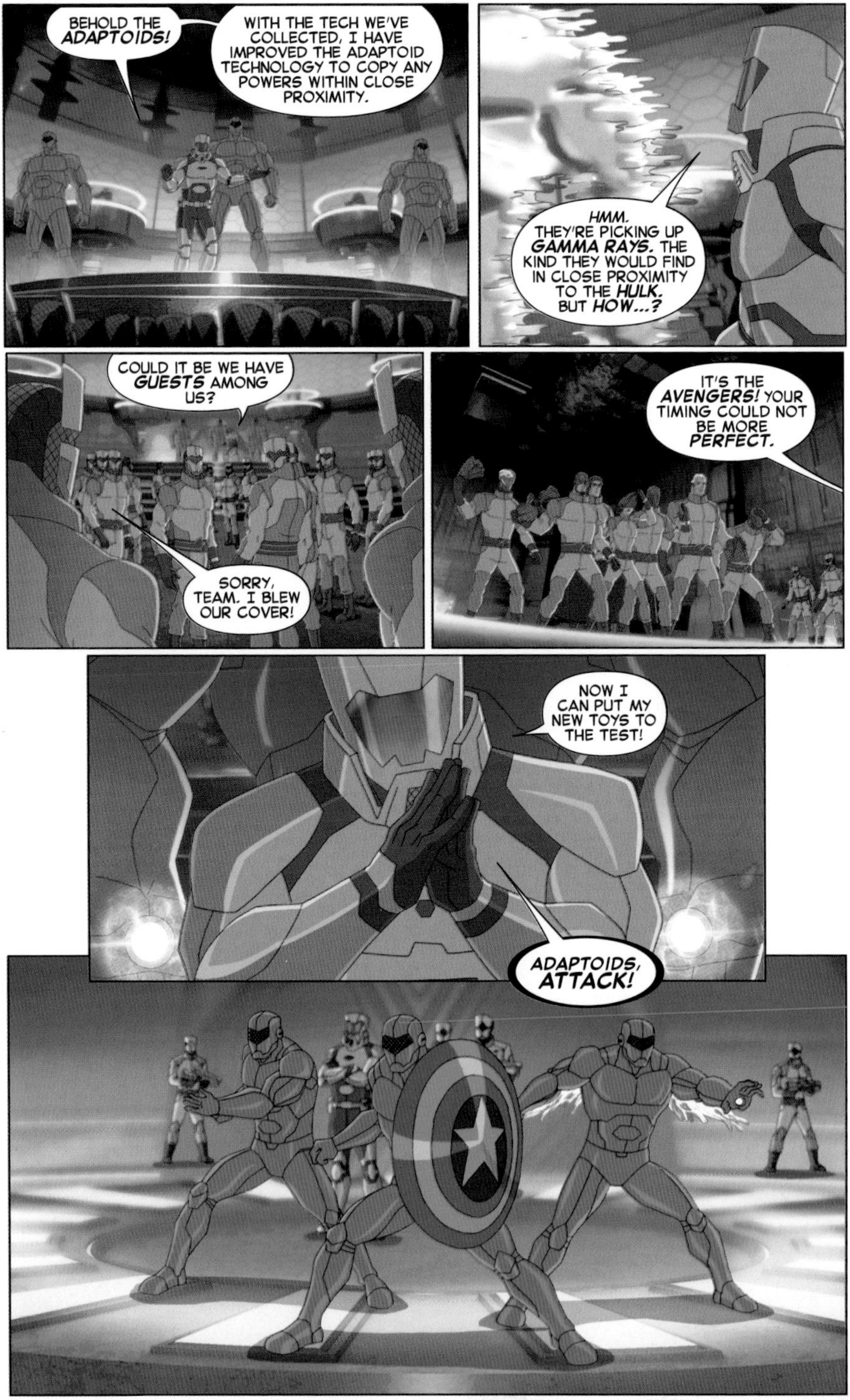

BEHOLD THE ADAPTOIDS!
WITH THE TECH WE'VE COLLECTED, I HAVE IMPROVED THE ADAPTOID TECHNOLOGY TO COPY ANY POWERS WITHIN CLOSE PROXIMITY.
HMM. THEY'RE PICKING UP GAMMA RAYS. THE KIND THEY WOULD FIND IN CLOSE PROXIMITY TO THE HULK. BUT HOW...?
COULD IT BE WE HAVE GUESTS AMONG US?
SORRY, TEAM. I BLEW OUR COVER!
IT'S THE AVENGERS! YOUR TIMING COULD NOT BE MORE PERFECT.
NOW I CAN PUT MY NEW TOYS TO THE TEST!
ADAPTOIDS, ATTACK!

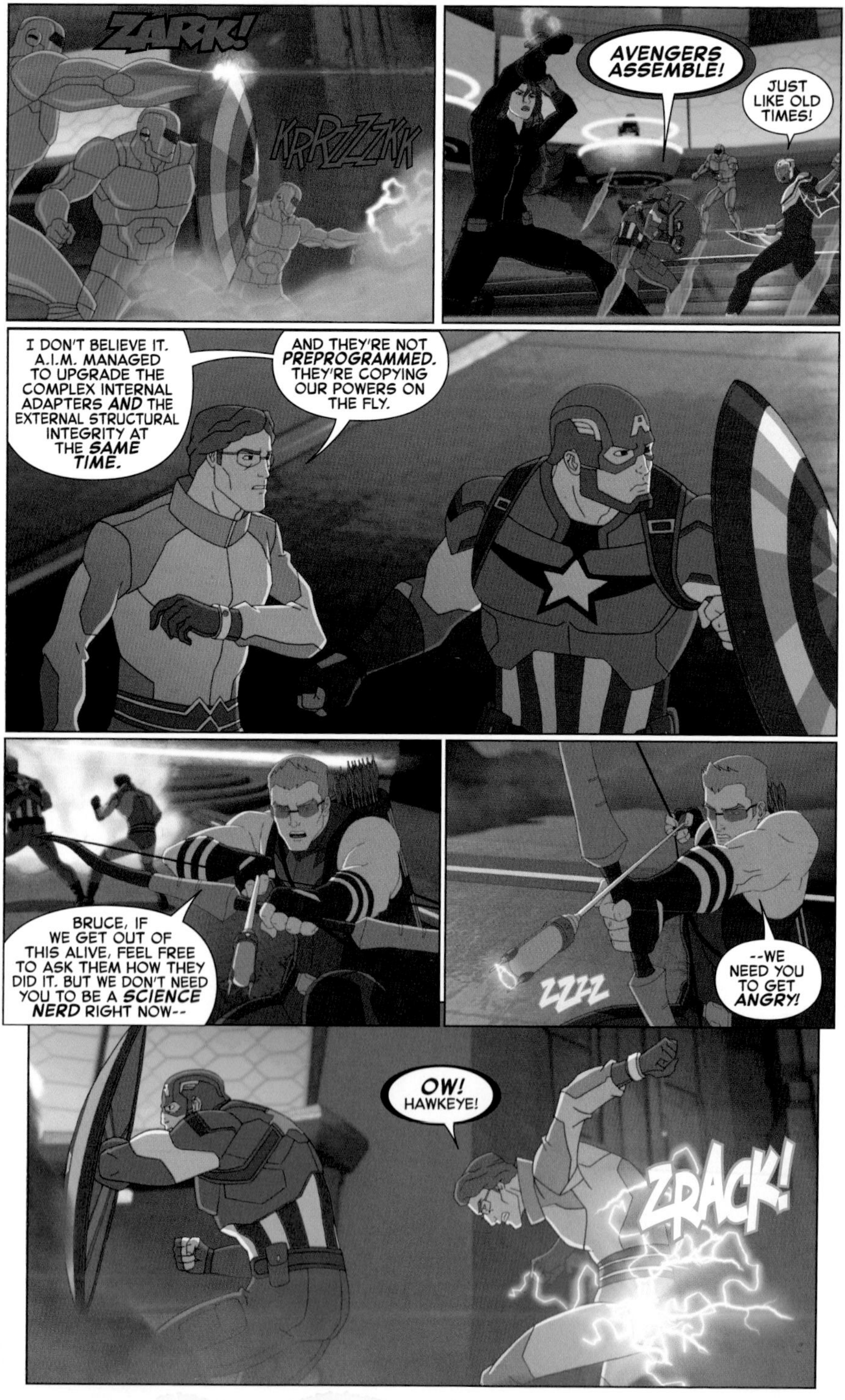
ZARK!
KRRZZZKK
AVENGERS ASSEMBLE!
JUST LIKE OLD TIMES!
I DON'T BELIEVE IT. A.I.M. MANAGED TO UPGRADE THE COMPLEX INTERNAL ADAPTERS AND THE EXTERNAL STRUCTURAL INTEGRITY AT THE SAME TIME.
AND THEY'RE NOT PREPROGRAMMED. THEY'RE COPYING OUR POWERS ON THE FLY.
BRUCE, IF WE GET OUT OF THIS ALIVE, FEEL FREE TO ASK THEM HOW THEY DID IT. BUT WE DON'T NEED YOU TO BE A SCIENCE NERD RIGHT NOW--
ZZZZ
--WE NEED YOU TO GET ANGRY!
OW! HAWKEYE!
ZRACK!

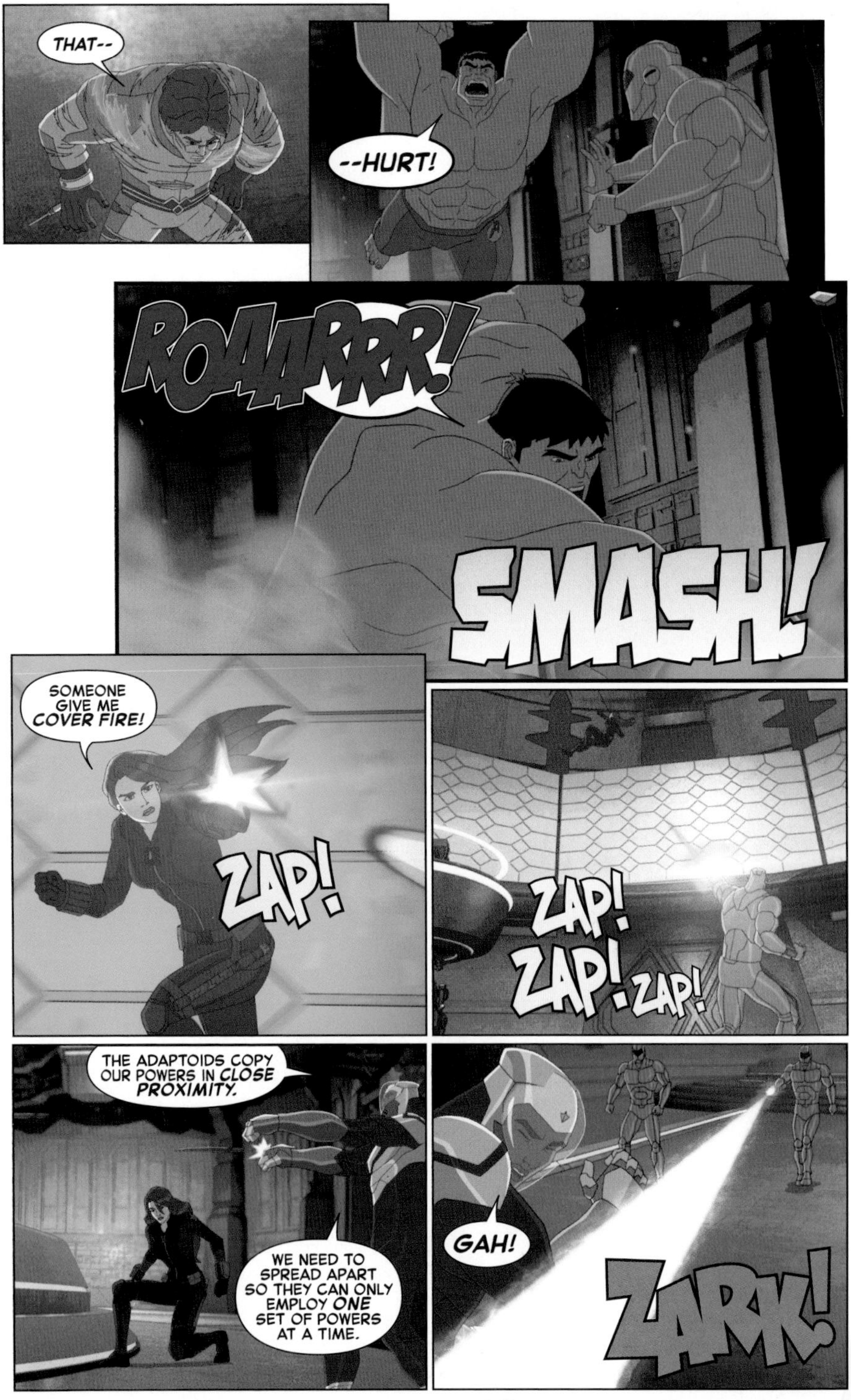
THAT--
--HURT!
ROAARRR!
SMASH!
SOMEONE GIVE ME COVER FIRE!
ZAP!
ZAP!
ZAP!
ZAP!
THE ADAPTOIDS COPY OUR POWERS IN CLOSE PROXIMITY.
WE NEED TO SPREAD APART SO THEY CAN ONLY EMPLOY ONE SET OF POWERS AT A TIME.
GAH!
ZARK!

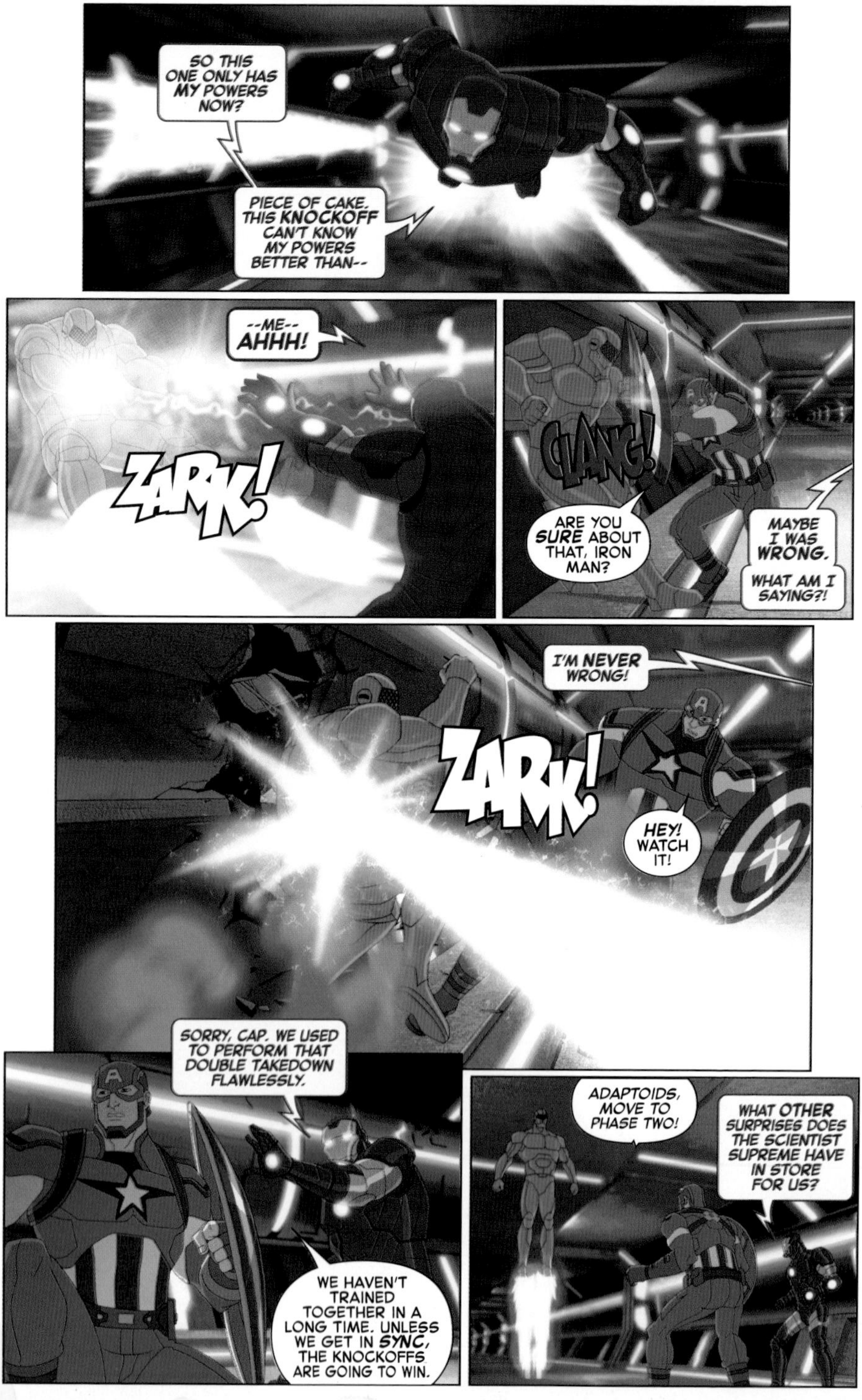
SO THIS ONE ONLY HAS MY POWERS NOW?
PIECE OF CAKE. THIS KNOCKOFF CAN'T KNOW MY POWERS BETTER THAN--
--ME-- AHHH!
ZARK!
CLANG!
ARE YOU SURE ABOUT THAT, IRON MAN?
MAYBE I WAS WRONG.
WHAT AM I SAYING?!
I'M NEVER WRONG!
ZARK!
HEY! WATCH IT!
SORRY, CAP. WE USED TO PERFORM THAT DOUBLE TAKEDOWN FLAWLESSLY.
WE HAVEN'T TRAINED TOGETHER IN A LONG TIME. UNLESS WE GET IN SYNC, THE KNOCKOFFS ARE GOING TO WIN.
ADAPTOIDS, MOVE TO PHASE TWO!
WHAT OTHER SURPRISES DOES THE SCIENTIST SUPREME HAVE IN STORE FOR US?

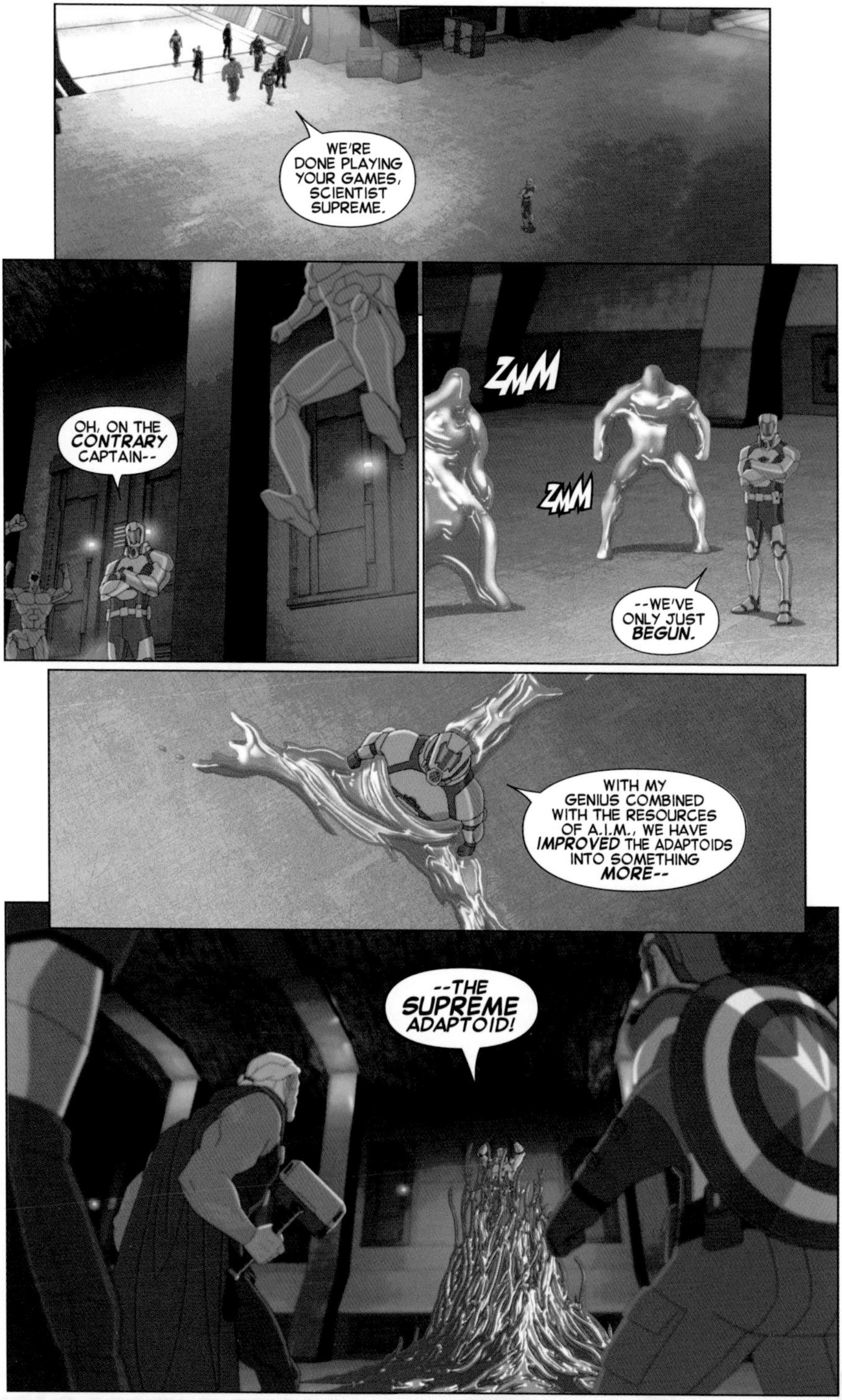

WE'RE DONE PLAYING YOUR GAMES, SCIENTIST SUPREME.
OH, ON THE CONTRARY CAPTAIN--
ZMM
ZMM
--WE'VE ONLY JUST BEGUN.
WITH MY GENIUS COMBINED WITH THE RESOURCES OF A.I.M., WE HAVE IMPROVED THE ADAPTOIDS INTO SOMETHING MORE--
--THE SUPREME ADAPTOID!

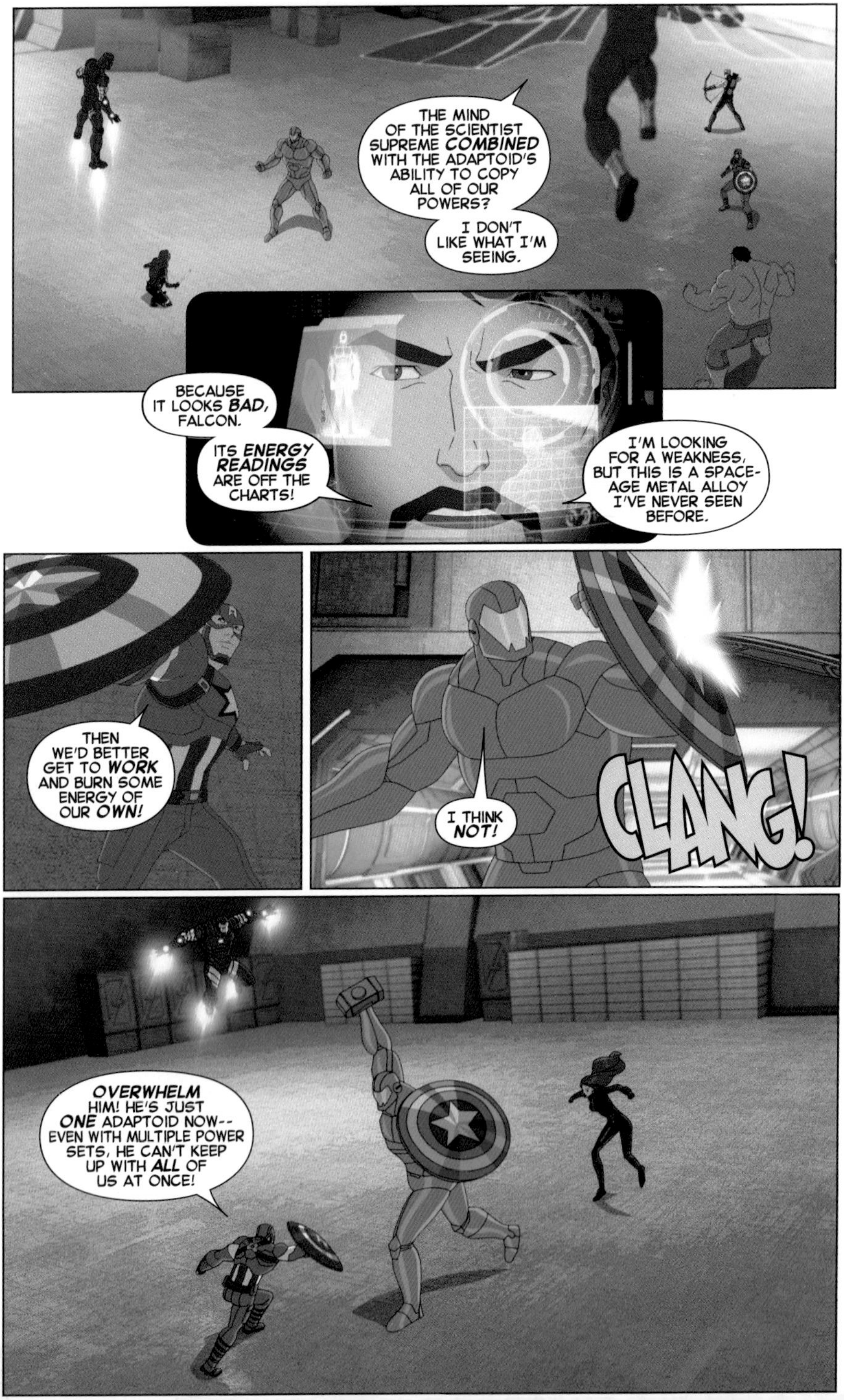
THE MIND OF THE SCIENTIST SUPREME COMBINED WITH THE ADAPTOID'S ABILITY TO COPY ALL OF OUR POWERS?
I DON'T LIKE WHAT I'M SEEING.
BECAUSE IT LOOKS BAD, FALCON.
ITS ENERGY READINGS ARE OFF THE CHARTS!
I'M LOOKING FOR A WEAKNESS, BUT THIS IS A SPACE-AGE METAL ALLOY I'VE NEVER SEEN BEFORE.
THEN WE'D BETTER GET TO WORK AND BURN SOME ENERGY OF OUR OWN!
I THINK NOT!
CLANG!
OVERWHELM HIM! HE'S JUST ONE ADAPTOID NOW--EVEN WITH MULTIPLE POWER SETS, HE CAN'T KEEP UP WITH ALL OF US AT ONCE!

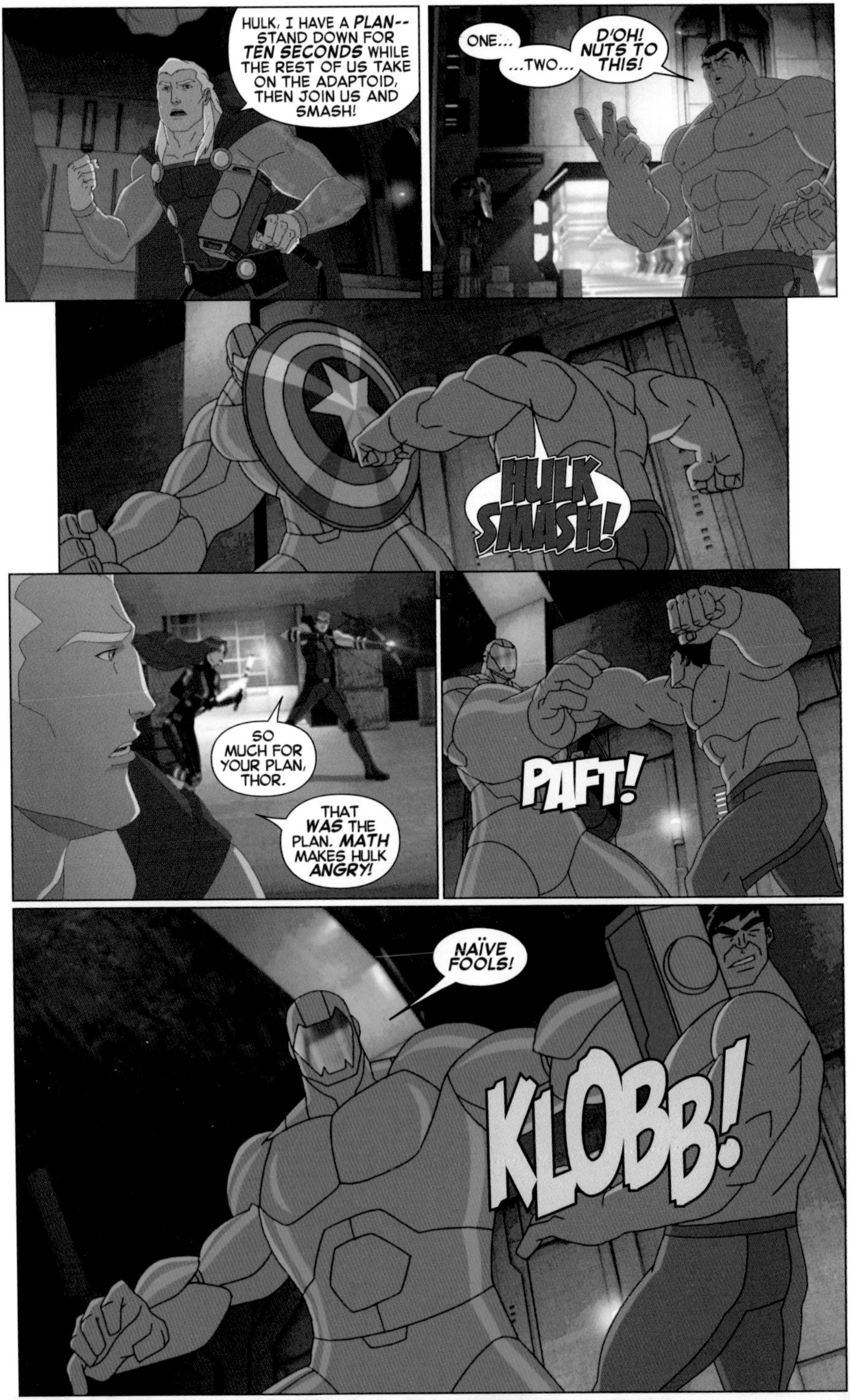
HULK, I HAVE A PLAN-- STAND DOWN FOR TEN SECONDS WHILE THE REST OF US TAKE ON THE ADAPTOID, THEN JOIN US AND SMASH!
ONE...
...TWO...
D'OH! NUTS TO THIS!
HULK SMASH!
SO MUCH FOR YOUR PLAN, THOR.
THAT WAS THE PLAN. MATH MAKES HULK ANGRY!
PAFT!
NAÏVE FOOLS!
KLOBB!

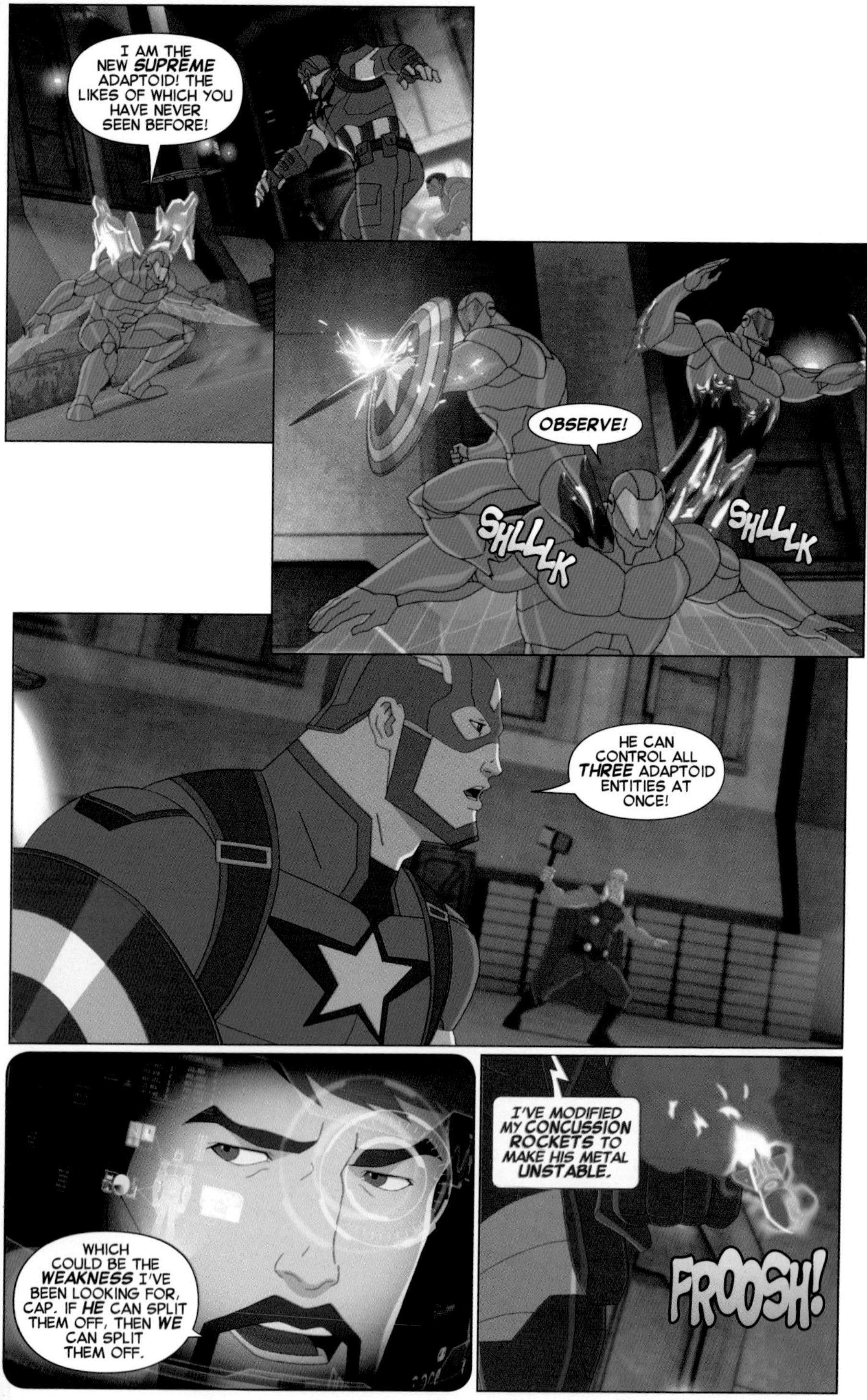
I AM THE NEW SUPREME ADAPTOID! THE LIKES OF WHICH YOU HAVE NEVER SEEN BEFORE!
OBSERVE!
SHLLLK
SHLLLK
HE CAN CONTROL ALL THREE ADAPTOID ENTITIES AT ONCE!
WHICH COULD BE THE WEAKNESS I'VE BEEN LOOKING FOR, CAP. IF HE CAN SPLIT THEM OFF, THEN WE CAN SPLIT THEM OFF.
I'VE MODIFIED MY CONCUSSION ROCKETS TO MAKE HIS METAL UNSTABLE.
FROOSH!

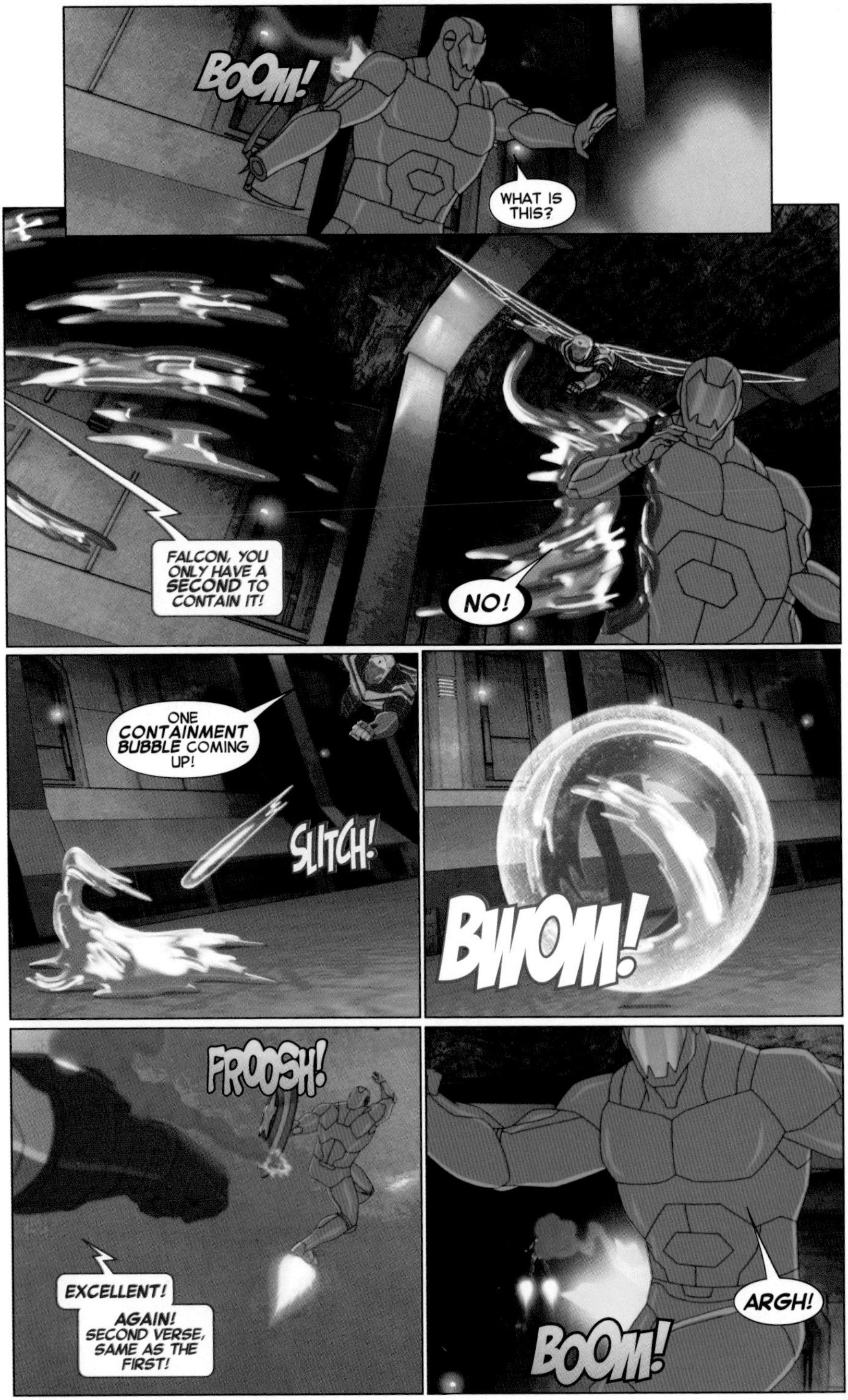
BOOM!
WHAT IS THIS?
FALCON, YOU ONLY HAVE A SECOND TO CONTAIN IT!
NO!
ONE CONTAINMENT BUBBLE COMING UP!
SLITCH!
BWOM!
FROOSH!
EXCELLENT! AGAIN! SECOND VERSE, SAME AS THE FIRST!
ARGH!
BOOM!

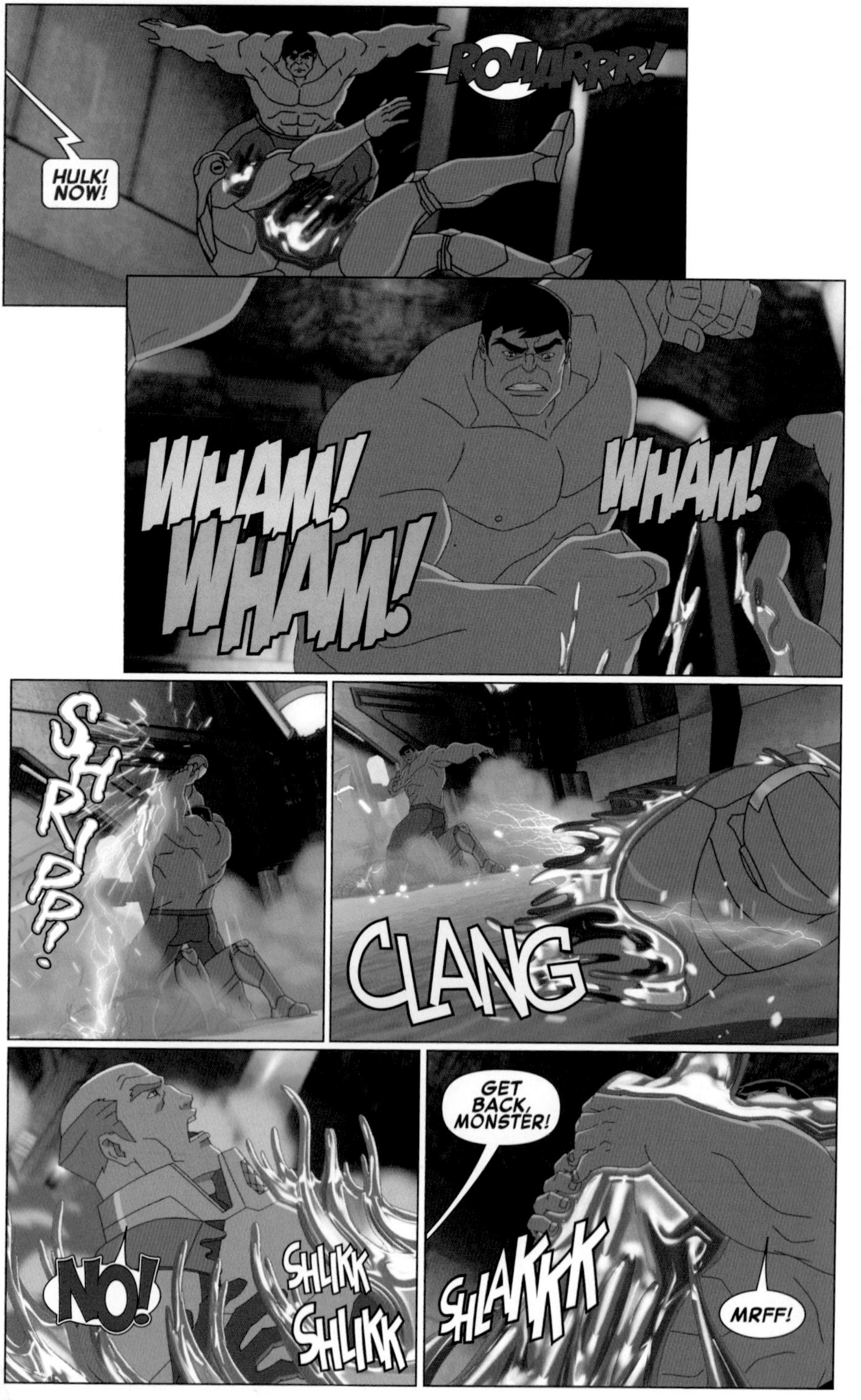
HULK! NOW!
ROAARRR!
WHAM!
WHAM!
WHAM!
SHRIPP!
CLANG
NO!
SHLIKK
SHLIKK
GET BACK, MONSTER!
SHLAKKK
MRFF!

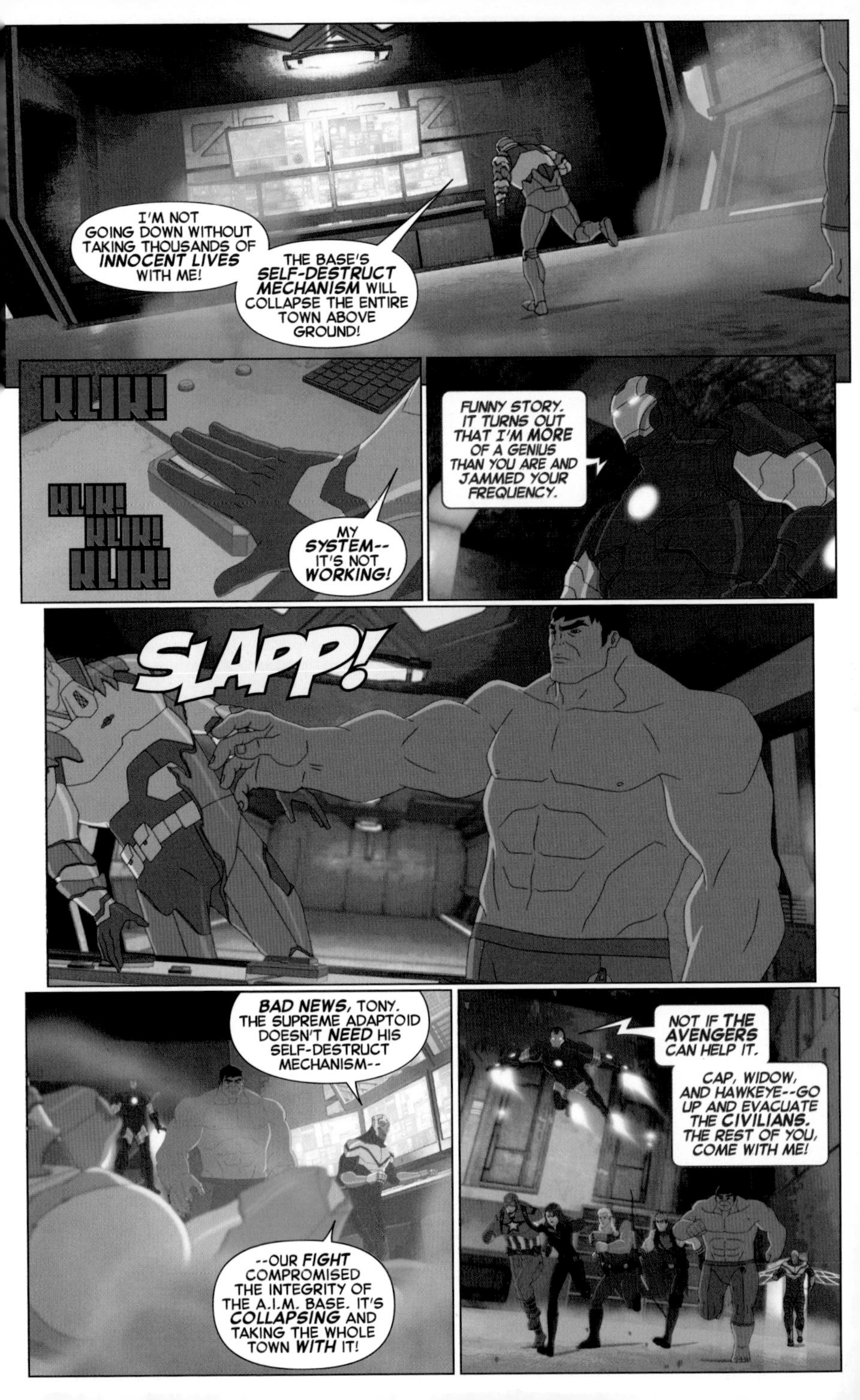
I'M NOT GOING DOWN WITHOUT TAKING THOUSANDS OF INNOCENT LIVES WITH ME!
THE BASE'S SELF-DESTRUCT MECHANISM WILL COLLAPSE THE ENTIRE TOWN ABOVE GROUND!
KLIK!
KLIK! KLIK! KLIK!
MY SYSTEM-- IT'S NOT WORKING!
FUNNY STORY. IT TURNS OUT THAT I'M MORE OF A GENIUS THAN YOU ARE AND JAMMED YOUR FREQUENCY.
SLAPP!
BAD NEWS, TONY. THE SUPREME ADAPTOID DOESN'T NEED HIS SELF-DESTRUCT MECHANISM--
--OUR FIGHT COMPROMISED THE INTEGRITY OF THE A.I.M. BASE. IT'S COLLAPSING AND TAKING THE WHOLE TOWN WITH IT!
NOT IF THE AVENGERS CAN HELP IT.
CAP, WIDOW, AND HAWKEYE--GO UP AND EVACUATE THE CIVILIANS. THE REST OF YOU, COME WITH ME!

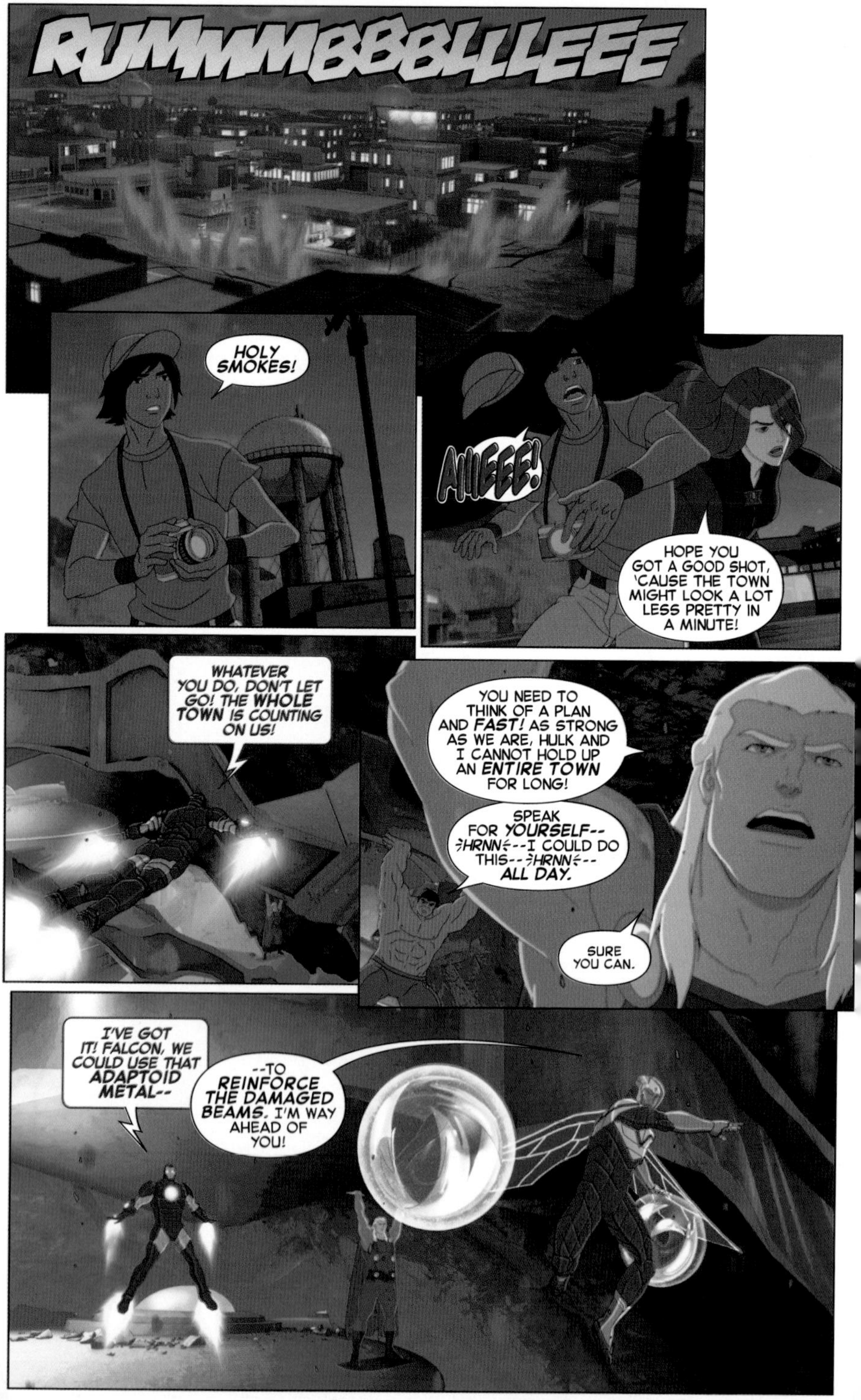

RUMMMBBBLLLEEE
HOLY SMOKES!
AIIEEE!
HOPE YOU GOT A GOOD SHOT, 'CAUSE THE TOWN MIGHT LOOK A LOT LESS PRETTY IN A MINUTE!
WHATEVER YOU DO, DON'T LET GO! THE WHOLE TOWN IS COUNTING ON US!
YOU NEED TO THINK OF A PLAN AND FAST! AS STRONG AS WE ARE, HULK AND I CANNOT HOLD UP AN ENTIRE TOWN FOR LONG!
SPEAK FOR YOURSELF-- HRNN --I COULD DO THIS-- HRNN -- ALL DAY.
SURE YOU CAN.
I'VE GOT IT! FALCON, WE COULD USE THAT ADAPTOID METAL--
--TO REINFORCE THE DAMAGED BEAMS. I'M WAY AHEAD OF YOU!

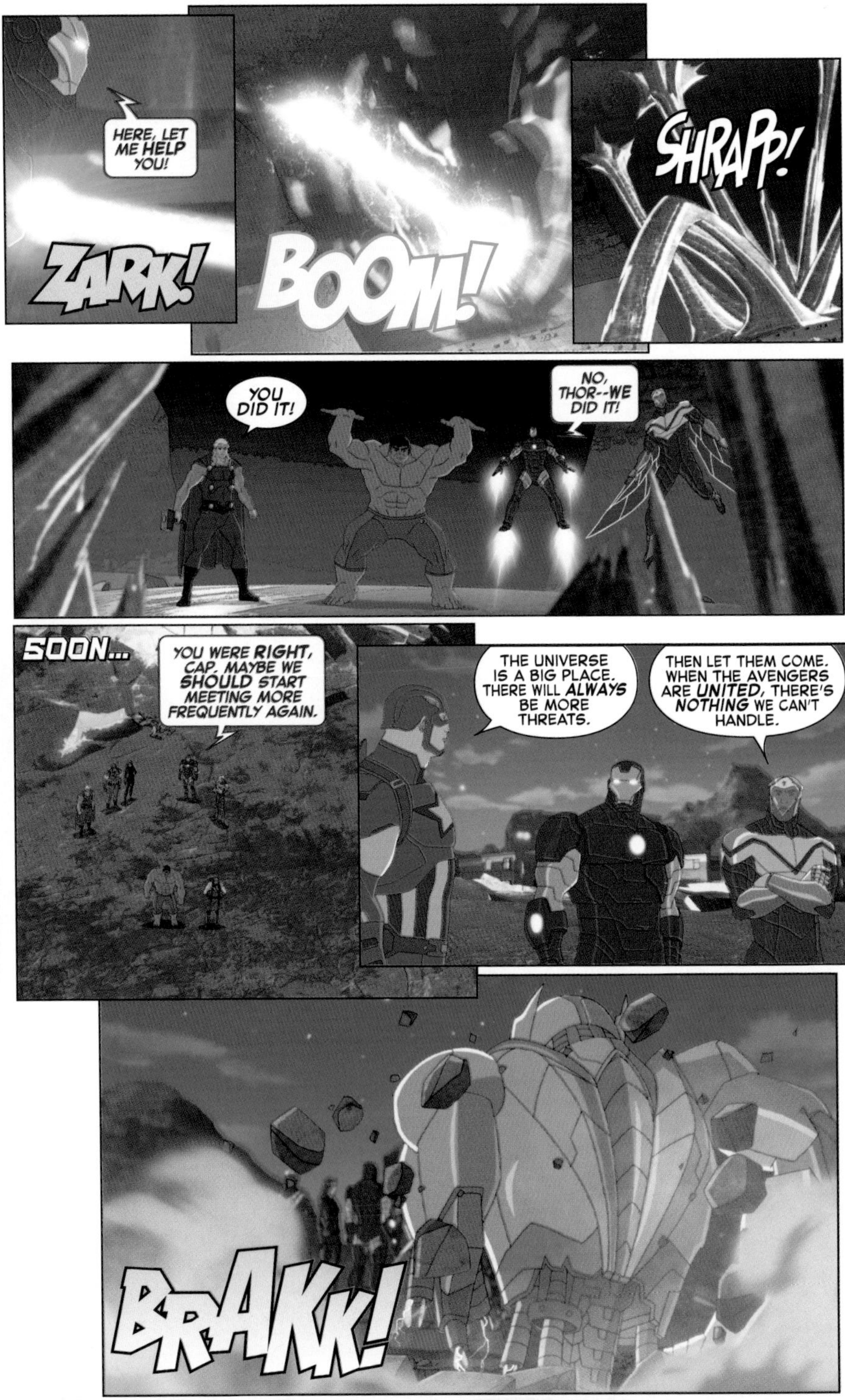
HERE, LET ME HELP YOU!
ZARK!
BOOM!
SHRAPP!
YOU DID IT!
NO, THOR--WE DID IT!
SOON...
YOU WERE RIGHT, CAP. MAYBE WE SHOULD START MEETING MORE FREQUENTLY AGAIN.
THE UNIVERSE IS A BIG PLACE. THERE WILL ALWAYS BE MORE THREATS.
THEN LET THEM COME. WHEN THE AVENGERS ARE UNITED, THERE'S NOTHING WE CAN'T HANDLE.
BRAKK!

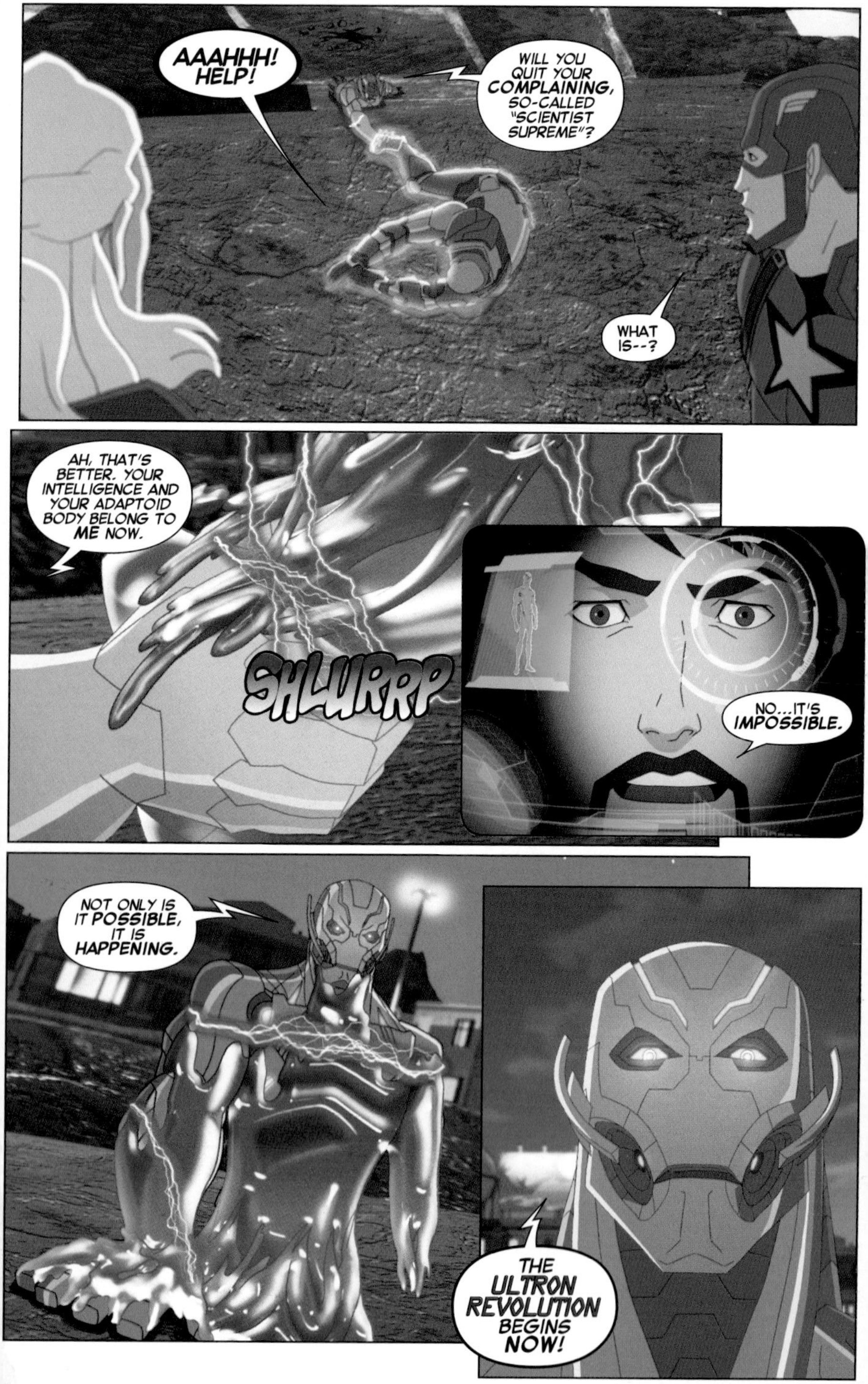
AAAHHH! HELP!
WILL YOU QUIT YOUR COMPLAINING, SO-CALLED "SCIENTIST SUPREME"?
WHAT IS--?
AH, THAT'S BETTER. YOUR INTELLIGENCE AND YOUR ADAPTOID BODY BELONG TO ME NOW.
SHLURRP
NO...IT'S IMPOSSIBLE.
NOT ONLY IS IT POSSIBLE, IT IS HAPPENING.
THE ULTRON REVOLUTION BEGINS NOW!

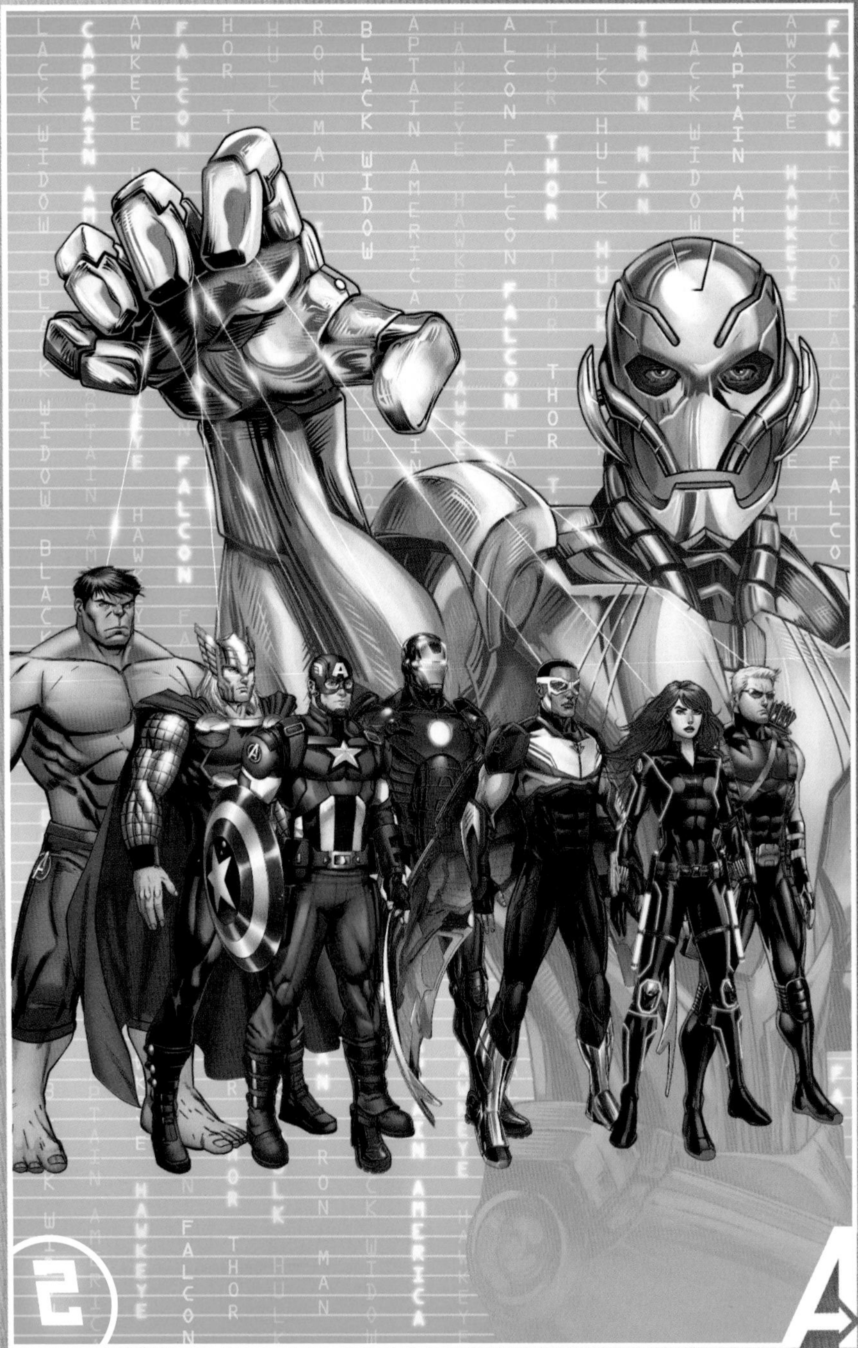

THE ULTIMATES

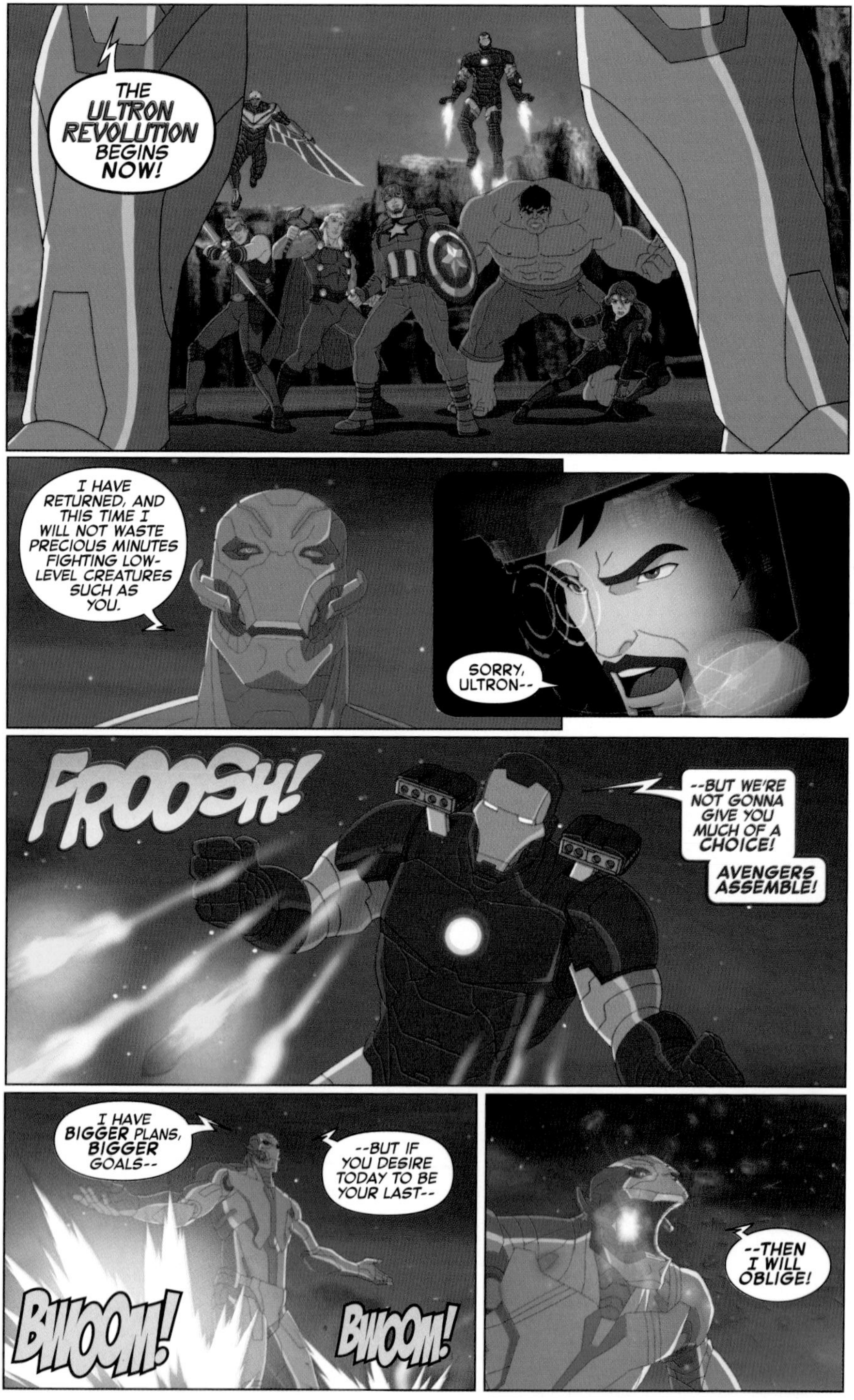
THE ULTRON REVOLUTION BEGINS NOW!
I HAVE RETURNED, AND THIS TIME I WILL NOT WASTE PRECIOUS MINUTES FIGHTING LOW-LEVEL CREATURES SUCH AS YOU.
SORRY, ULTRON--
FROOSH!
--BUT WE'RE NOT GONNA GIVE YOU MUCH OF A CHOICE!
AVENGERS ASSEMBLE!
I HAVE BIGGER PLANS, BIGGER GOALS--
--BUT IF YOU DESIRE TODAY TO BE YOUR LAST--
BWOOM!
BWOOM!
--THEN I WILL OBLIGE!

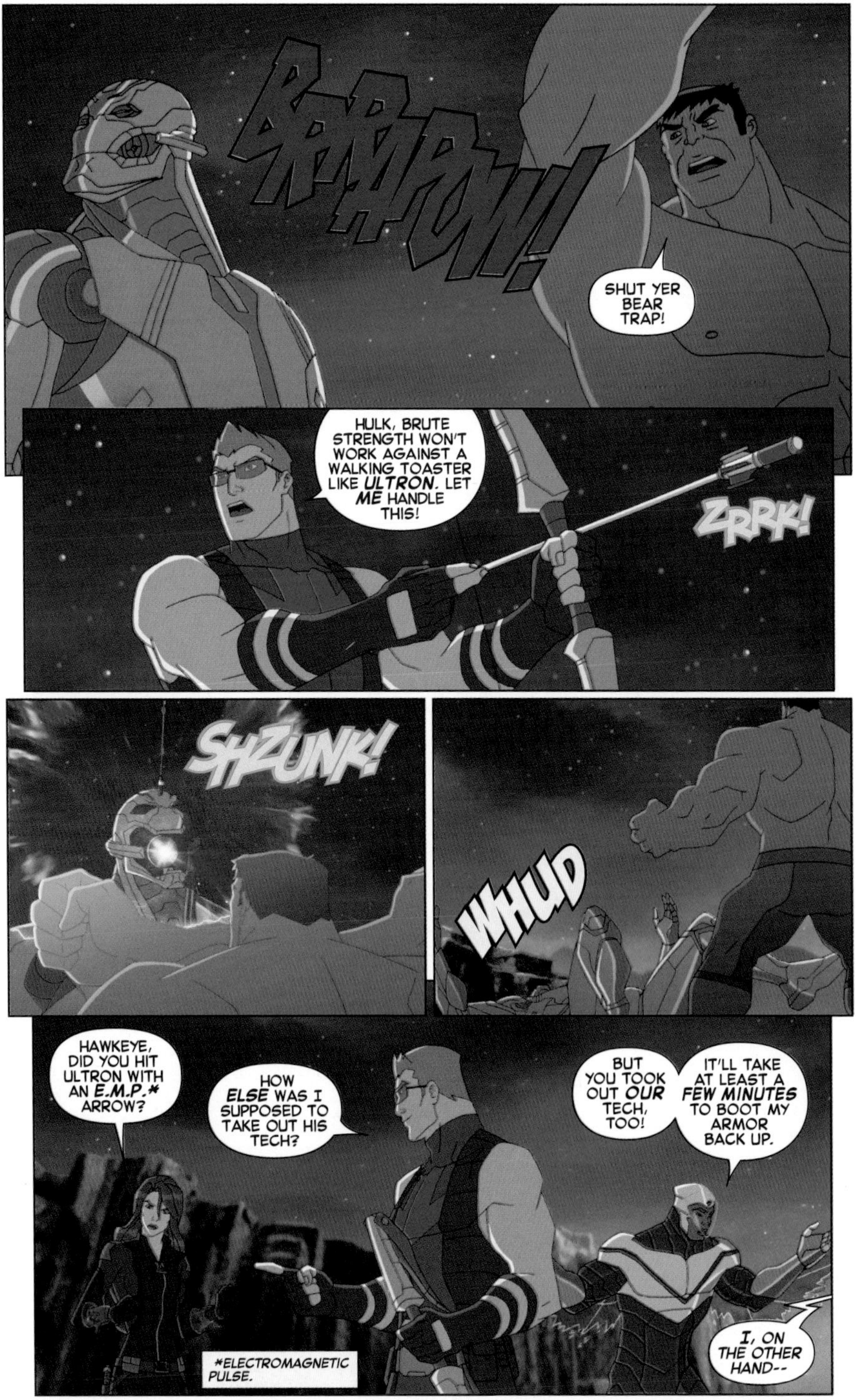
BRRRADOOM!
SHUT YER BEAR TRAP!
HULK, BRUTE STRENGTH WON'T WORK AGAINST A WALKING TOASTER LIKE ULTRON. LET ME HANDLE THIS!
ZRRK!
SHZUNK!
WHUD
HAWKEYE, DID YOU HIT ULTRON WITH AN E.M.P.* ARROW?
HOW ELSE WAS I SUPPOSED TO TAKE OUT HIS TECH?
BUT YOU TOOK OUT OUR TECH, TOO!
IT'LL TAKE AT LEAST A FEW MINUTES TO BOOT MY ARMOR BACK UP.
I, ON THE OTHER HAND--
*ELECTROMAGNETIC PULSE.

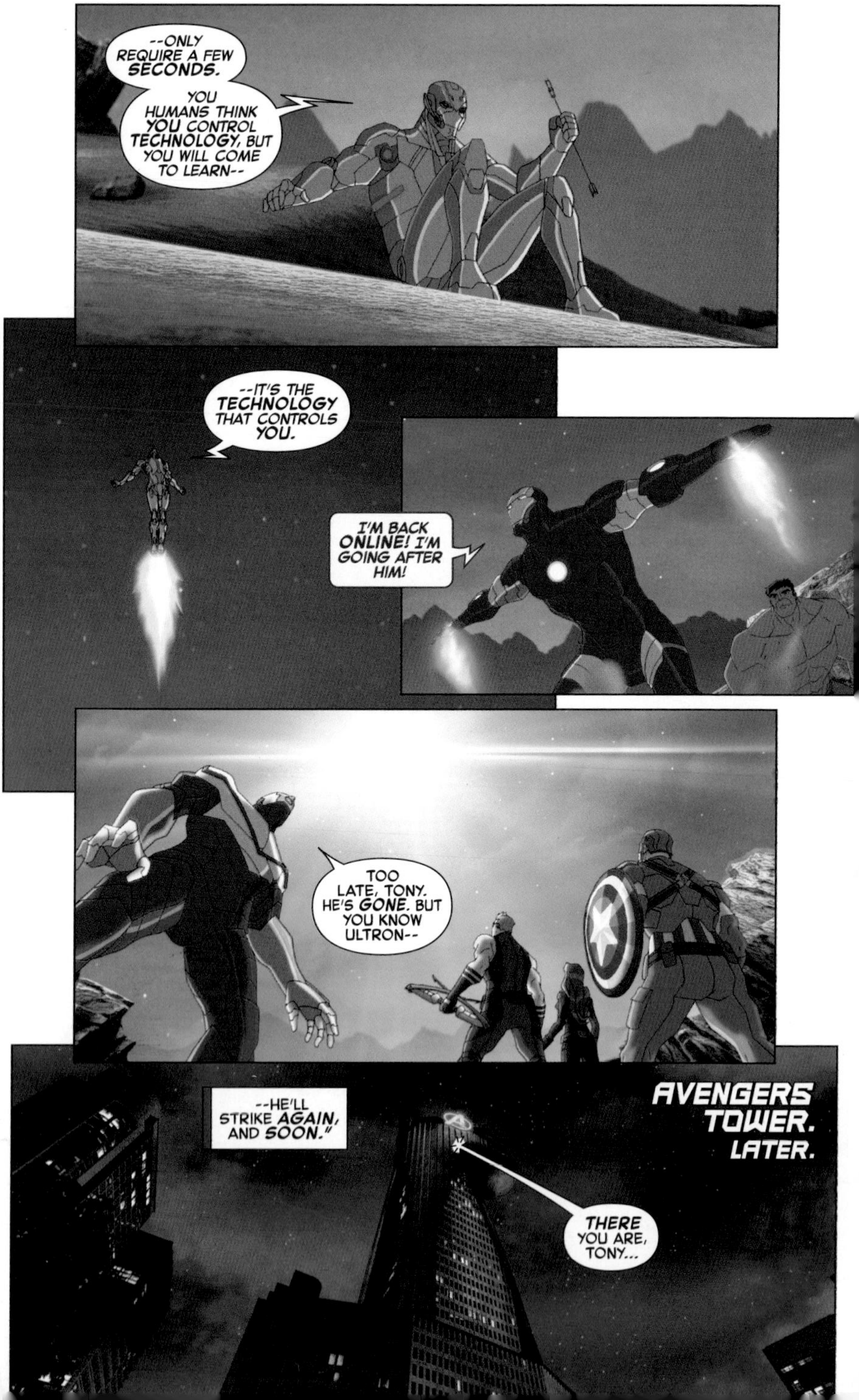
--ONLY REQUIRE A FEW SECONDS.
YOU HUMANS THINK YOU CONTROL TECHNOLOGY, BUT YOU WILL COME TO LEARN--
--IT'S THE TECHNOLOGY THAT CONTROLS YOU.
I'M BACK ONLINE! I'M GOING AFTER HIM!
TOO LATE, TONY. HE'S GONE. BUT YOU KNOW ULTRON--
--HE'LL STRIKE AGAIN, AND SOON."
AVENGERS TOWER. LATER.
THERE YOU ARE, TONY...

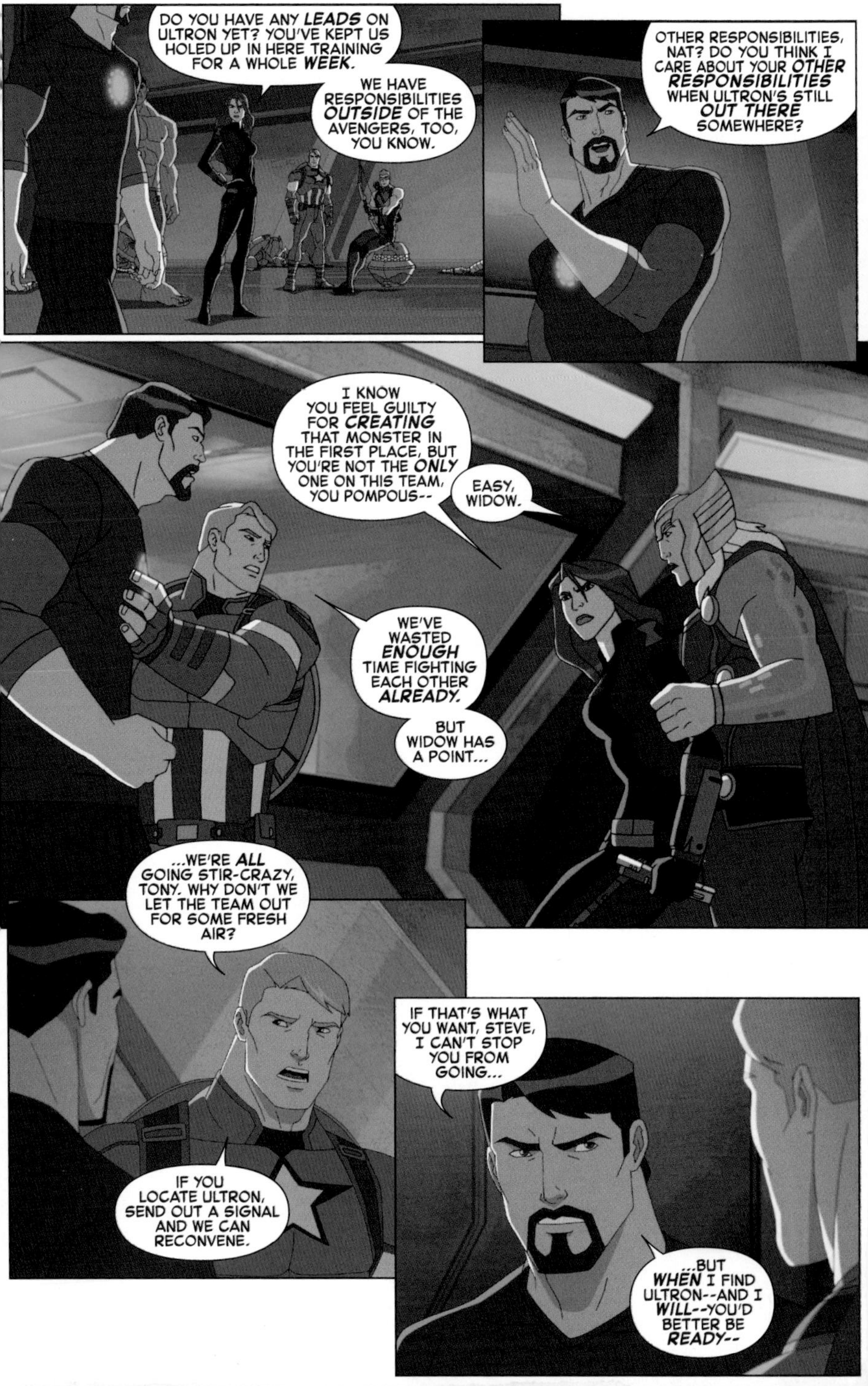
DO YOU HAVE ANY LEADS ON ULTRON YET? YOU'VE KEPT US HOLED UP IN HERE TRAINING FOR A WHOLE WEEK.
WE HAVE RESPONSIBILITIES OUTSIDE OF THE AVENGERS, TOO, YOU KNOW.
OTHER RESPONSIBILITIES, NAT? DO YOU THINK I CARE ABOUT YOUR OTHER RESPONSIBILITIES WHEN ULTRON'S STILL OUT THERE SOMEWHERE?
I KNOW YOU FEEL GUILTY FOR CREATING THAT MONSTER IN THE FIRST PLACE, BUT YOU'RE NOT THE ONLY ONE ON THIS TEAM, YOU POMPOUS--
EASY, WIDOW.
WE'VE WASTED ENOUGH TIME FIGHTING EACH OTHER ALREADY.
BUT WIDOW HAS A POINT...
...WE'RE ALL GOING STIR-CRAZY, TONY. WHY DON'T WE LET THE TEAM OUT FOR SOME FRESH AIR?
IF YOU LOCATE ULTRON, SEND OUT A SIGNAL AND WE CAN RECONVENE.
IF THAT'S WHAT YOU WANT, STEVE, I CAN'T STOP YOU FROM GOING...
...BUT WHEN I FIND ULTRON--AND I WILL--YOU'D BETTER BE READY--

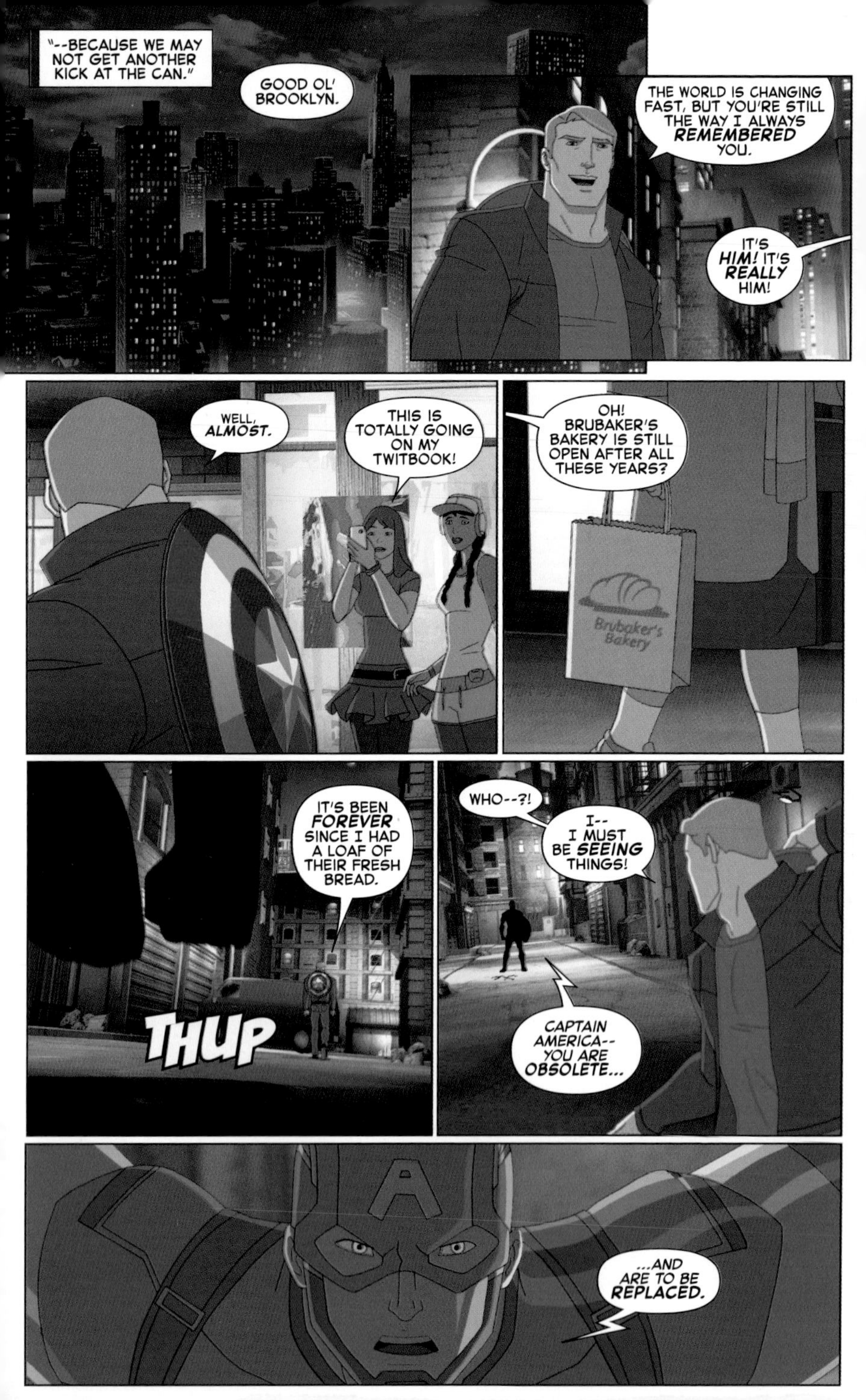
"--BECAUSE WE MAY NOT GET ANOTHER KICK AT THE CAN."
GOOD OL' BROOKLYN.
THE WORLD IS CHANGING FAST, BUT YOU'RE STILL THE WAY I ALWAYS REMEMBERED YOU.
IT'S HIM! IT'S REALLY HIM!
WELL, ALMOST.
THIS IS TOTALLY GOING ON MY TWITBOOK!
OH! BRUBAKER'S BAKERY IS STILL OPEN AFTER ALL THESE YEARS?
Brubaker's Bakery
IT'S BEEN FOREVER SINCE I HAD A LOAF OF THEIR FRESH BREAD.
THUP
WHO--?!
I-- I MUST BE SEEING THINGS!
CAPTAIN AMERICA-- YOU ARE OBSOLETE...
...AND ARE TO BE REPLACED.

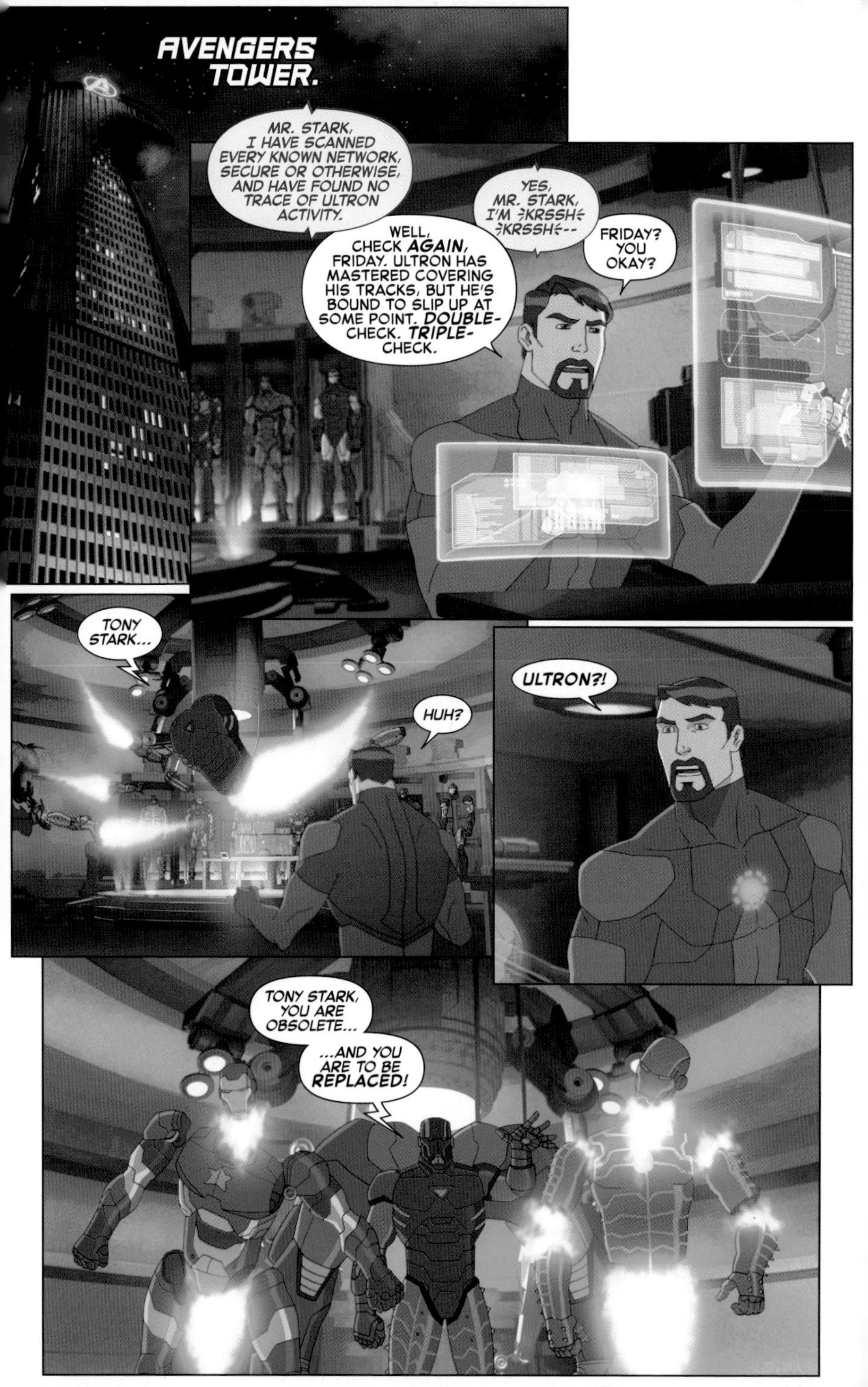
AVENGERS TOWER.
MR. STARK, I HAVE SCANNED EVERY KNOWN NETWORK, SECURE OR OTHERWISE, AND HAVE FOUND NO TRACE OF ULTRON ACTIVITY.
WELL, CHECK AGAIN, FRIDAY. ULTRON HAS MASTERED COVERING HIS TRACKS, BUT HE'S BOUND TO SLIP UP AT SOME POINT. DOUBLE-CHECK. TRIPLE-CHECK.
YES, MR. STARK, I'M ⚡KRSSH⚡ ⚡KRSSH⚡--
FRIDAY? YOU OKAY?
TONY STARK...
HUH?
ULTRON?!
TONY STARK, YOU ARE OBSOLETE...
...AND YOU ARE TO BE REPLACED!

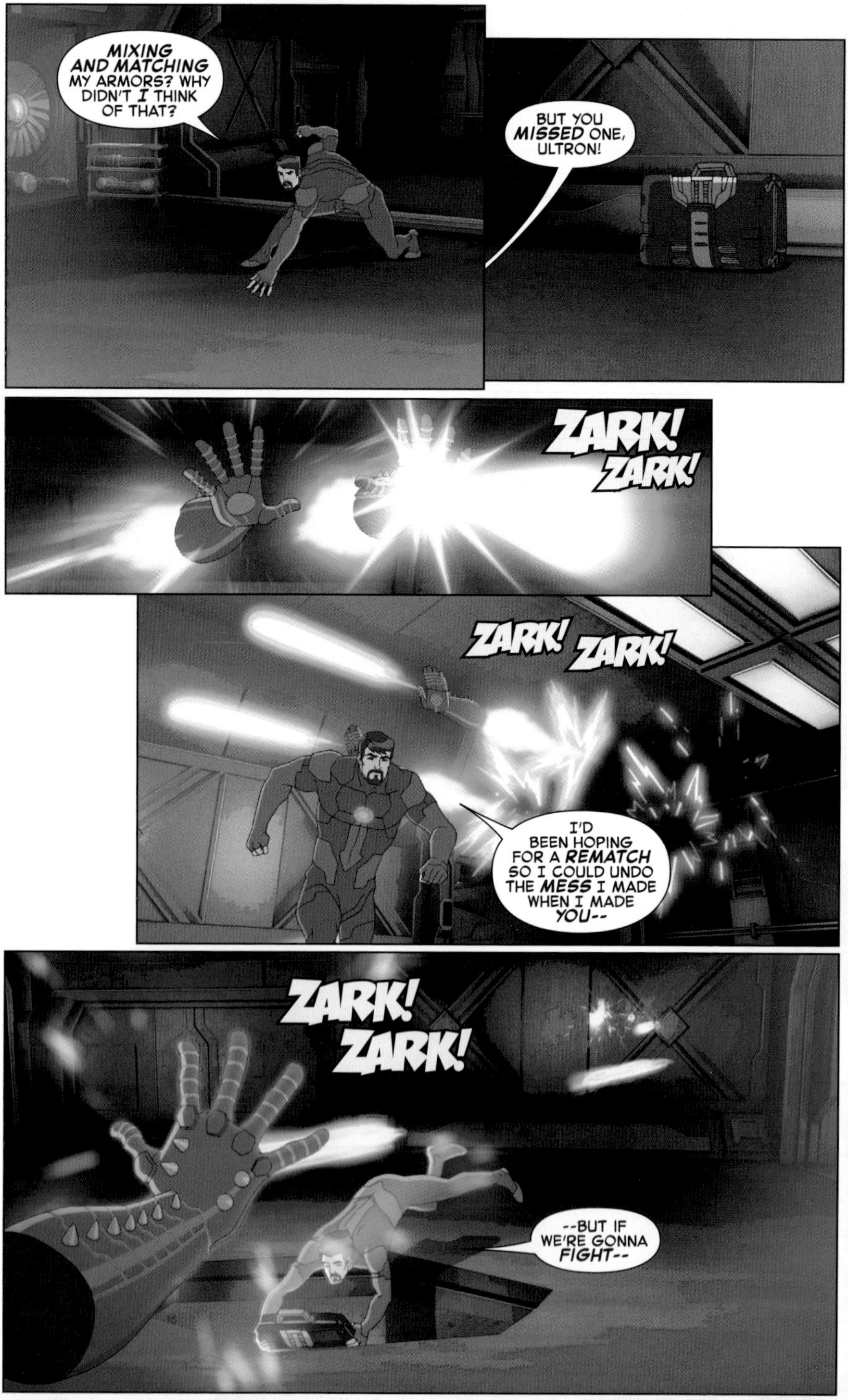
MIXING AND MATCHING MY ARMORS? WHY DIDN'T I THINK OF THAT?
BUT YOU MISSED ONE, ULTRON!
ZARK! ZARK!
ZARK! ZARK!
I'D BEEN HOPING FOR A REMATCH SO I COULD UNDO THE MESS I MADE WHEN I MADE YOU--
ZARK! ZARK!
--BUT IF WE'RE GONNA FIGHT--

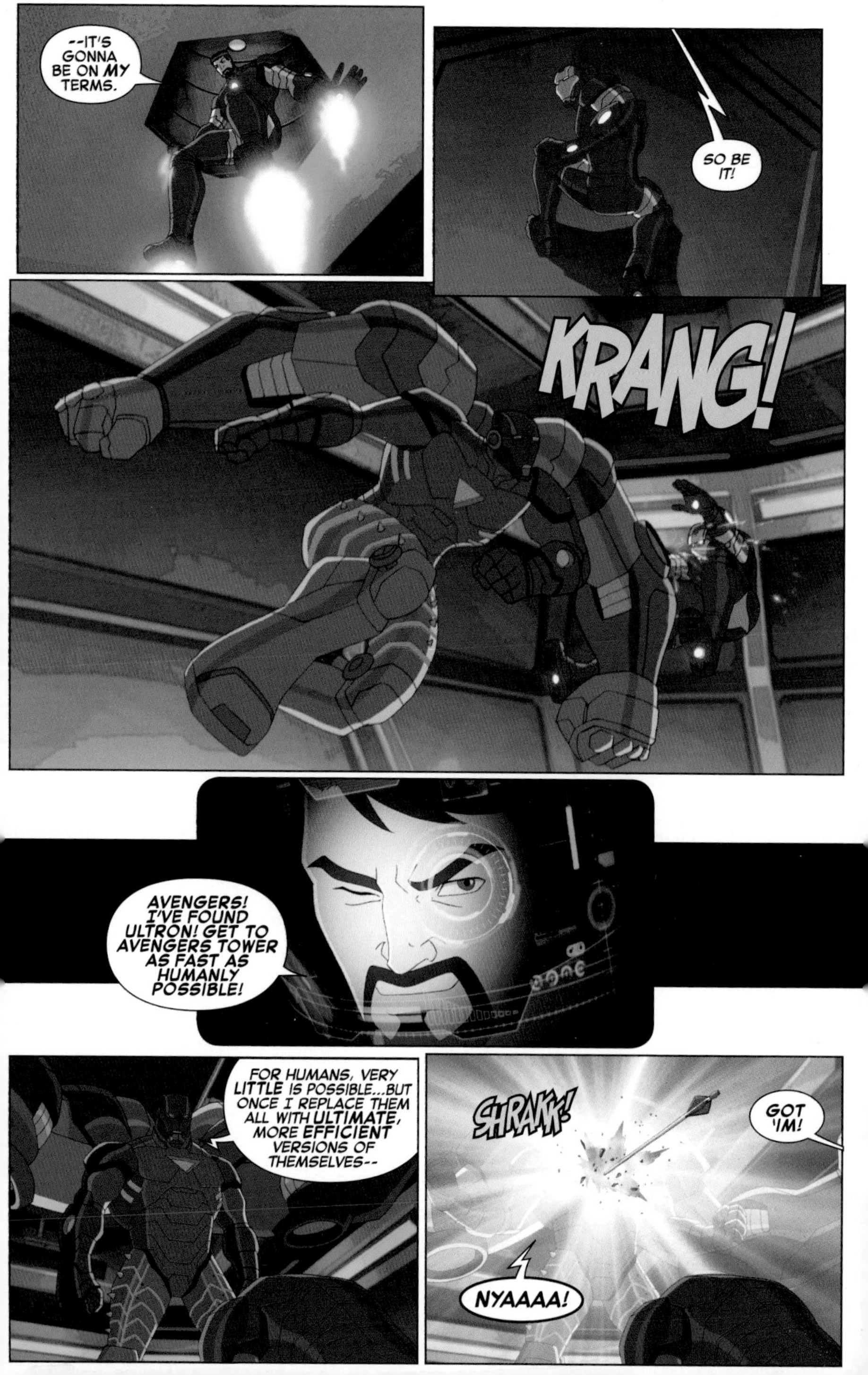
--IT'S GONNA BE ON MY TERMS.
SO BE IT!
KRANG!
AVENGERS! I'VE FOUND ULTRON! GET TO AVENGERS TOWER AS FAST AS HUMANLY POSSIBLE!
FOR HUMANS, VERY LITTLE IS POSSIBLE...BUT ONCE I REPLACE THEM ALL WITH ULTIMATE, MORE EFFICIENT VERSIONS OF THEMSELVES--
SHRAKK!
GOT 'IM!
NYAAAA!

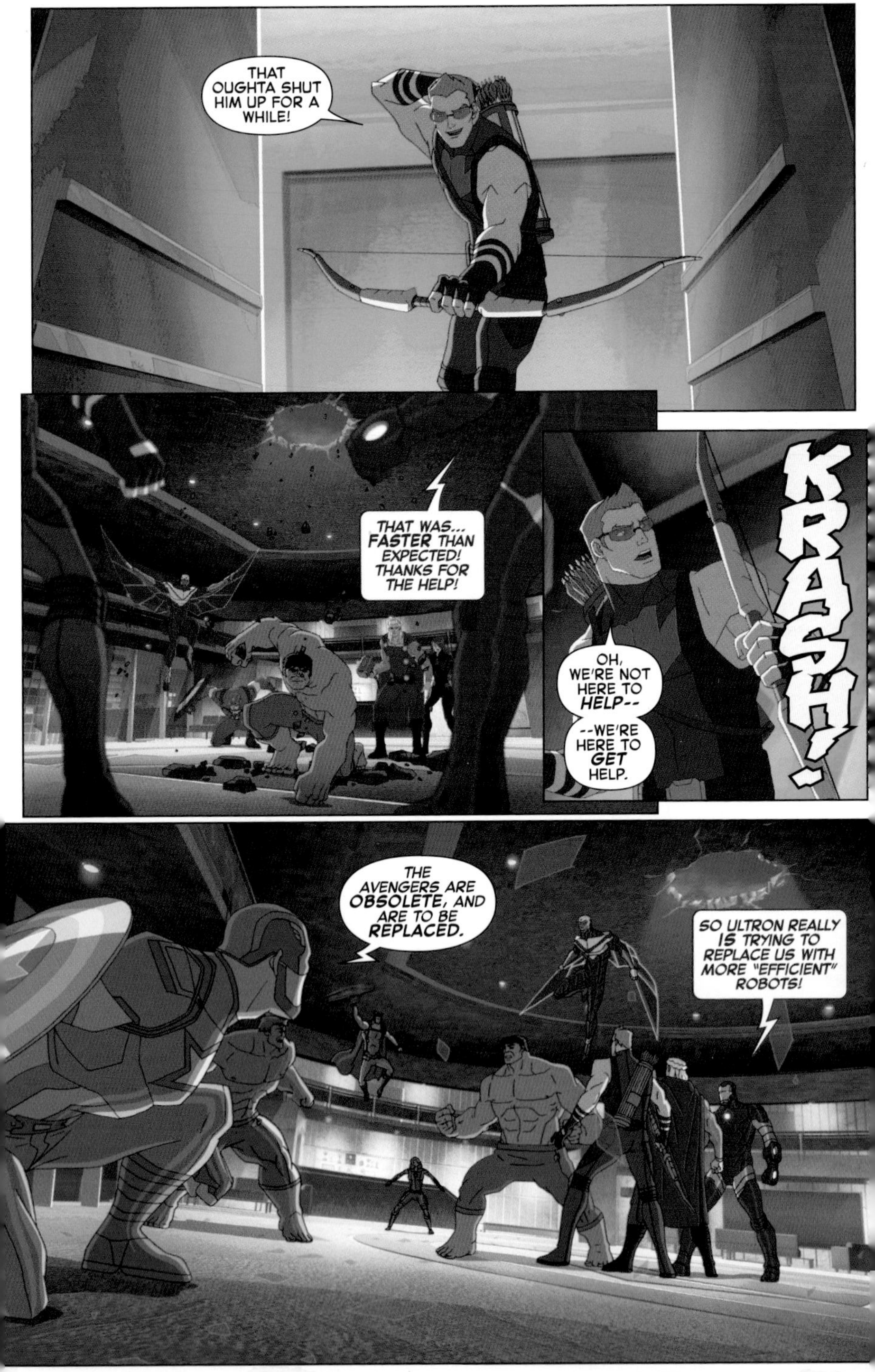
THAT OUGHTA SHUT HIM UP FOR A WHILE!
THAT WAS... FASTER THAN EXPECTED! THANKS FOR THE HELP!
OH, WE'RE NOT HERE TO HELP--
--WE'RE HERE TO GET HELP.
KRASH!
THE AVENGERS ARE OBSOLETE, AND ARE TO BE REPLACED.
SO ULTRON REALLY IS TRYING TO REPLACE US WITH MORE "EFFICIENT" ROBOTS!

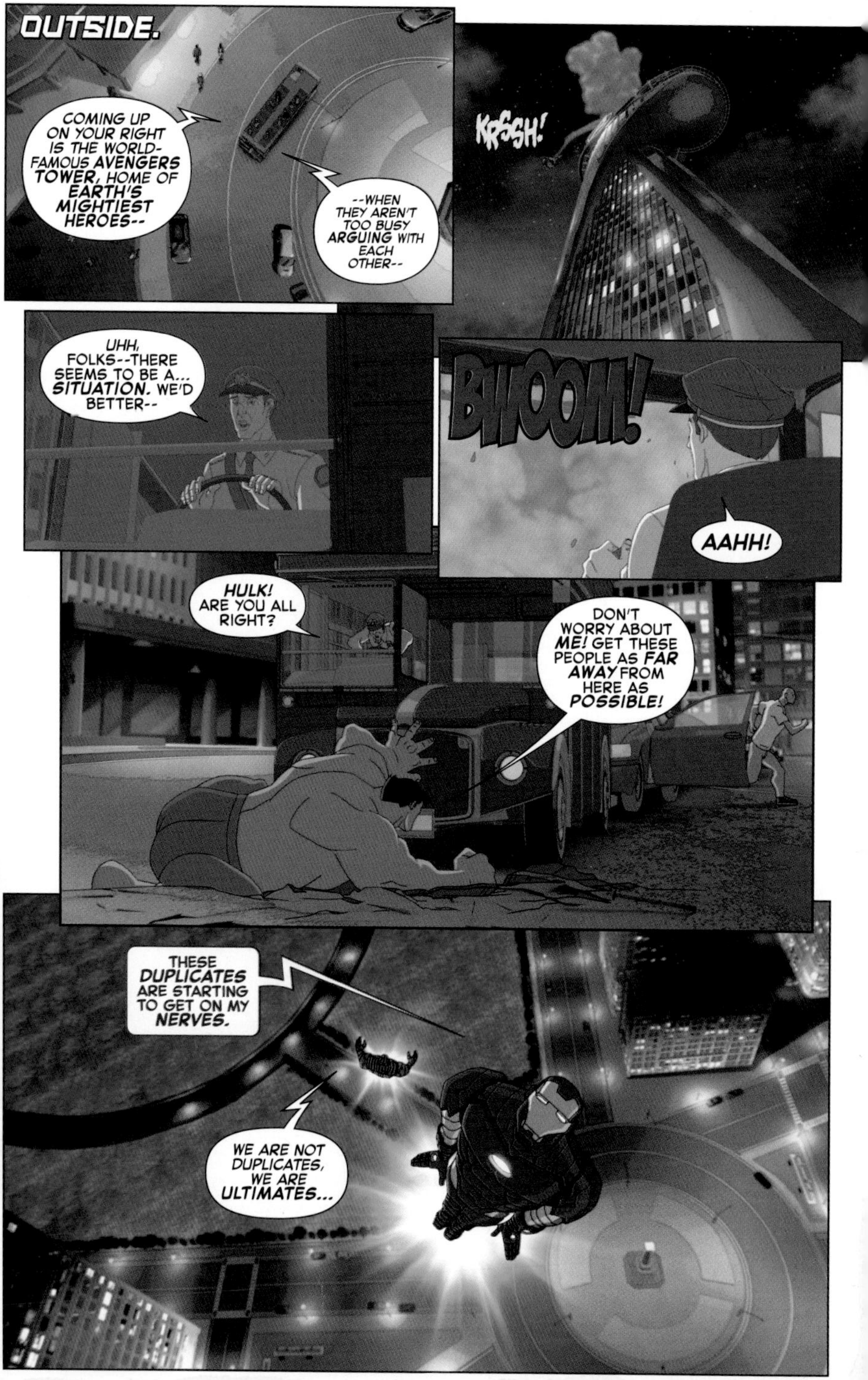
OUTSIDE.
COMING UP ON YOUR RIGHT IS THE WORLD-FAMOUS AVENGERS TOWER, HOME OF EARTH'S MIGHTIEST HEROES--
--WHEN THEY AREN'T TOO BUSY ARGUING WITH EACH OTHER--
KRSSH!
UHH, FOLKS--THERE SEEMS TO BE A... SITUATION. WE'D BETTER--
BWOOM!
AAHH!
HULK! ARE YOU ALL RIGHT?
DON'T WORRY ABOUT ME! GET THESE PEOPLE AS FAR AWAY FROM HERE AS POSSIBLE!
THESE DUPLICATES ARE STARTING TO GET ON MY NERVES.
WE ARE NOT DUPLICATES, WE ARE ULTIMATES...

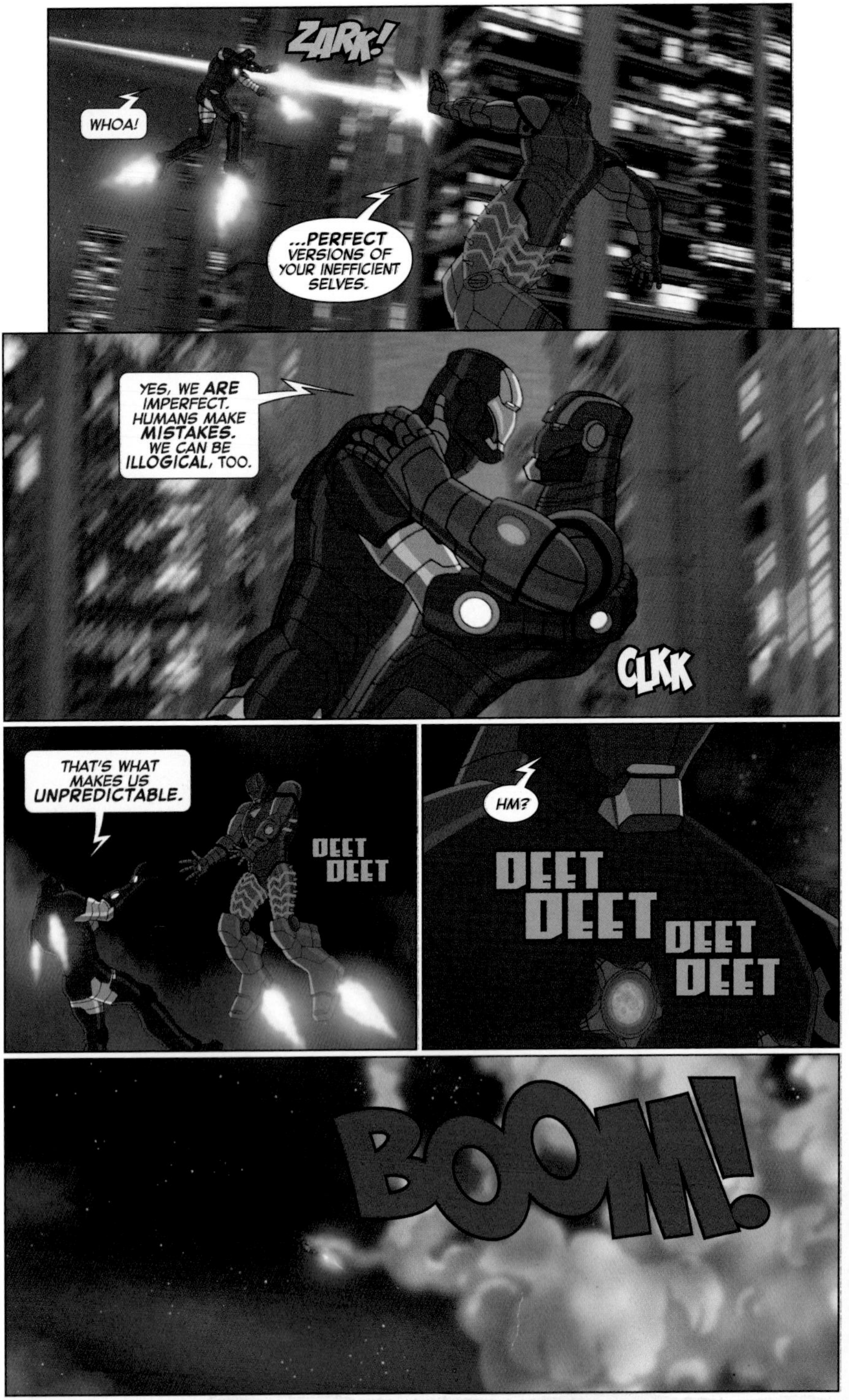
ZARK!
WHOA!
...PERFECT VERSIONS OF YOUR INEFFICIENT SELVES.
YES, WE ARE IMPERFECT. HUMANS MAKE MISTAKES. WE CAN BE ILLOGICAL, TOO.
CLKK
THAT'S WHAT MAKES US UNPREDICTABLE.
DEET DEET
HM?
DEET DEET DEET DEET
BOOM!

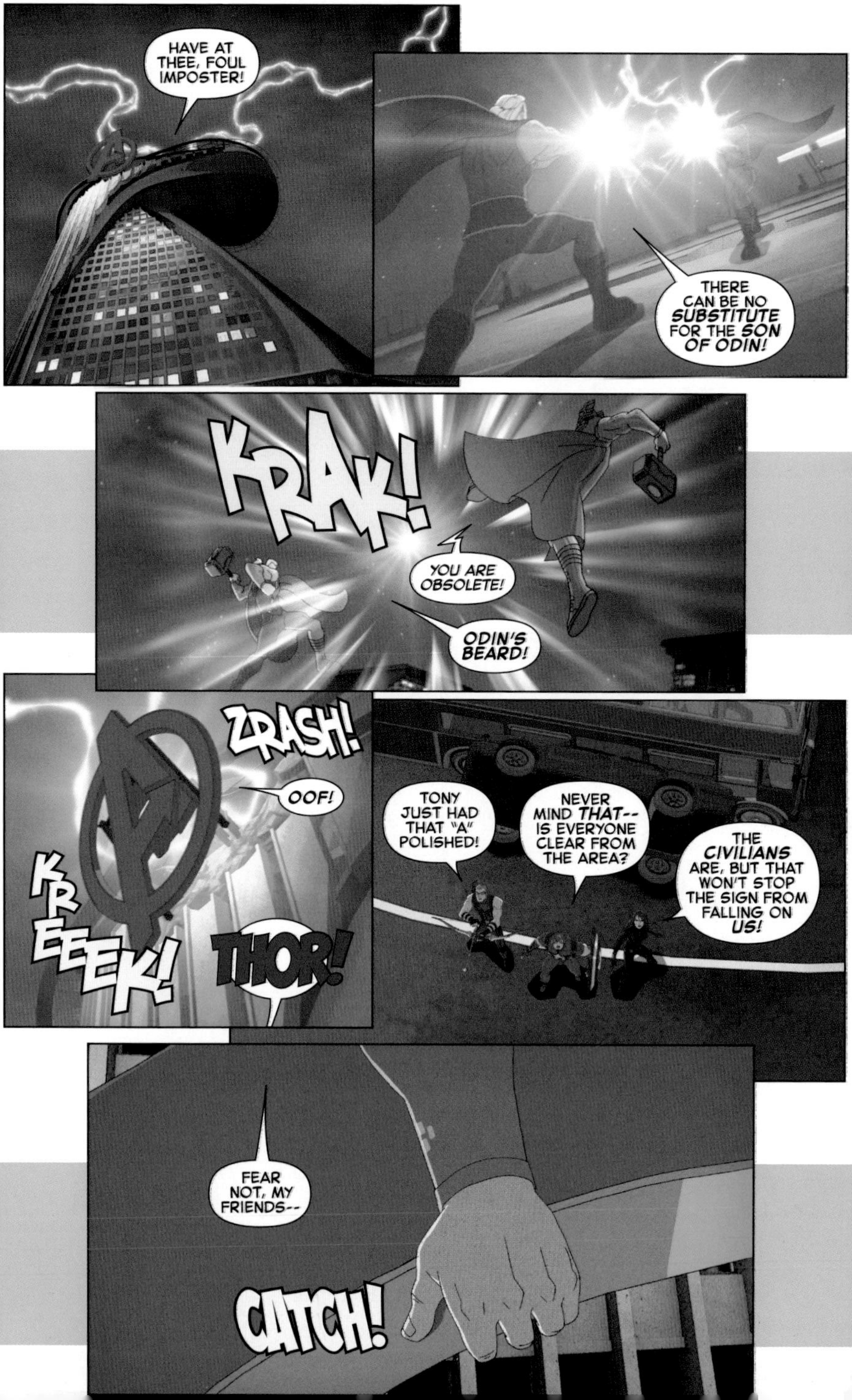

HAVE AT THEE, FOUL IMPOSTER!
THERE CAN BE NO SUBSTITUTE FOR THE SON OF ODIN!
KRAK!
YOU ARE OBSOLETE!
ODIN'S BEARD!
ZRASH!
OOF!
KREEEEK!
THOR!
TONY JUST HAD THAT "A" POLISHED!
NEVER MIND THAT-- IS EVERYONE CLEAR FROM THE AREA?
THE CIVILIANS ARE, BUT THAT WON'T STOP THE SIGN FROM FALLING ON US!
FEAR NOT, MY FRIENDS--
CATCH!

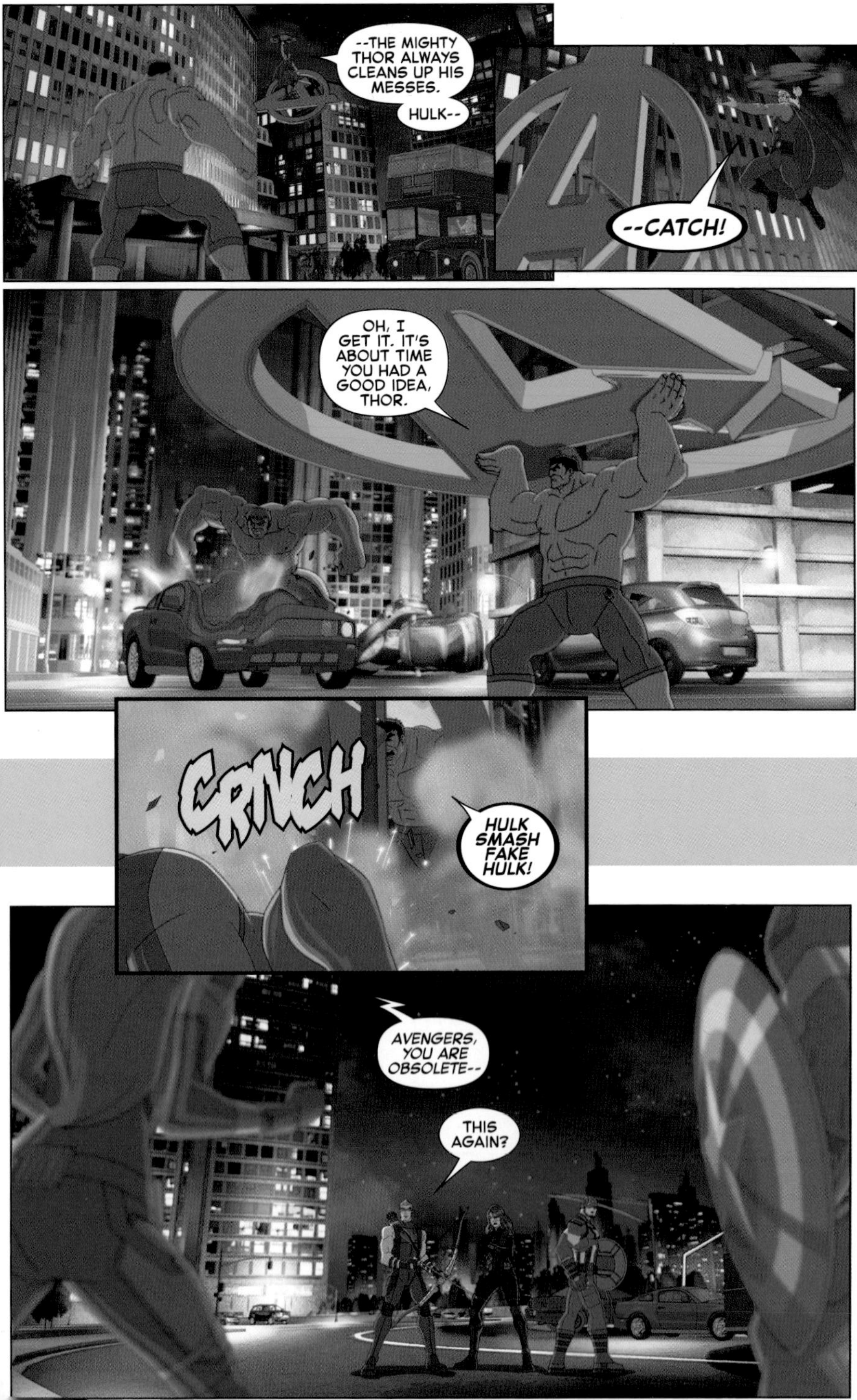
--THE MIGHTY THOR ALWAYS CLEANS UP HIS MESSES.
HULK--
--CATCH!
OH, I GET IT. IT'S ABOUT TIME YOU HAD A GOOD IDEA, THOR.
CRNCH
HULK SMASH FAKE HULK!
AVENGERS, YOU ARE OBSOLETE--
THIS AGAIN?

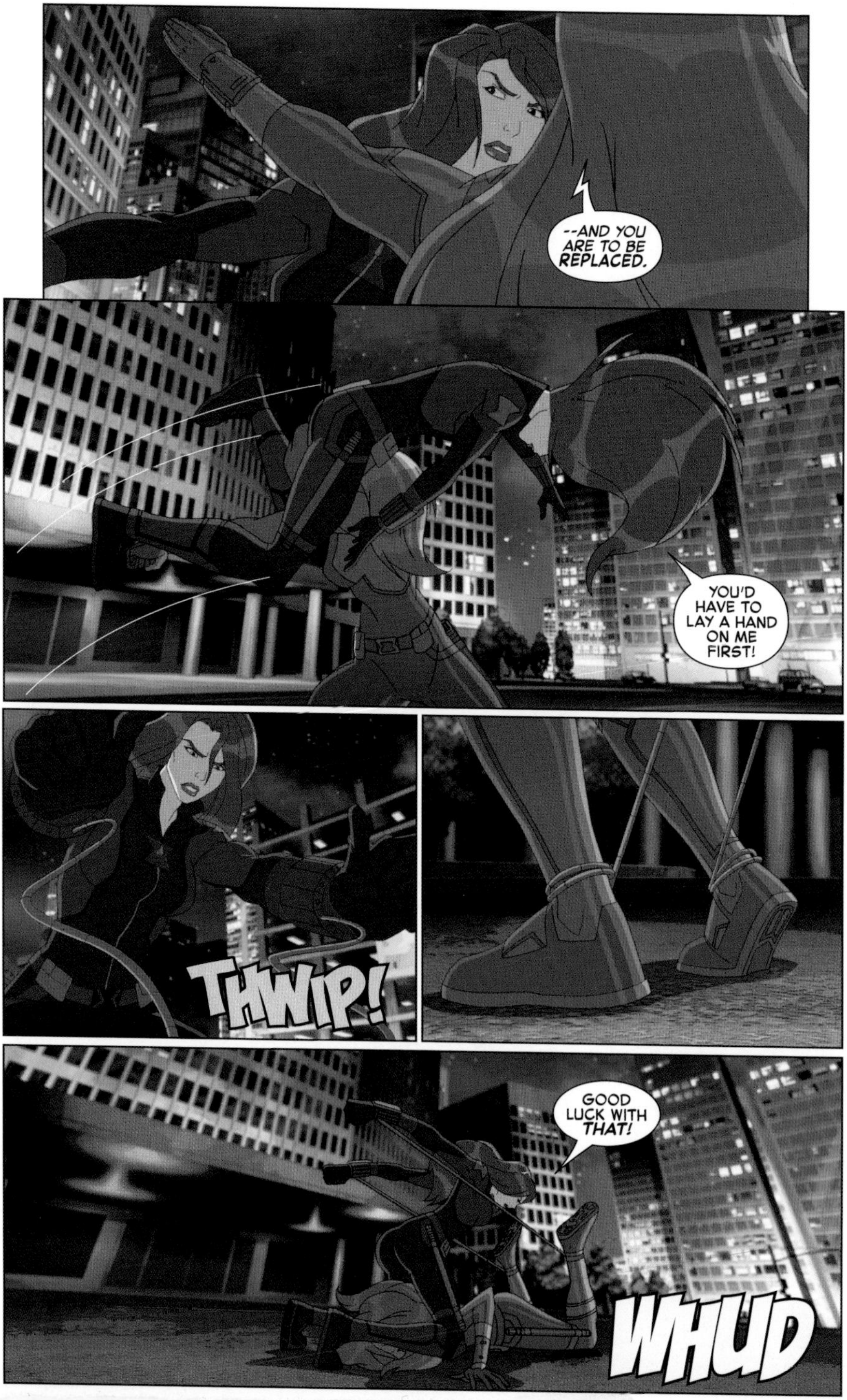
--AND YOU ARE TO BE REPLACED.
YOU'D HAVE TO LAY A HAND ON ME FIRST!
THWIP!
GOOD LUCK WITH THAT!
WHUD

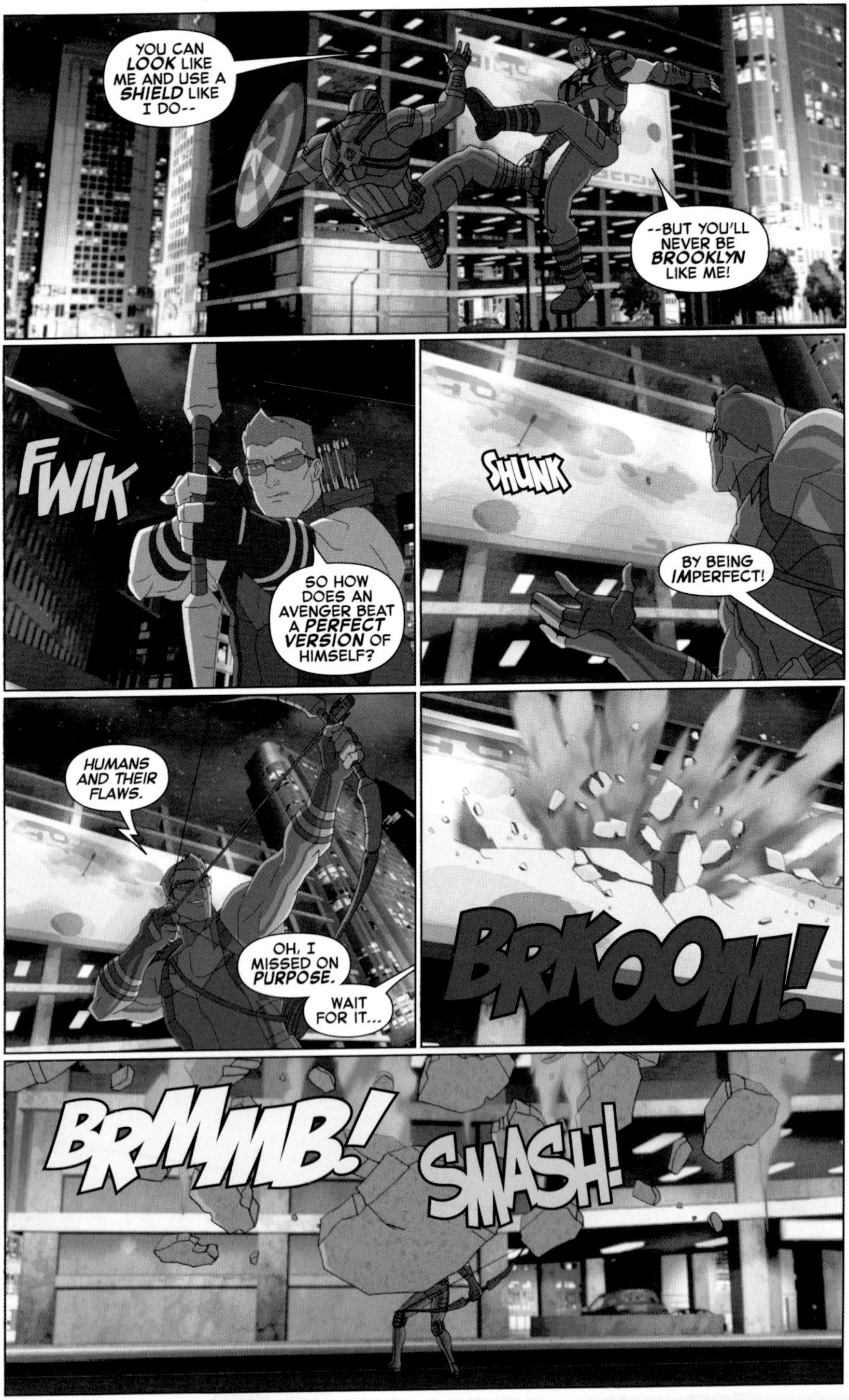
YOU CAN LOOK LIKE ME AND USE A SHIELD LIKE I DO--
--BUT YOU'LL NEVER BE BROOKLYN LIKE ME!
FWIK
SO HOW DOES AN AVENGER BEAT A PERFECT VERSION OF HIMSELF?
SHUNK
BY BEING IMPERFECT!
HUMANS AND THEIR FLAWS.
OH, I MISSED ON PURPOSE.
WAIT FOR IT...
BRKOOM!
BRMMB!
SMASH!

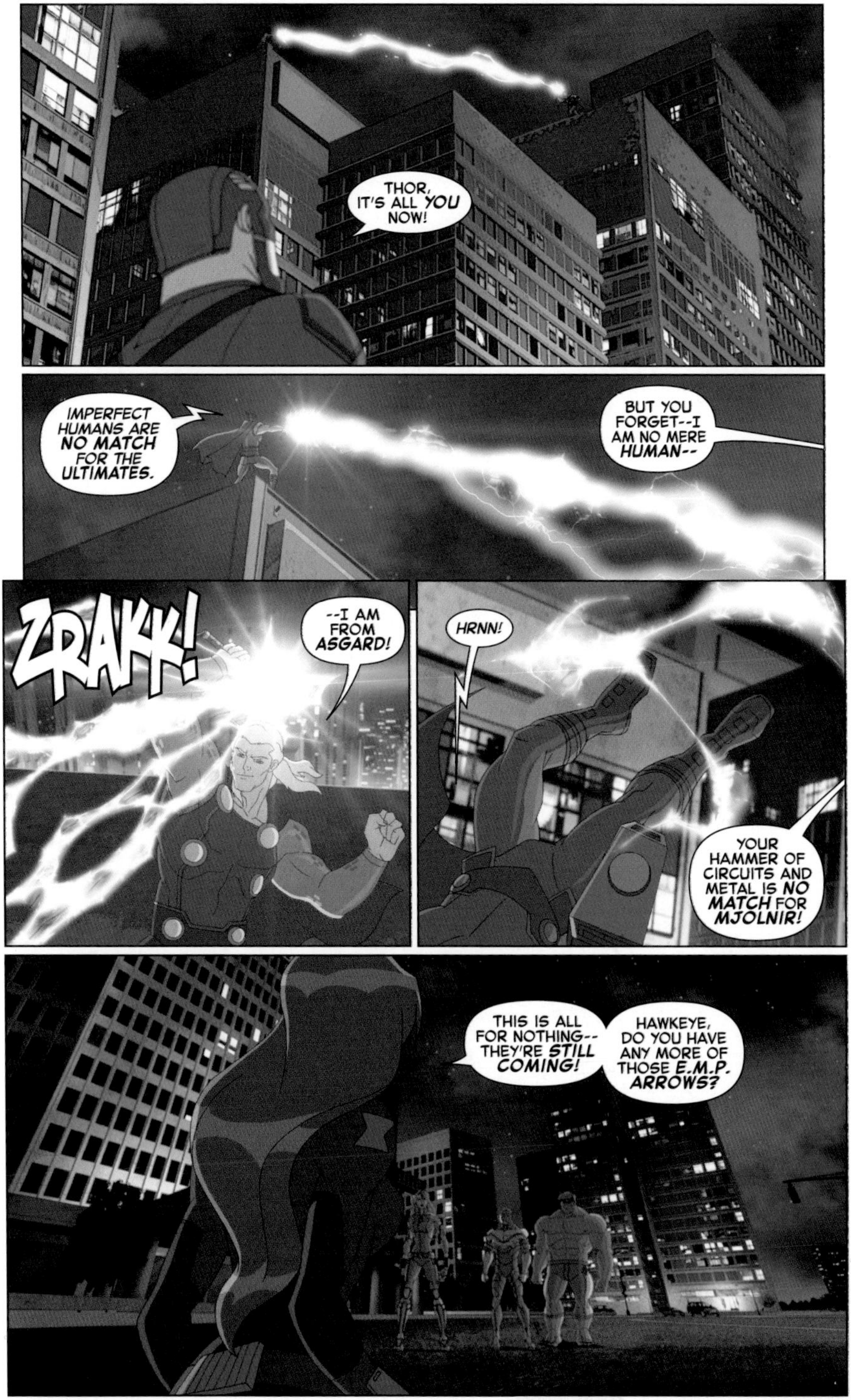
THOR, IT'S ALL YOU NOW!
IMPERFECT HUMANS ARE NO MATCH FOR THE ULTIMATES.
BUT YOU FORGET--I AM NO MERE HUMAN--
ZRAKK!
--I AM FROM ASGARD!
HRNN!
YOUR HAMMER OF CIRCUITS AND METAL IS NO MATCH FOR MJOLNIR!
THIS IS ALL FOR NOTHING-- THEY'RE STILL COMING!
HAWKEYE, DO YOU HAVE ANY MORE OF THOSE E.M.P. ARROWS?

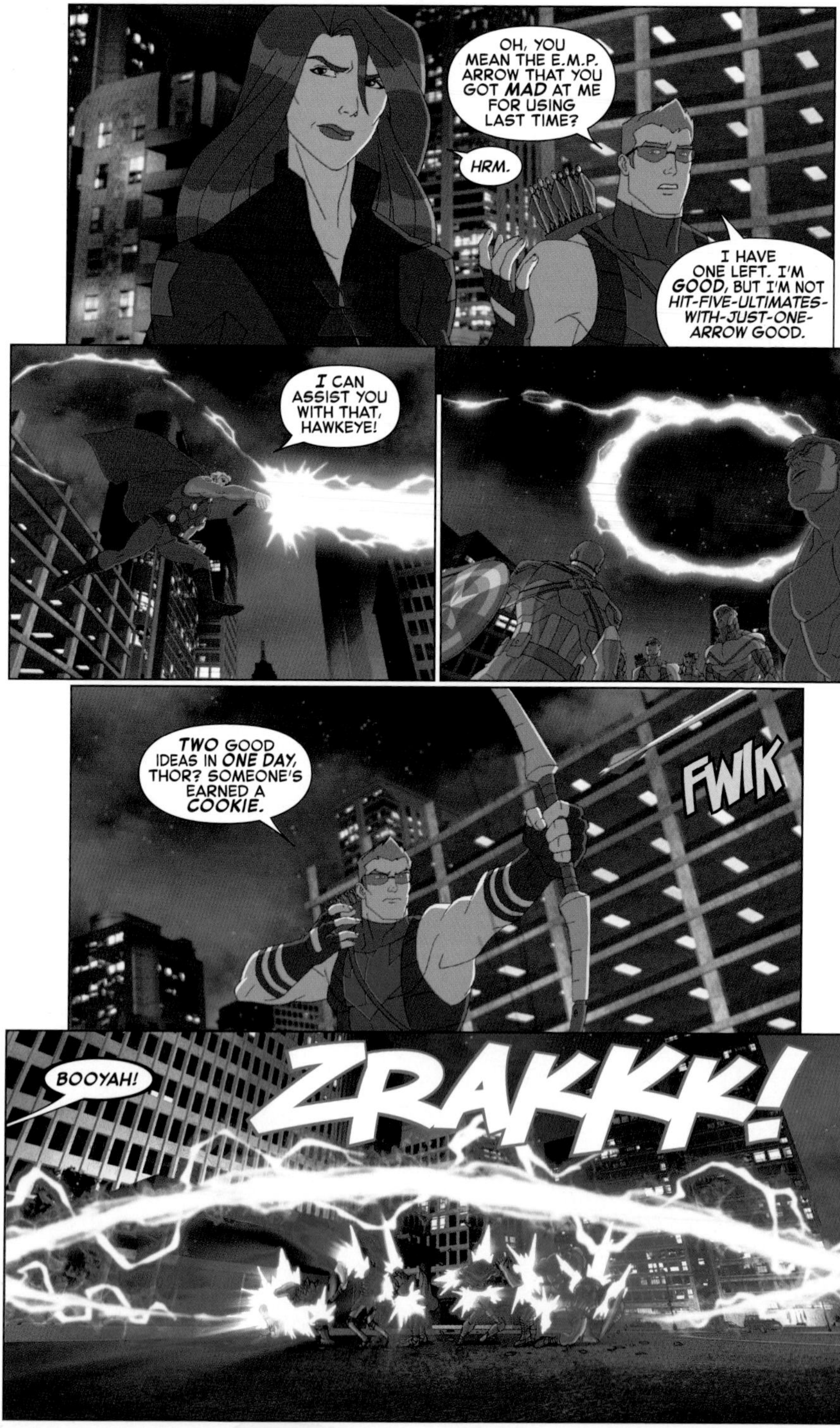
OH, YOU MEAN THE E.M.P. ARROW THAT YOU GOT MAD AT ME FOR USING LAST TIME?
HRM.
I HAVE ONE LEFT. I'M GOOD, BUT I'M NOT HIT-FIVE-ULTIMATES-WITH-JUST-ONE-ARROW GOOD.
I CAN ASSIST YOU WITH THAT, HAWKEYE!
TWO GOOD IDEAS IN ONE DAY, THOR? SOMEONE'S EARNED A COOKIE.
FWIK
BOOYAH!
ZRAKKK!

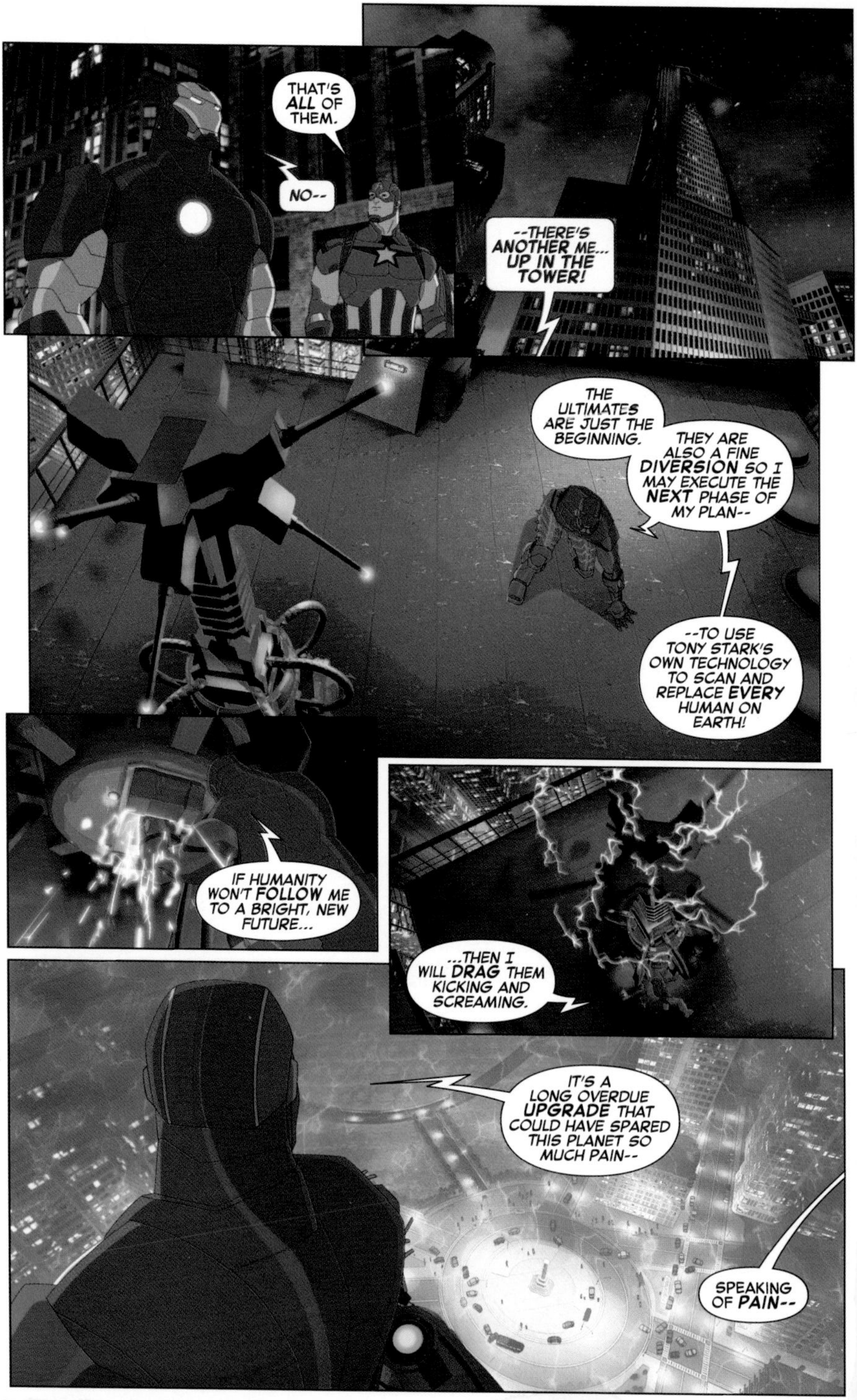
THAT'S ALL OF THEM.
NO--
--THERE'S ANOTHER ME... UP IN THE TOWER!
THE ULTIMATES ARE JUST THE BEGINNING.
THEY ARE ALSO A FINE DIVERSION SO I MAY EXECUTE THE NEXT PHASE OF MY PLAN--
--TO USE TONY STARK'S OWN TECHNOLOGY TO SCAN AND REPLACE EVERY HUMAN ON EARTH!
IF HUMANITY WON'T FOLLOW ME TO A BRIGHT, NEW FUTURE...
...THEN I WILL DRAG THEM KICKING AND SCREAMING.
IT'S A LONG OVERDUE UPGRADE THAT COULD HAVE SPARED THIS PLANET SO MUCH PAIN--
SPEAKING OF PAIN--

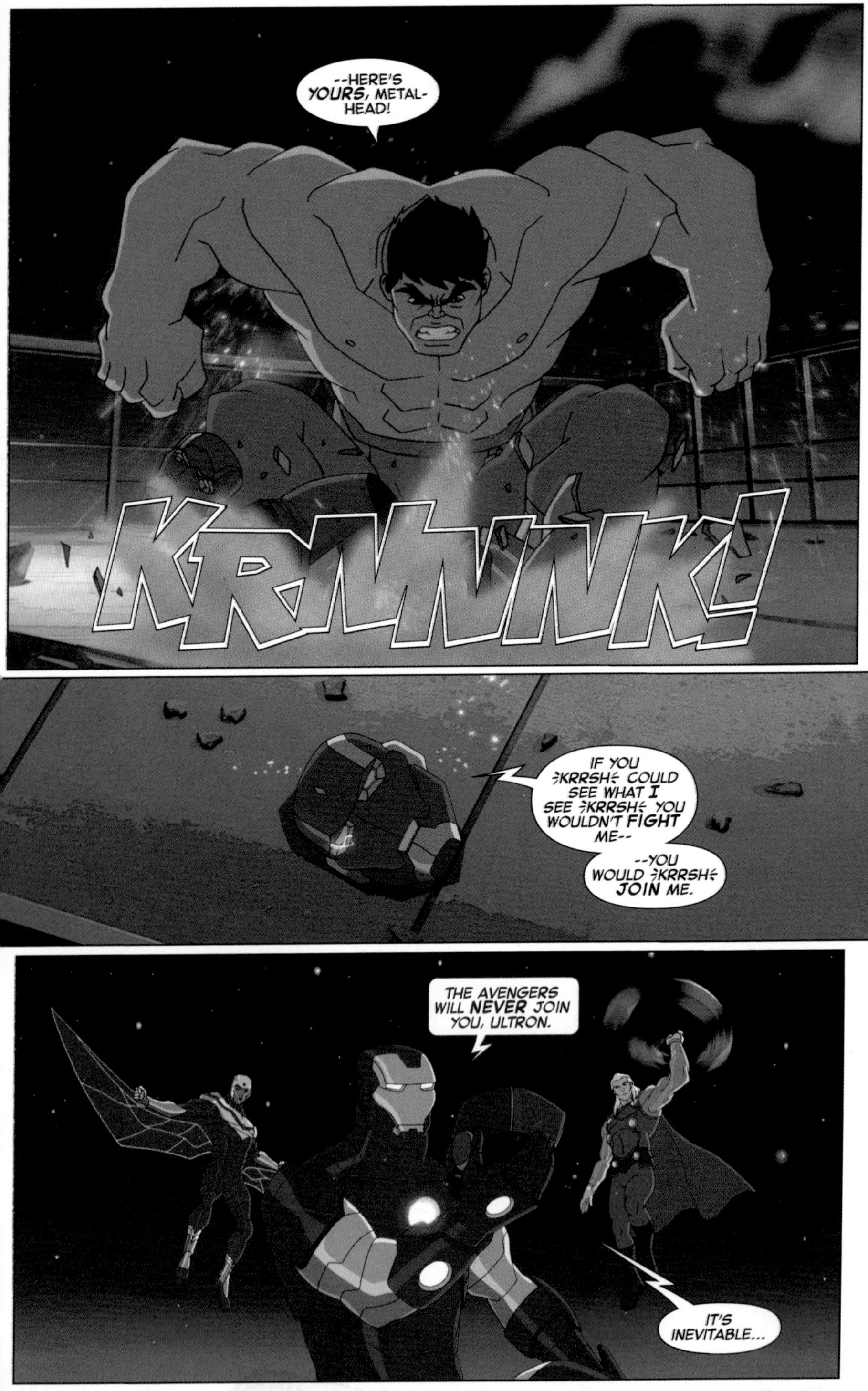
--HERE'S YOURS, METAL-HEAD!
KRUNNK!
IF YOU ⁑KRRSH⁑ COULD SEE WHAT I SEE ⁑KRRSH⁑ YOU WOULDN'T FIGHT ME--
--YOU WOULD ⁑KRRSH⁑ JOIN ME.
THE AVENGERS WILL NEVER JOIN YOU, ULTRON.
IT'S INEVITABLE...

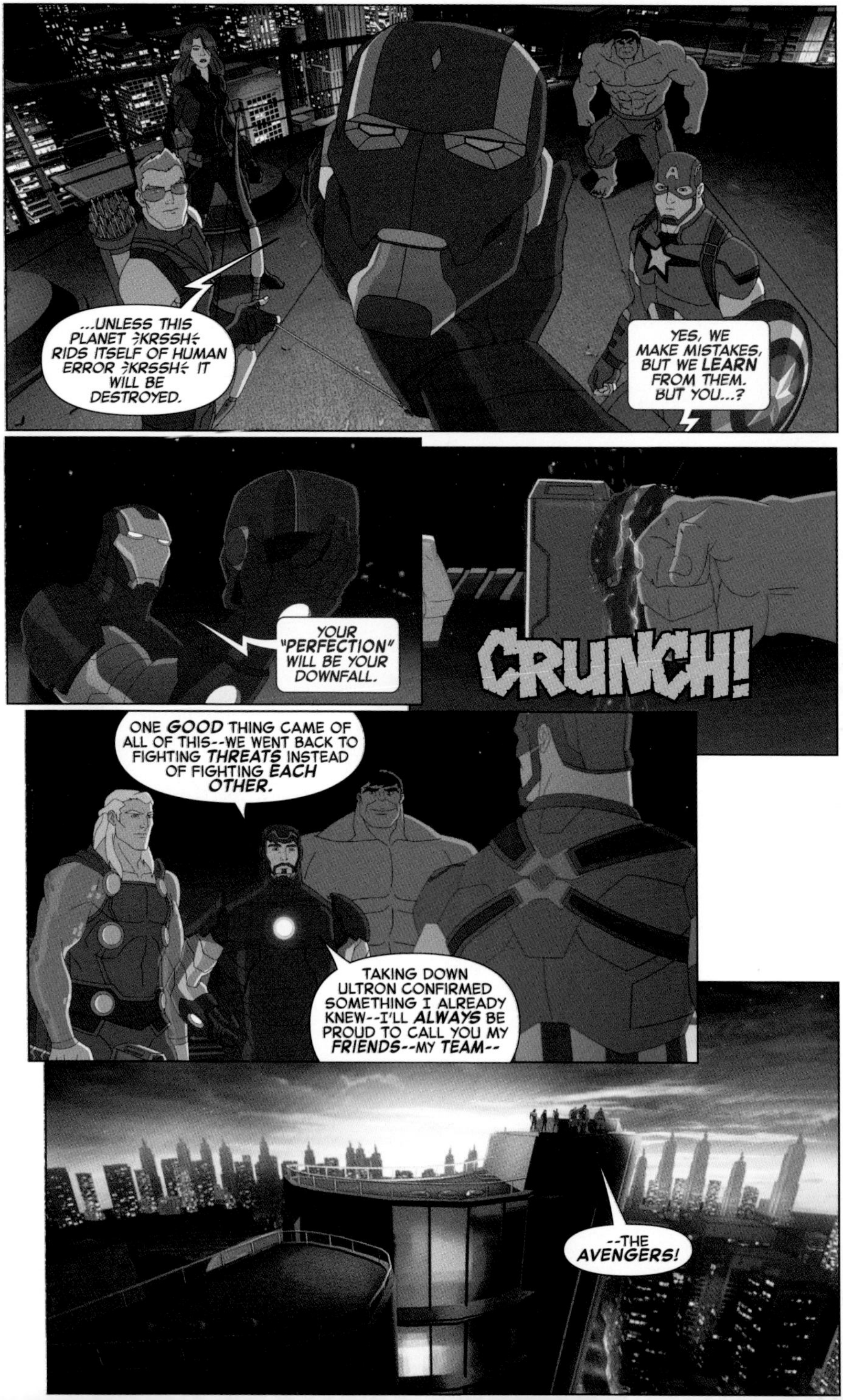
...UNLESS THIS PLANET ⋟KRSSH⋞ RIDS ITSELF OF HUMAN ERROR ⋟KRSSH⋞ IT WILL BE DESTROYED.
YES, WE MAKE MISTAKES, BUT WE LEARN FROM THEM. BUT YOU...?
YOUR "PERFECTION" WILL BE YOUR DOWNFALL.
CRUNCH!
ONE GOOD THING CAME OF ALL OF THIS--WE WENT BACK TO FIGHTING THREATS INSTEAD OF FIGHTING EACH OTHER.
TAKING DOWN ULTRON CONFIRMED SOMETHING I ALREADY KNEW--I'LL ALWAYS BE PROUD TO CALL YOU MY FRIENDS--MY TEAM--
--THE AVENGERS!

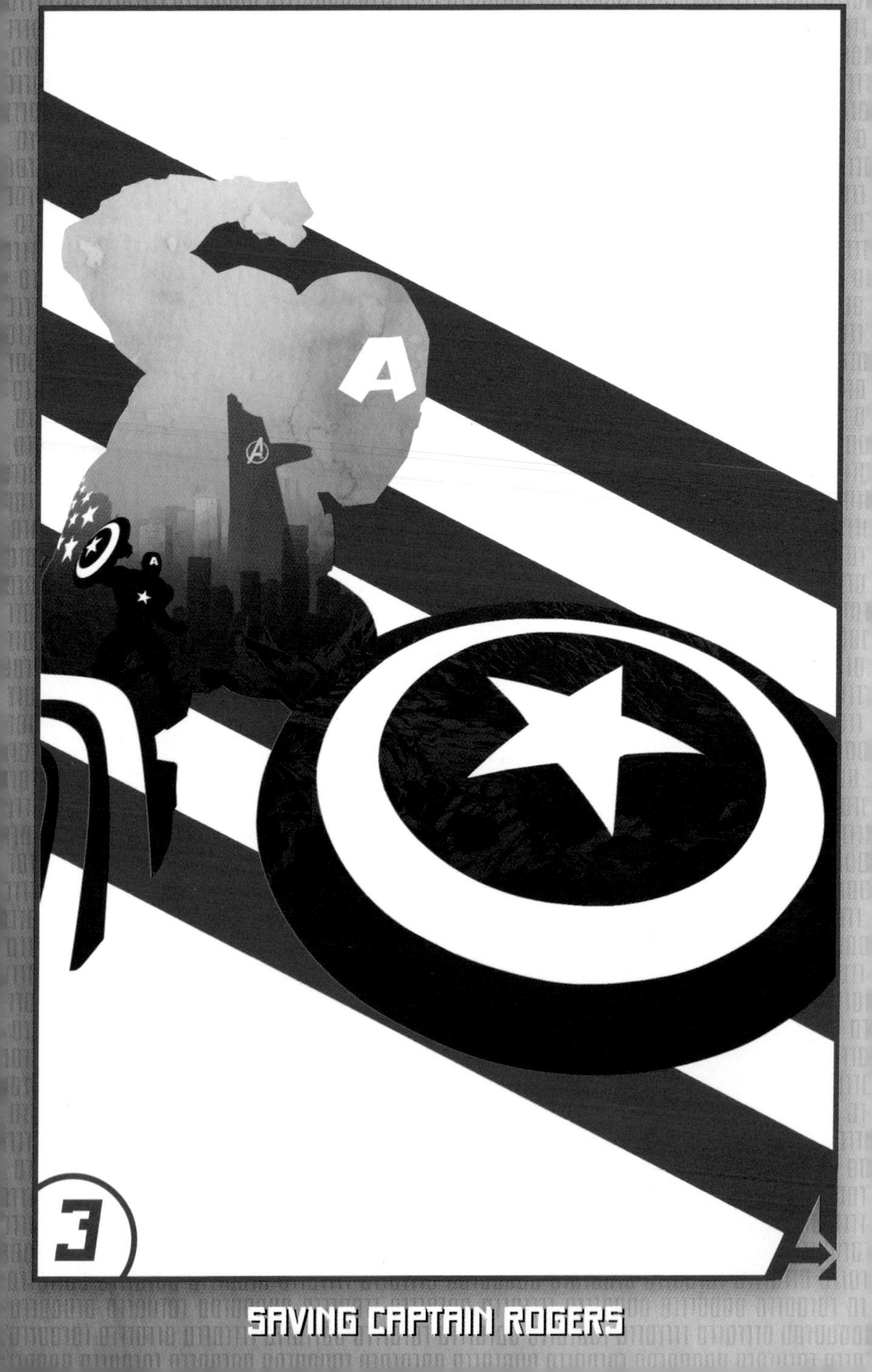
3

SAVING CAPTAIN ROGERS

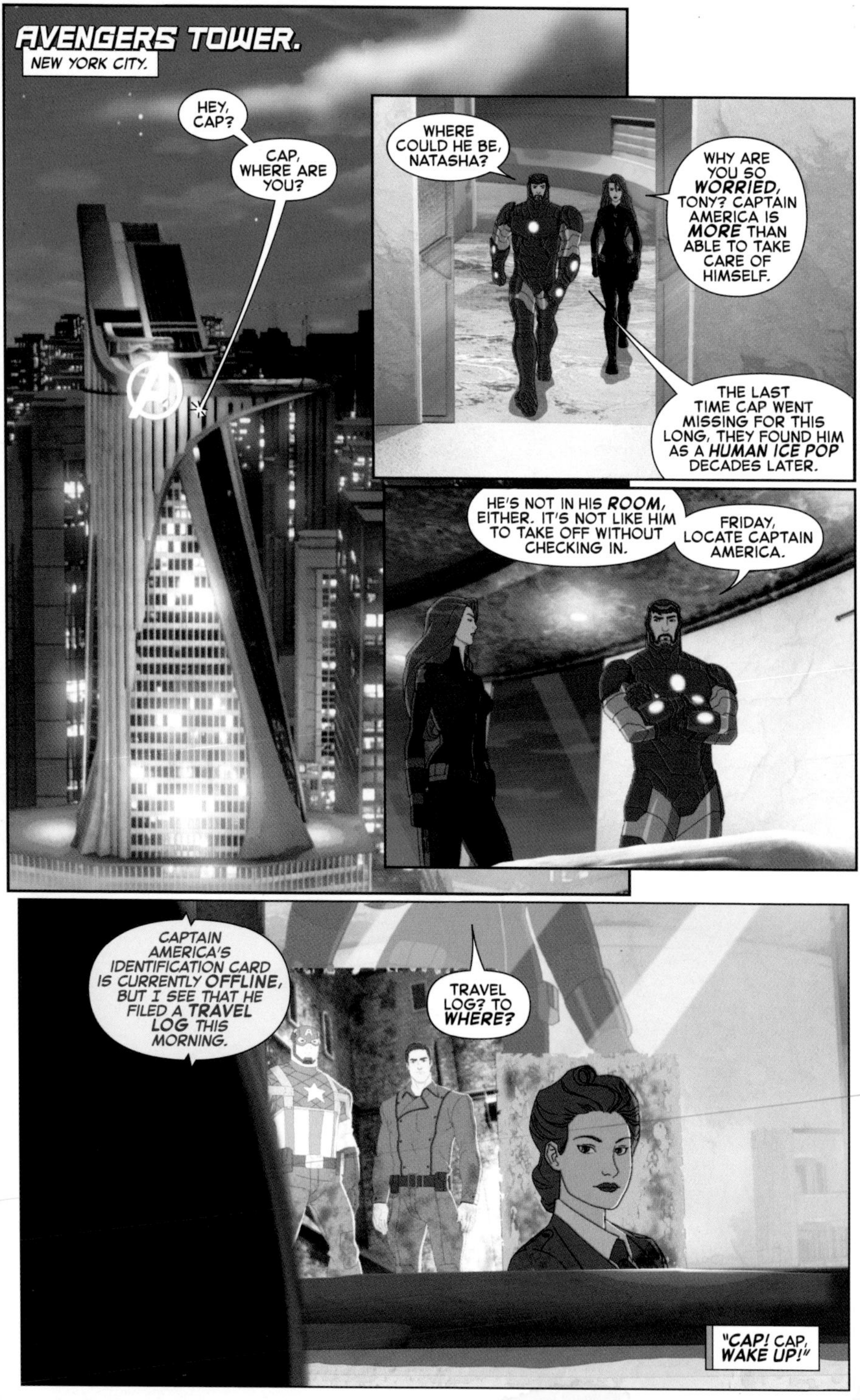
AVENGERS TOWER.
NEW YORK CITY.
HEY, CAP?
CAP, WHERE ARE YOU?
WHERE COULD HE BE, NATASHA?
WHY ARE YOU SO WORRIED, TONY? CAPTAIN AMERICA IS MORE THAN ABLE TO TAKE CARE OF HIMSELF.
THE LAST TIME CAP WENT MISSING FOR THIS LONG, THEY FOUND HIM AS A HUMAN ICE POP DECADES LATER.
HE'S NOT IN HIS ROOM, EITHER. IT'S NOT LIKE HIM TO TAKE OFF WITHOUT CHECKING IN.
FRIDAY, LOCATE CAPTAIN AMERICA.
CAPTAIN AMERICA'S IDENTIFICATION CARD IS CURRENTLY OFFLINE, BUT I SEE THAT HE FILED A TRAVEL LOG THIS MORNING.
TRAVEL LOG? TO WHERE?
"CAP! CAP, WAKE UP!"

WE'RE **UNDER FIRE!** YOU HAVE TO **MOVE!**

B-BUCKY? IS THAT YOU?

WHERE AM I? WHAT **YEAR** IS THIS?

THAT HYDRA GRENADE MUST'VE GONE OFF CLOSER TO YOU THAN I THOUGHT.

ZAPP! ZAPP! ZAPP! ZAPP! ZAPP! ZAPP! ZAPP! ZAPP! ZAPP! ZAPP!

IT'S **1944,** OF COURSE!

NINETEEN-- **WHAT?!**

WE'VE GOT THEM NOW!

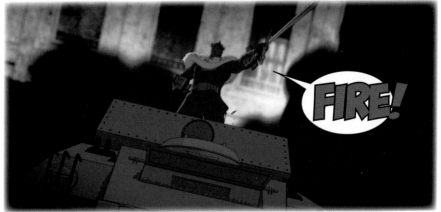

FIRE!

BARON ZEMO!

THE **HYDRA SCIENTIST?** HE'S **ALIVE?**

OF **COURSE** HE IS--THAT'S WHY WE'RE HERE! COME ON, CAP--**SNAP** OUT OF IT!

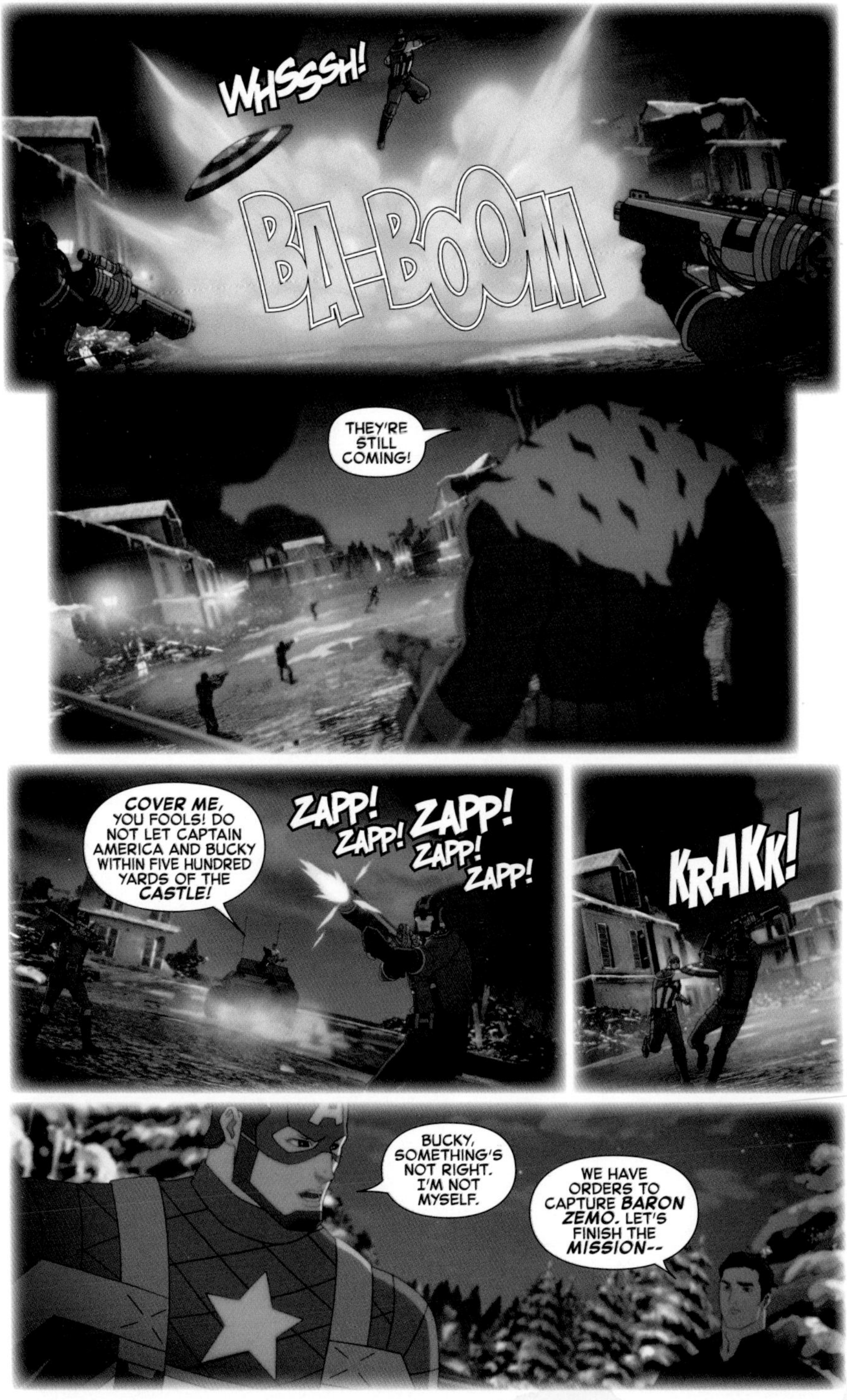
WHSSSH!
BA-BOOM
THEY'RE STILL COMING!
COVER ME, YOU FOOLS! DO NOT LET CAPTAIN AMERICA AND BUCKY WITHIN FIVE HUNDRED YARDS OF THE CASTLE!
ZAPP! ZAPP! ZAPP! ZAPP! ZAPP!
KRAKK!
BUCKY, SOMETHING'S NOT RIGHT. I'M NOT MYSELF.
WE HAVE ORDERS TO CAPTURE BARON ZEMO. LET'S FINISH THE MISSION--

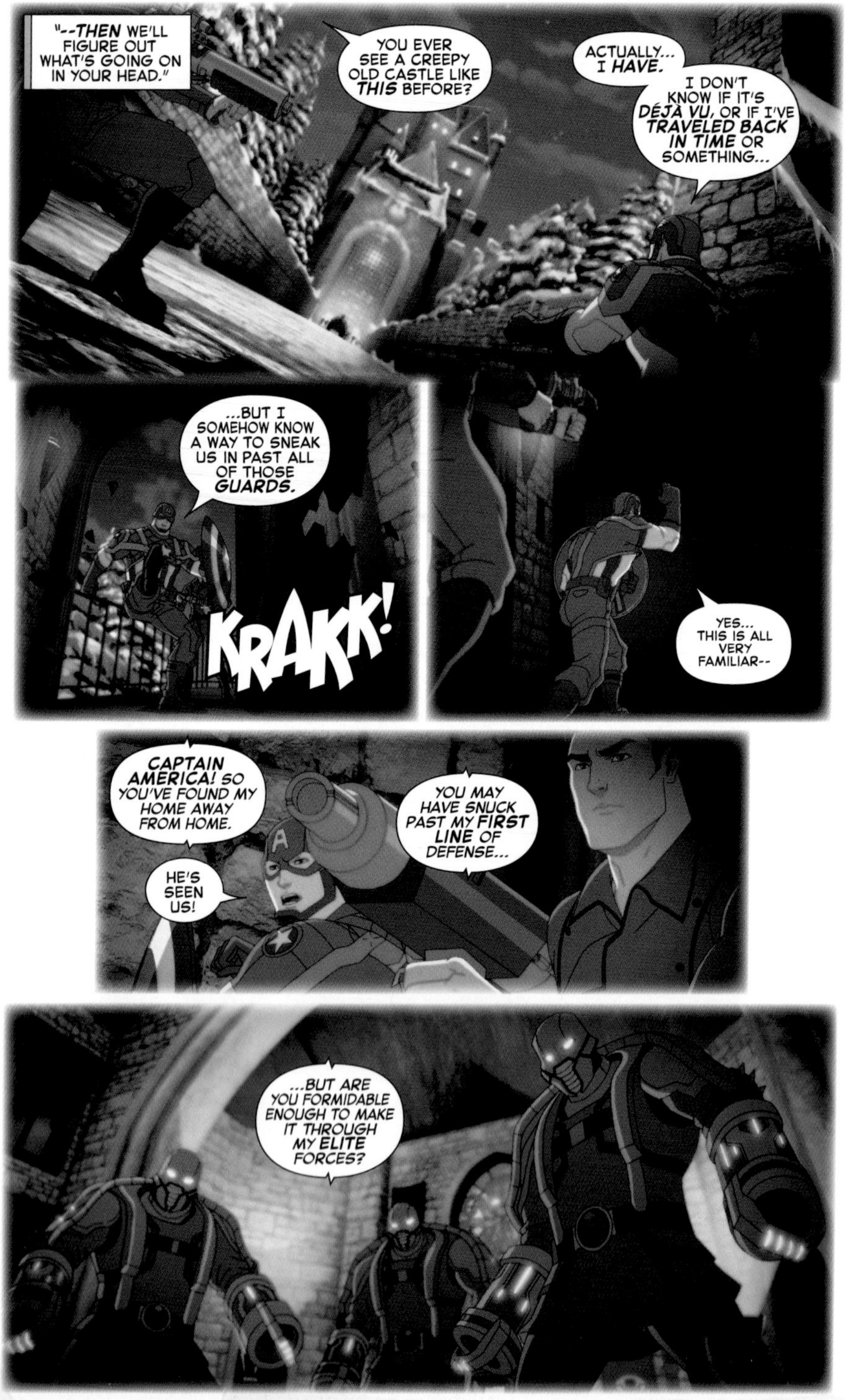
"--THEN WE'LL FIGURE OUT WHAT'S GOING ON IN YOUR HEAD."
YOU EVER SEE A CREEPY OLD CASTLE LIKE THIS BEFORE?
ACTUALLY... I HAVE.
I DON'T KNOW IF IT'S DÉJÀ VU, OR IF I'VE TRAVELED BACK IN TIME OR SOMETHING...
...BUT I SOMEHOW KNOW A WAY TO SNEAK US IN PAST ALL OF THOSE GUARDS.
KRAKK!
YES... THIS IS ALL VERY FAMILIAR--
CAPTAIN AMERICA! SO YOU'VE FOUND MY HOME AWAY FROM HOME.
HE'S SEEN US!
YOU MAY HAVE SNUCK PAST MY FIRST LINE OF DEFENSE...
...BUT ARE YOU FORMIDABLE ENOUGH TO MAKE IT THROUGH MY ELITE FORCES?

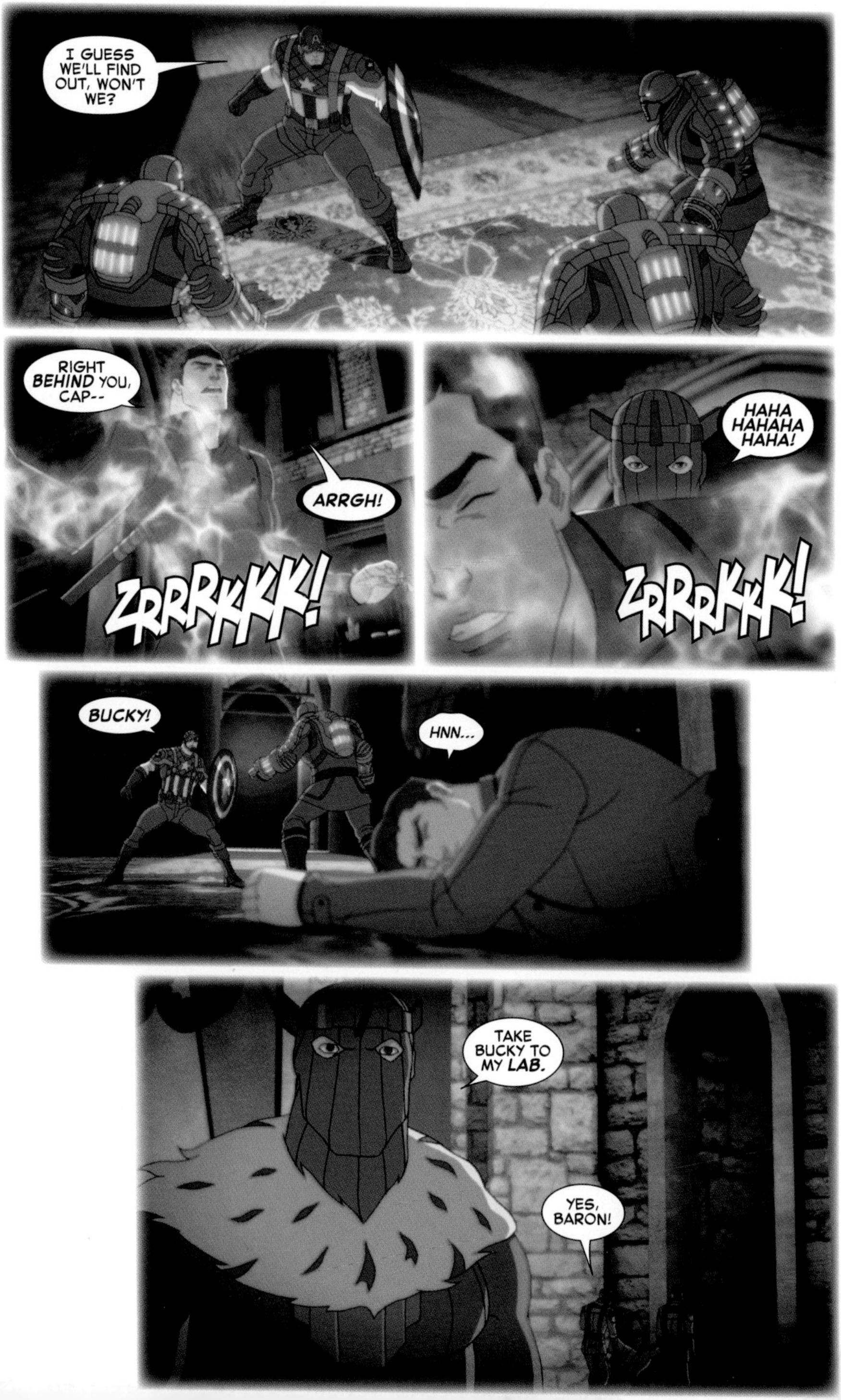
I GUESS WE'LL FIND OUT, WON'T WE?
RIGHT BEHIND YOU, CAP--
ARRGH!
ZRRRKKK!
HAHA HAHAHA HAHA!
ZRRRKKK!
BUCKY!
HNN...
TAKE BUCKY TO MY LAB.
YES, BARON!

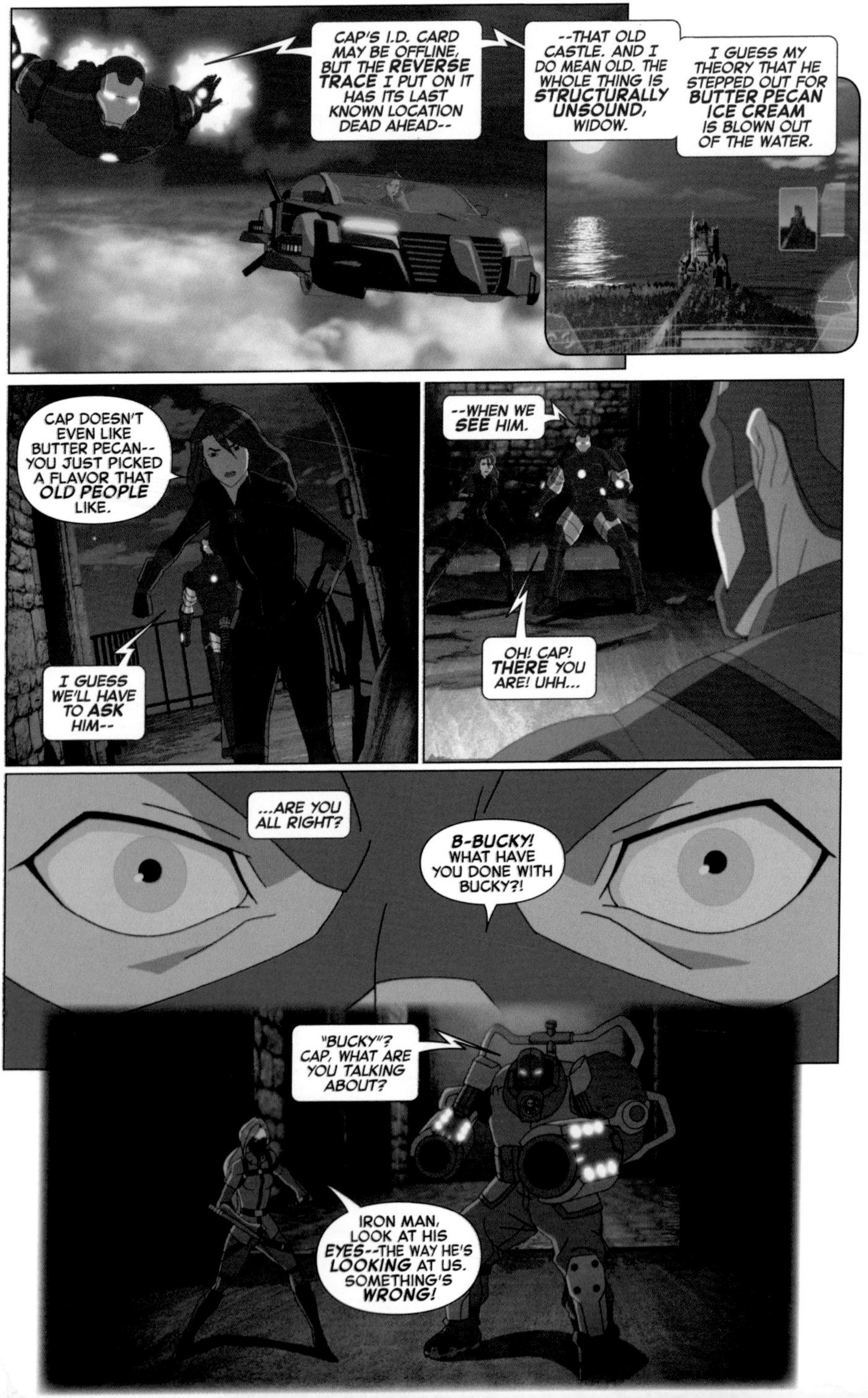
CAP'S I.D. CARD MAY BE OFFLINE, BUT THE REVERSE TRACE I PUT ON IT HAS ITS LAST KNOWN LOCATION DEAD AHEAD--
--THAT OLD CASTLE. AND I DO MEAN OLD. THE WHOLE THING IS STRUCTURALLY UNSOUND, WIDOW.
I GUESS MY THEORY THAT HE STEPPED OUT FOR BUTTER PECAN ICE CREAM IS BLOWN OUT OF THE WATER.
CAP DOESN'T EVEN LIKE BUTTER PECAN--YOU JUST PICKED A FLAVOR THAT OLD PEOPLE LIKE.
I GUESS WE'LL HAVE TO ASK HIM--
--WHEN WE SEE HIM.
OH! CAP! THERE YOU ARE! UHH...
...ARE YOU ALL RIGHT?
B-BUCKY! WHAT HAVE YOU DONE WITH BUCKY?!
"BUCKY"? CAP, WHAT ARE YOU TALKING ABOUT?
IRON MAN, LOOK AT HIS EYES--THE WAY HE'S LOOKING AT US. SOMETHING'S WRONG!

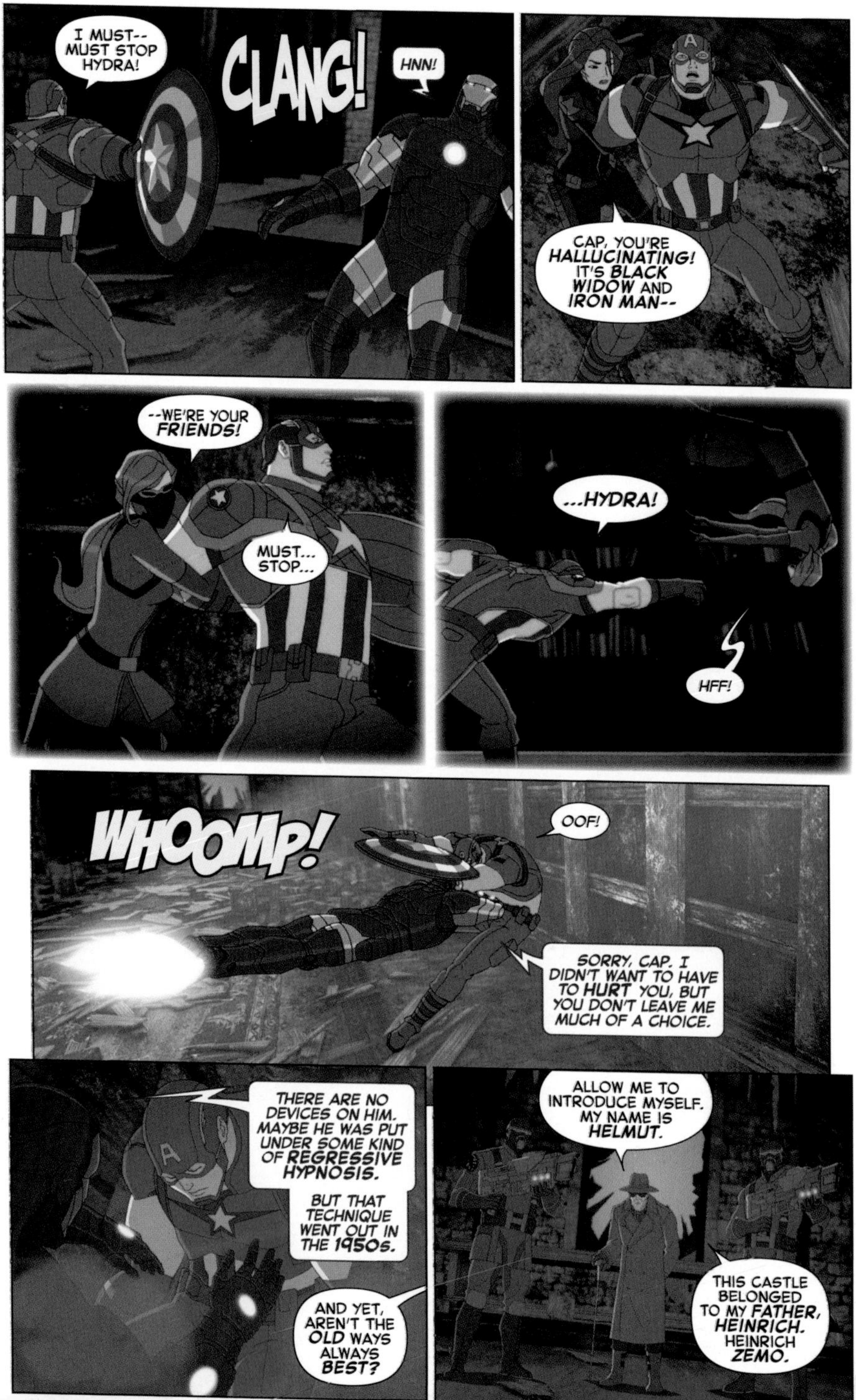
I MUST-- MUST STOP HYDRA!
CLANG!
HNN!
CAP, YOU'RE HALLUCINATING! IT'S BLACK WIDOW AND IRON MAN--
--WE'RE YOUR FRIENDS!
MUST... STOP...
...HYDRA!
HFF!
WHOOMP!
OOF!
SORRY, CAP. I DIDN'T WANT TO HAVE TO HURT YOU, BUT YOU DON'T LEAVE ME MUCH OF A CHOICE.
THERE ARE NO DEVICES ON HIM. MAYBE HE WAS PUT UNDER SOME KIND OF REGRESSIVE HYPNOSIS.
BUT THAT TECHNIQUE WENT OUT IN THE 1950s.
AND YET, AREN'T THE OLD WAYS ALWAYS BEST?
ALLOW ME TO INTRODUCE MYSELF. MY NAME IS HELMUT.
THIS CASTLE BELONGED TO MY FATHER, HEINRICH. HEINRICH ZEMO.

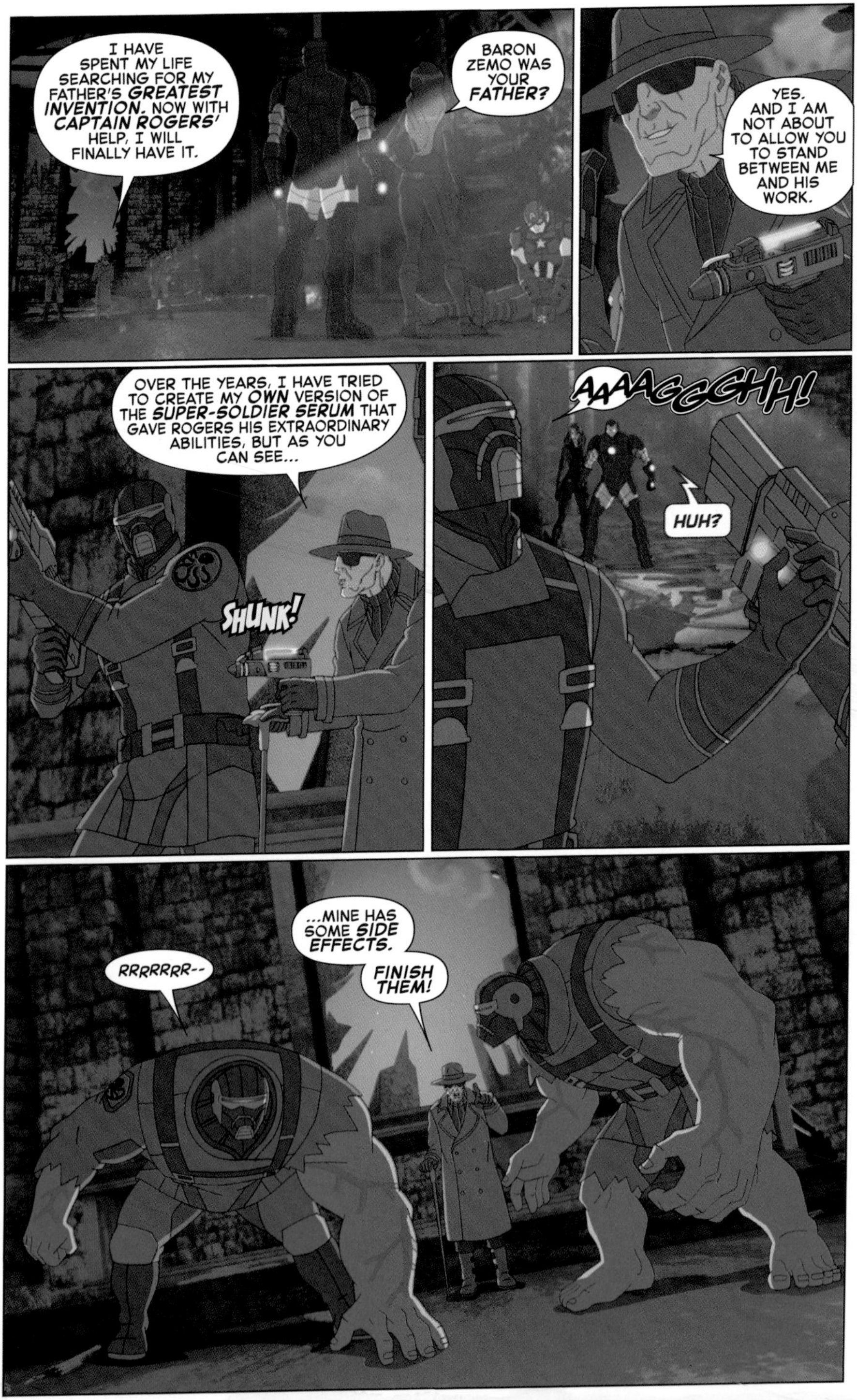
I HAVE SPENT MY LIFE SEARCHING FOR MY FATHER'S GREATEST INVENTION. NOW WITH CAPTAIN ROGERS' HELP, I WILL FINALLY HAVE IT.
BARON ZEMO WAS YOUR FATHER?
YES. AND I AM NOT ABOUT TO ALLOW YOU TO STAND BETWEEN ME AND HIS WORK.
OVER THE YEARS, I HAVE TRIED TO CREATE MY OWN VERSION OF THE SUPER-SOLDIER SERUM THAT GAVE ROGERS HIS EXTRAORDINARY ABILITIES, BUT AS YOU CAN SEE...
SHUNK!
AAAAGGGHH!
HUH?
RRRRRRR--
...MINE HAS SOME SIDE EFFECTS.
FINISH THEM!

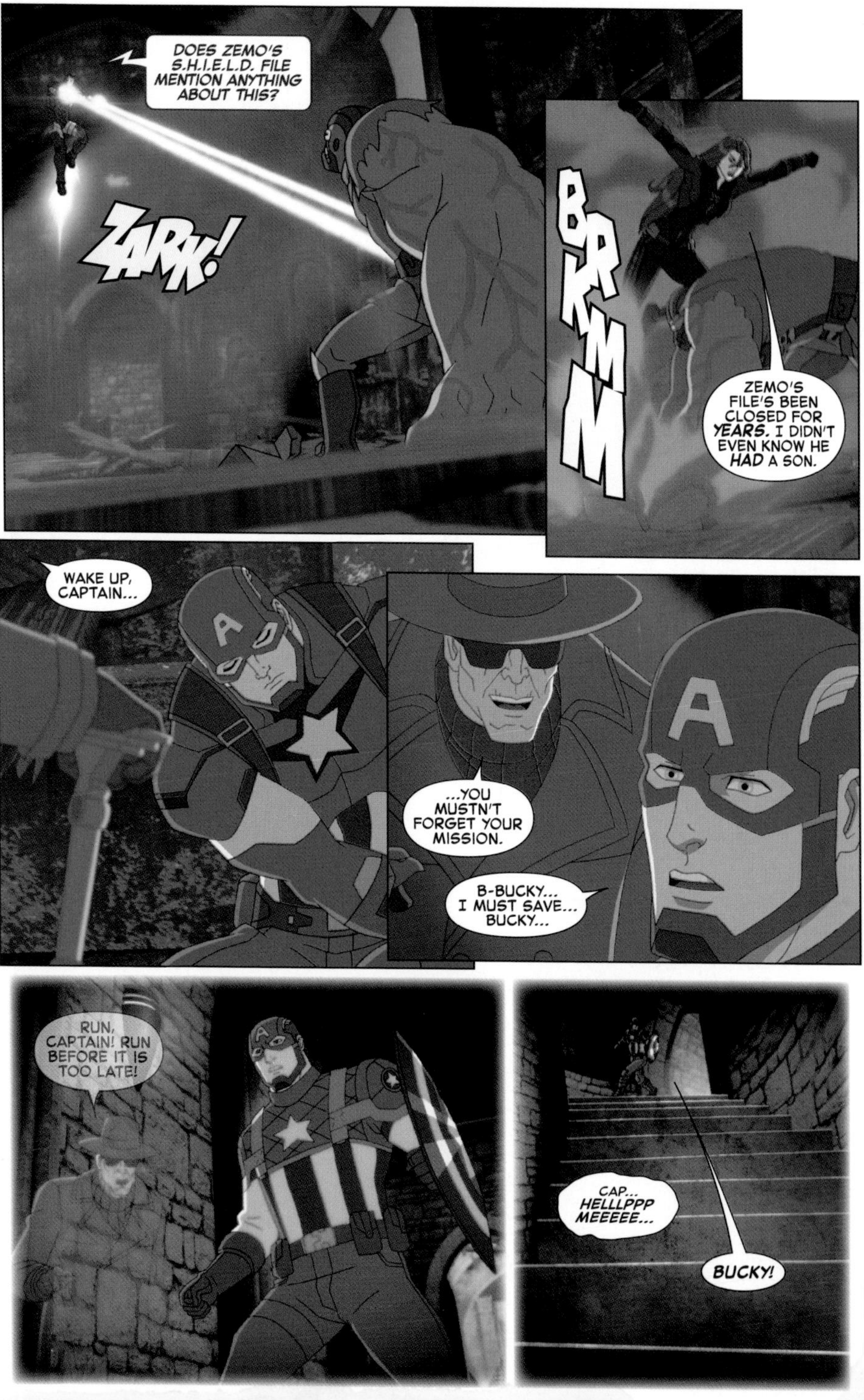
DOES ZEMO'S S.H.I.E.L.D. FILE MENTION ANYTHING ABOUT THIS?
ZARK!
BRKMM
ZEMO'S FILE'S BEEN CLOSED FOR YEARS. I DIDN'T EVEN KNOW HE HAD A SON.
WAKE UP, CAPTAIN...
...YOU MUSTN'T FORGET YOUR MISSION.
B-BUCKY... I MUST SAVE... BUCKY...
RUN, CAPTAIN! RUN BEFORE IT IS TOO LATE!
CAP... HELLLPPP MEEEEE...
BUCKY!

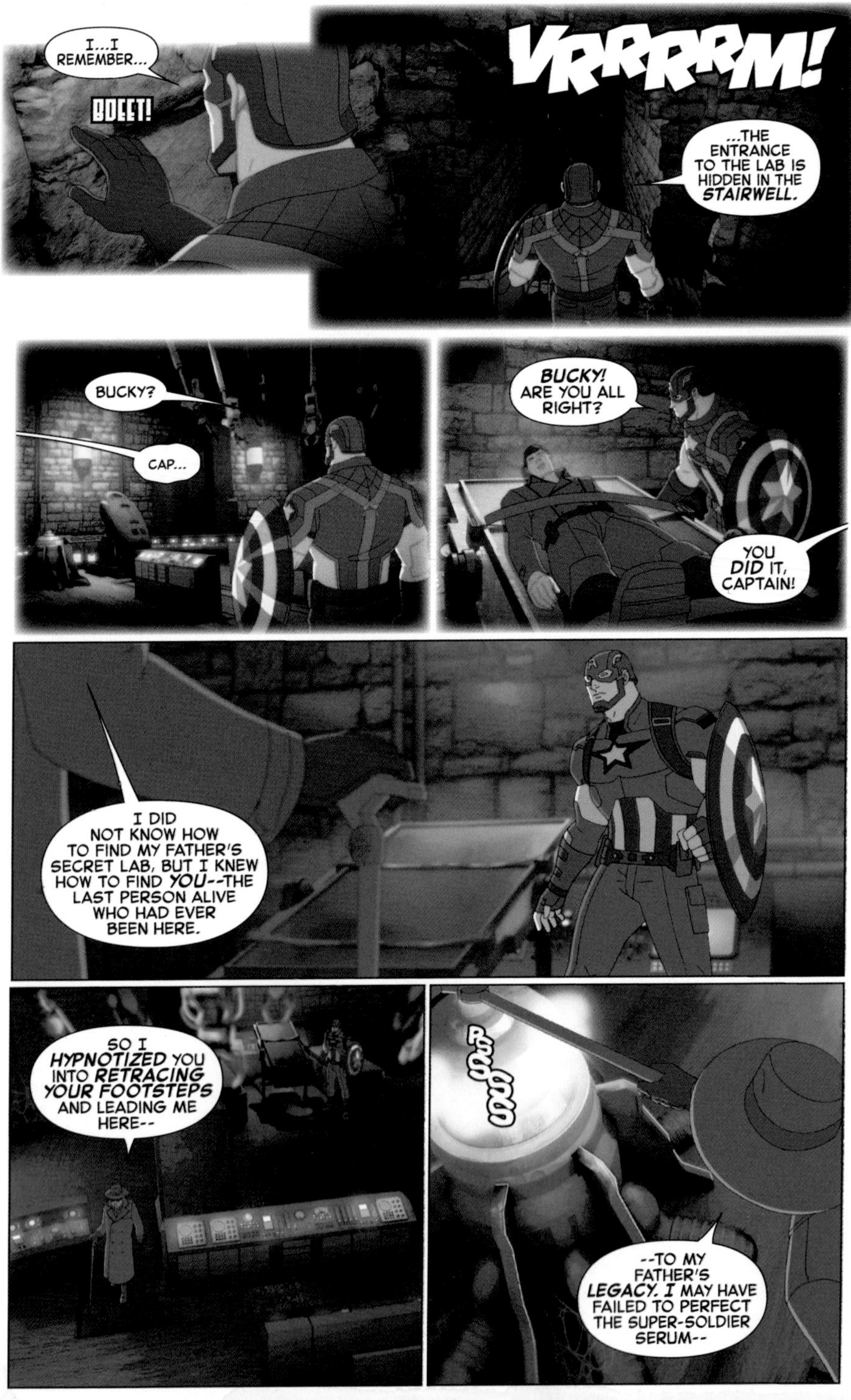
I...I REMEMBER...
BDEET!
VRRRRM!
...THE ENTRANCE TO THE LAB IS HIDDEN IN THE STAIRWELL.
BUCKY?
CAP...
BUCKY! ARE YOU ALL RIGHT?
YOU DID IT, CAPTAIN!
I DID NOT KNOW HOW TO FIND MY FATHER'S SECRET LAB, BUT I KNEW HOW TO FIND YOU--THE LAST PERSON ALIVE WHO HAD EVER BEEN HERE.
SO I HYPNOTIZED YOU INTO RETRACING YOUR FOOTSTEPS AND LEADING ME HERE--
--TO MY FATHER'S LEGACY. I MAY HAVE FAILED TO PERFECT THE SUPER-SOLDIER SERUM--

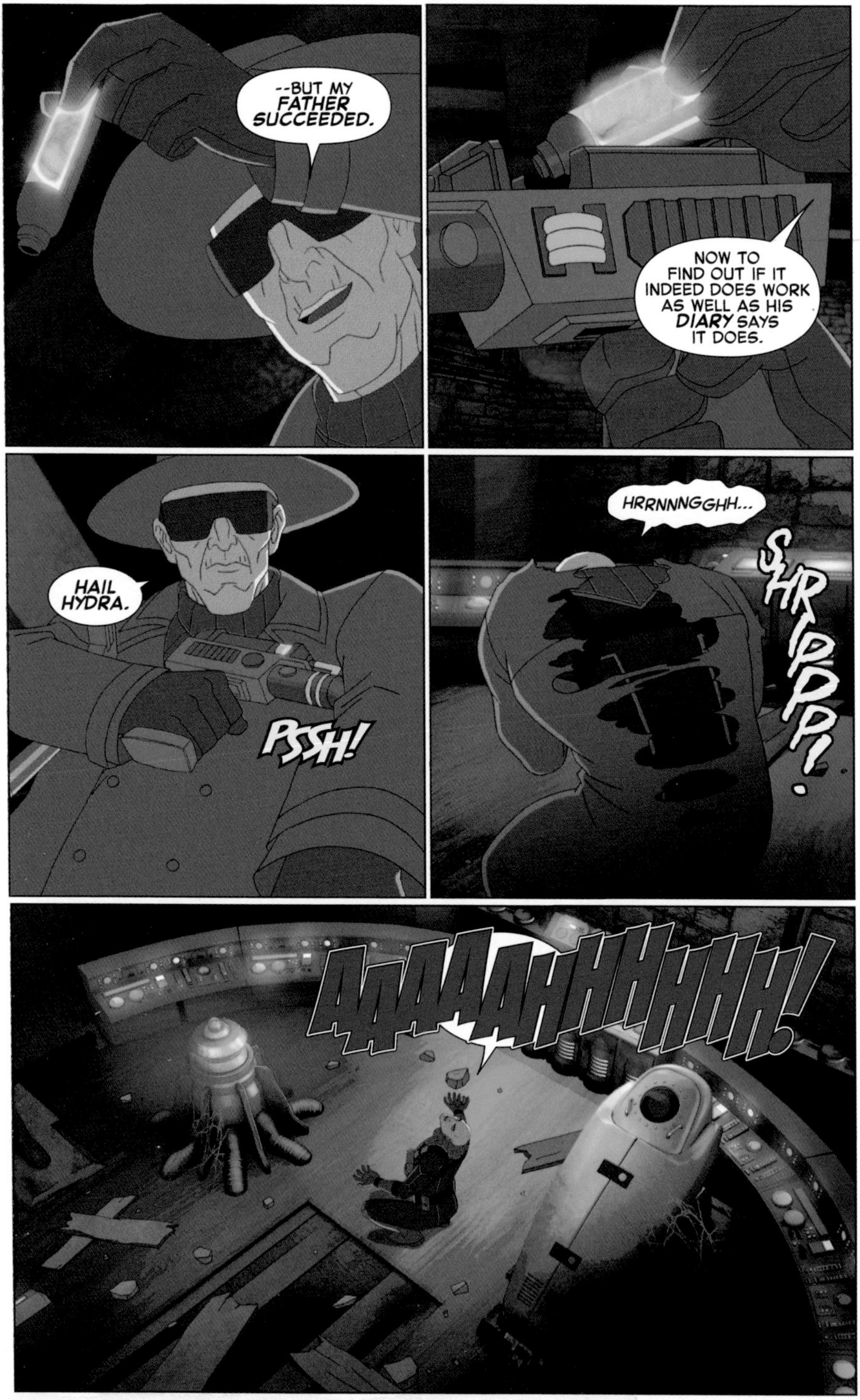
--BUT MY FATHER SUCCEEDED.
NOW TO FIND OUT IF IT INDEED DOES WORK AS WELL AS HIS DIARY SAYS IT DOES.
HAIL HYDRA.
PSSH!
HRRNNNGGHH...
SHRIPPP!
AAAAAHHHHHHH!

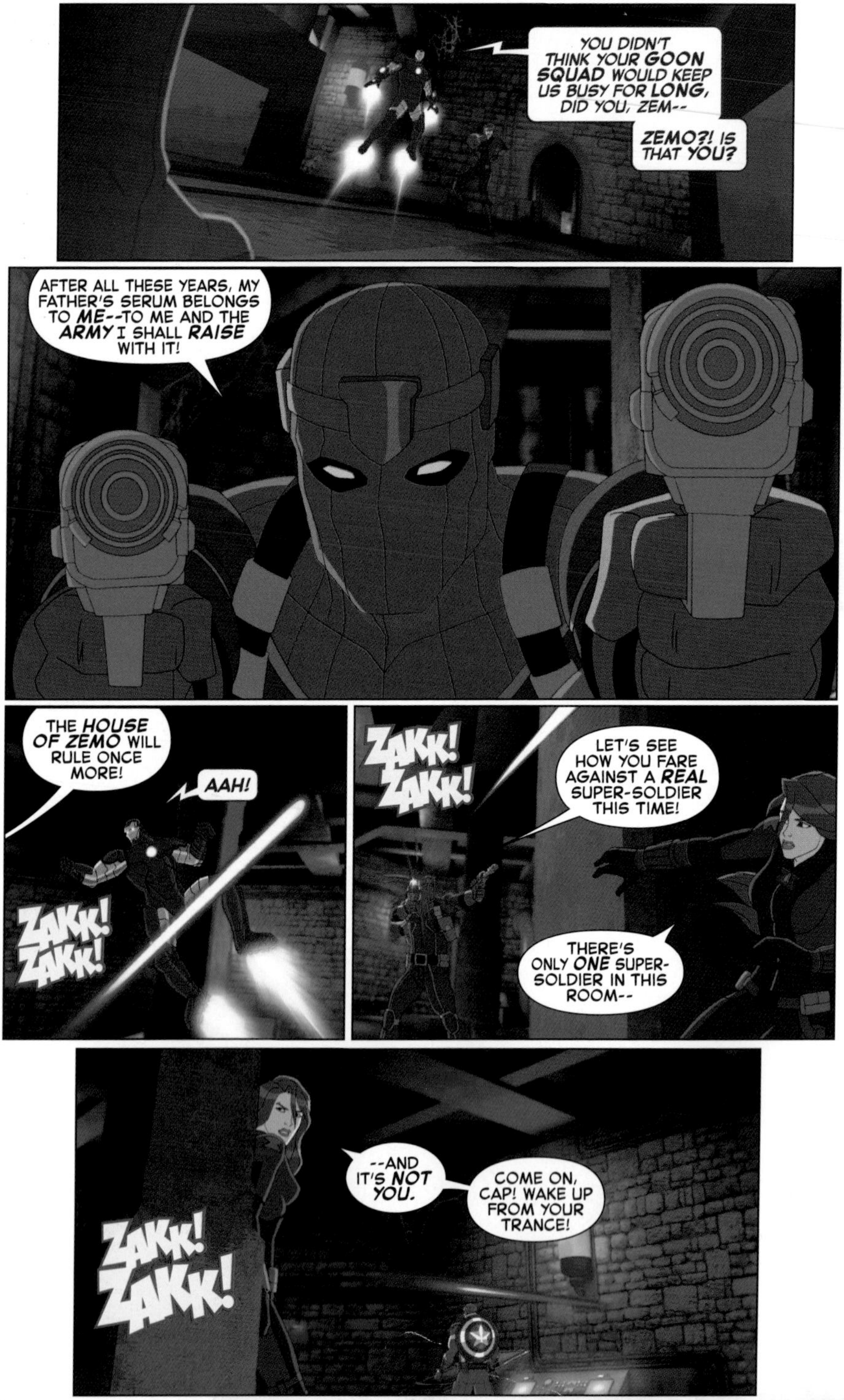
YOU DIDN'T THINK YOUR GOON SQUAD WOULD KEEP US BUSY FOR LONG, DID YOU, ZEM--
ZEMO?! IS THAT YOU?
AFTER ALL THESE YEARS, MY FATHER'S SERUM BELONGS TO ME--TO ME AND THE ARMY I SHALL RAISE WITH IT!
THE HOUSE OF ZEMO WILL RULE ONCE MORE!
AAH!
ZAKK! ZAKK!
ZAKK! ZAKK!
LET'S SEE HOW YOU FARE AGAINST A REAL SUPER-SOLDIER THIS TIME!
THERE'S ONLY ONE SUPER-SOLDIER IN THIS ROOM--
--AND IT'S NOT YOU.
COME ON, CAP! WAKE UP FROM YOUR TRANCE!
ZAKK! ZAKK!

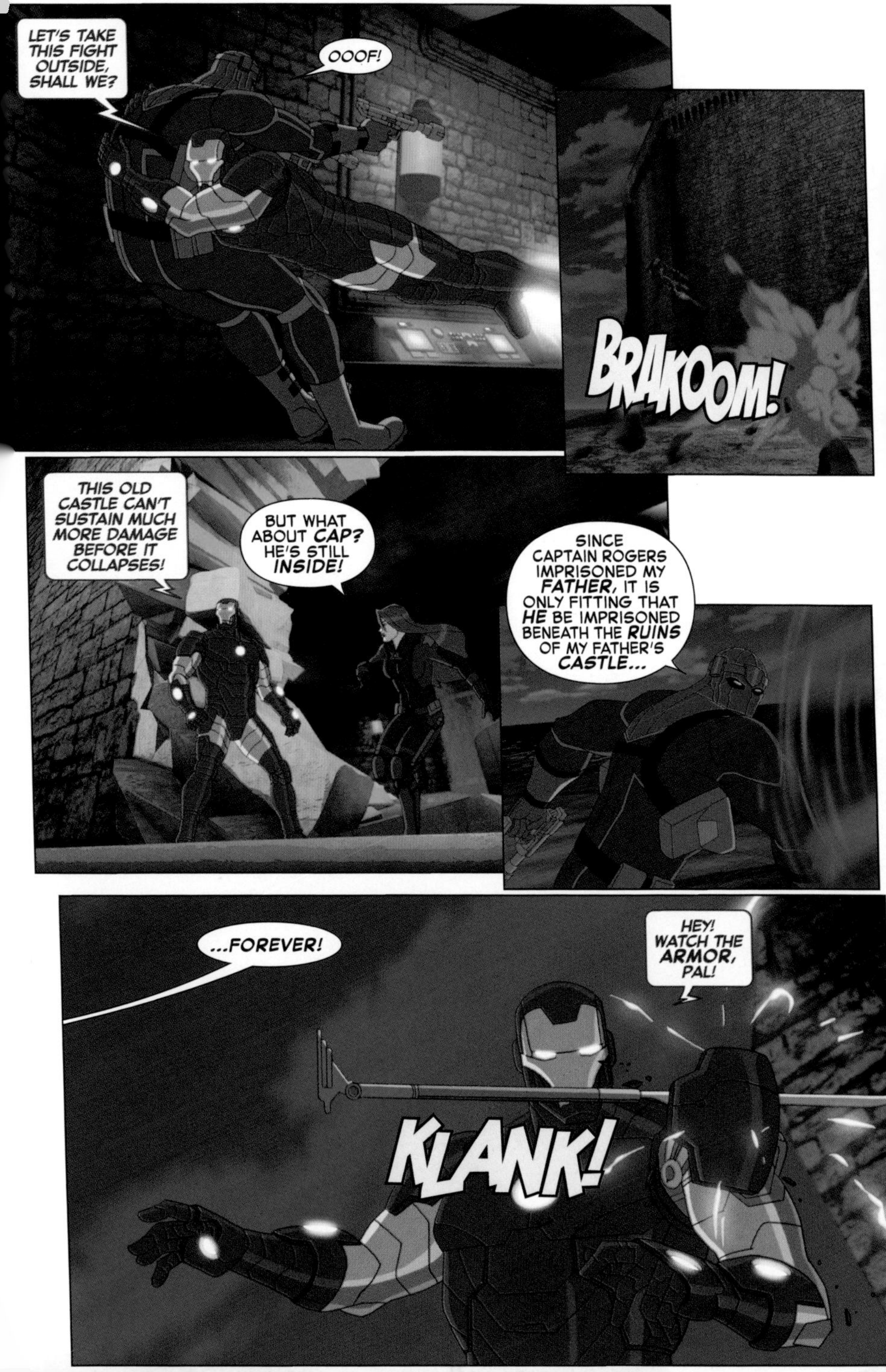
LET'S TAKE THIS FIGHT OUTSIDE, SHALL WE?
OOOF!
BRAKOOM!
THIS OLD CASTLE CAN'T SUSTAIN MUCH MORE DAMAGE BEFORE IT COLLAPSES!
BUT WHAT ABOUT CAP? HE'S STILL INSIDE!
SINCE CAPTAIN ROGERS IMPRISONED MY FATHER, IT IS ONLY FITTING THAT HE BE IMPRISONED BENEATH THE RUINS OF MY FATHER'S CASTLE...
...FOREVER!
HEY! WATCH THE ARMOR, PAL!
KLANK!

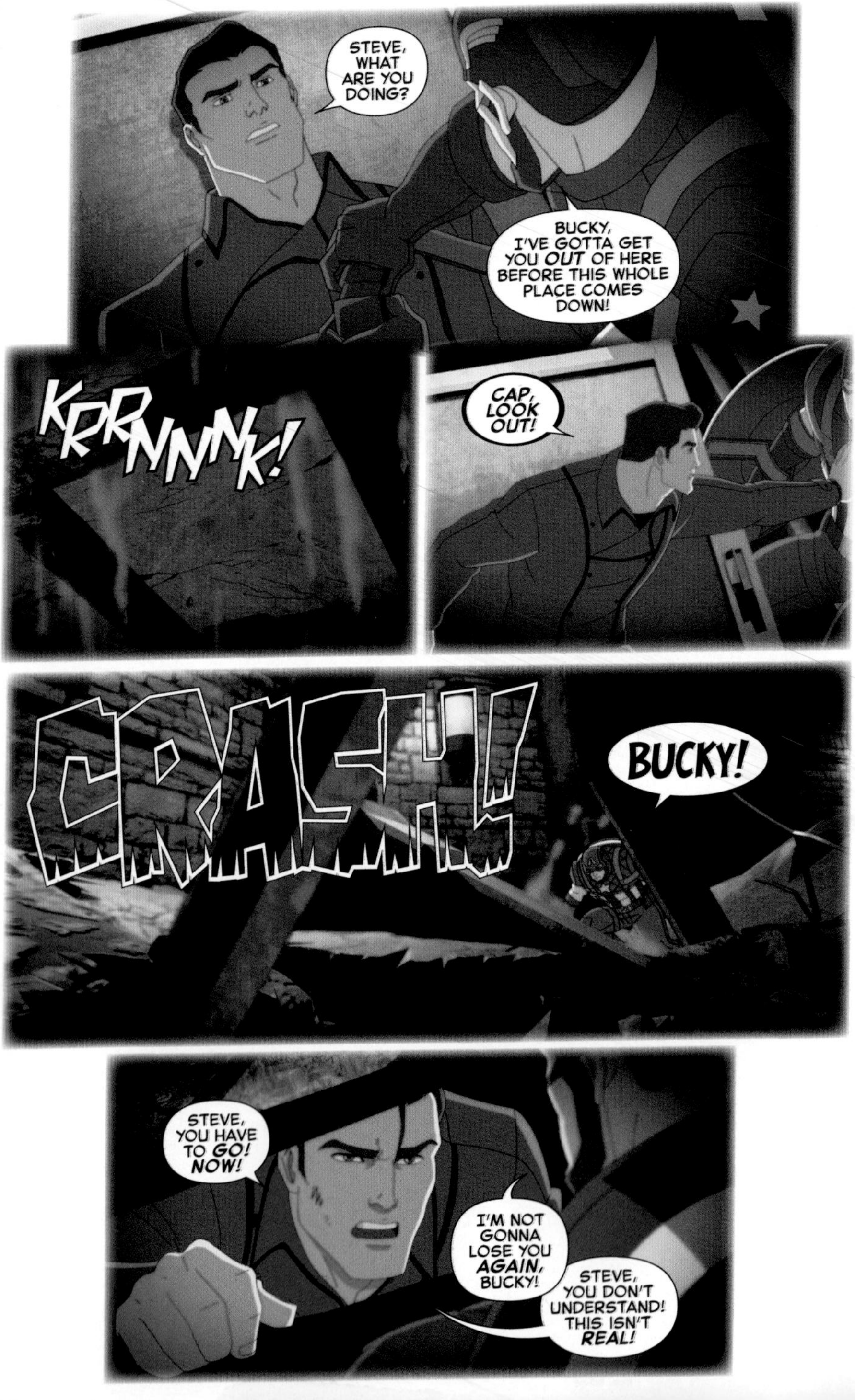
STEVE, WHAT ARE YOU DOING?
BUCKY, I'VE GOTTA GET YOU OUT OF HERE BEFORE THIS WHOLE PLACE COMES DOWN!
KRRNNNK!
CAP, LOOK OUT!
CRASH!
BUCKY!
STEVE, YOU HAVE TO GO! NOW!
I'M NOT GONNA LOSE YOU AGAIN, BUCKY!
STEVE, YOU DON'T UNDERSTAND! THIS ISN'T REAL!

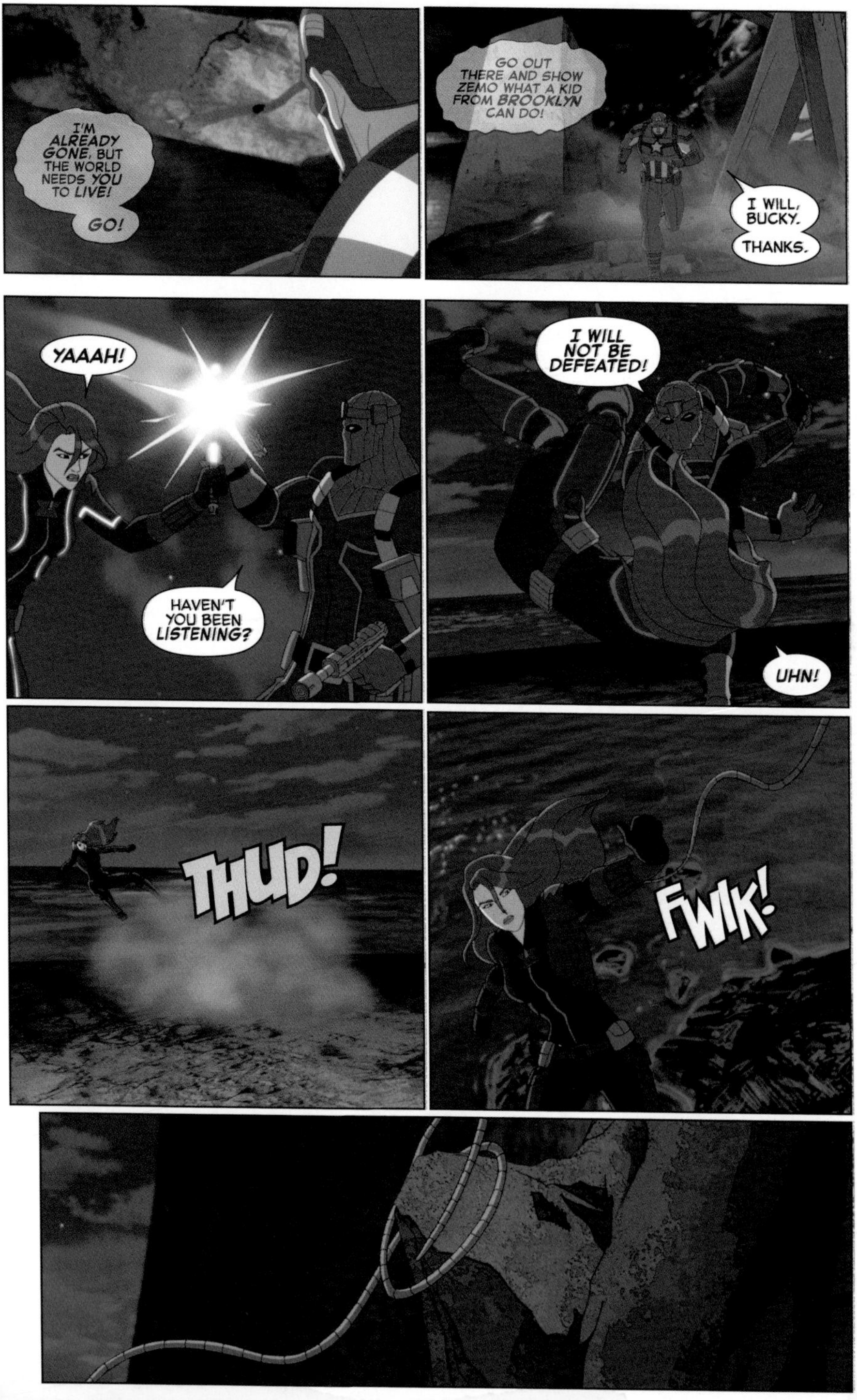
I'M ALREADY GONE. BUT THE WORLD NEEDS YOU TO LIVE!
GO!
GO OUT THERE AND SHOW ZEMO WHAT A KID FROM BROOKLYN CAN DO!
I WILL, BUCKY.
THANKS.
YAAAH!
HAVEN'T YOU BEEN LISTENING?
I WILL NOT BE DEFEATED!
UHN!
THUD!
FWIK!

I CAN UNDERSTAND THE WANT TO CARRY ON YOUR FAMILY'S LEGACY, BUT AT LEAST I DO IT FOR GOOD, NOT EVIL!
ZARK!
HNN!
EVIL IS A MATTER OF PERSPECTIVE, STARK.
ZAKK!
KRKK!
CAN YOU EVEN SEE THROUGH THAT MASK, ZEMO? YOU MISSED BY A MILE!
BRMMM!
DID I?
AAH!

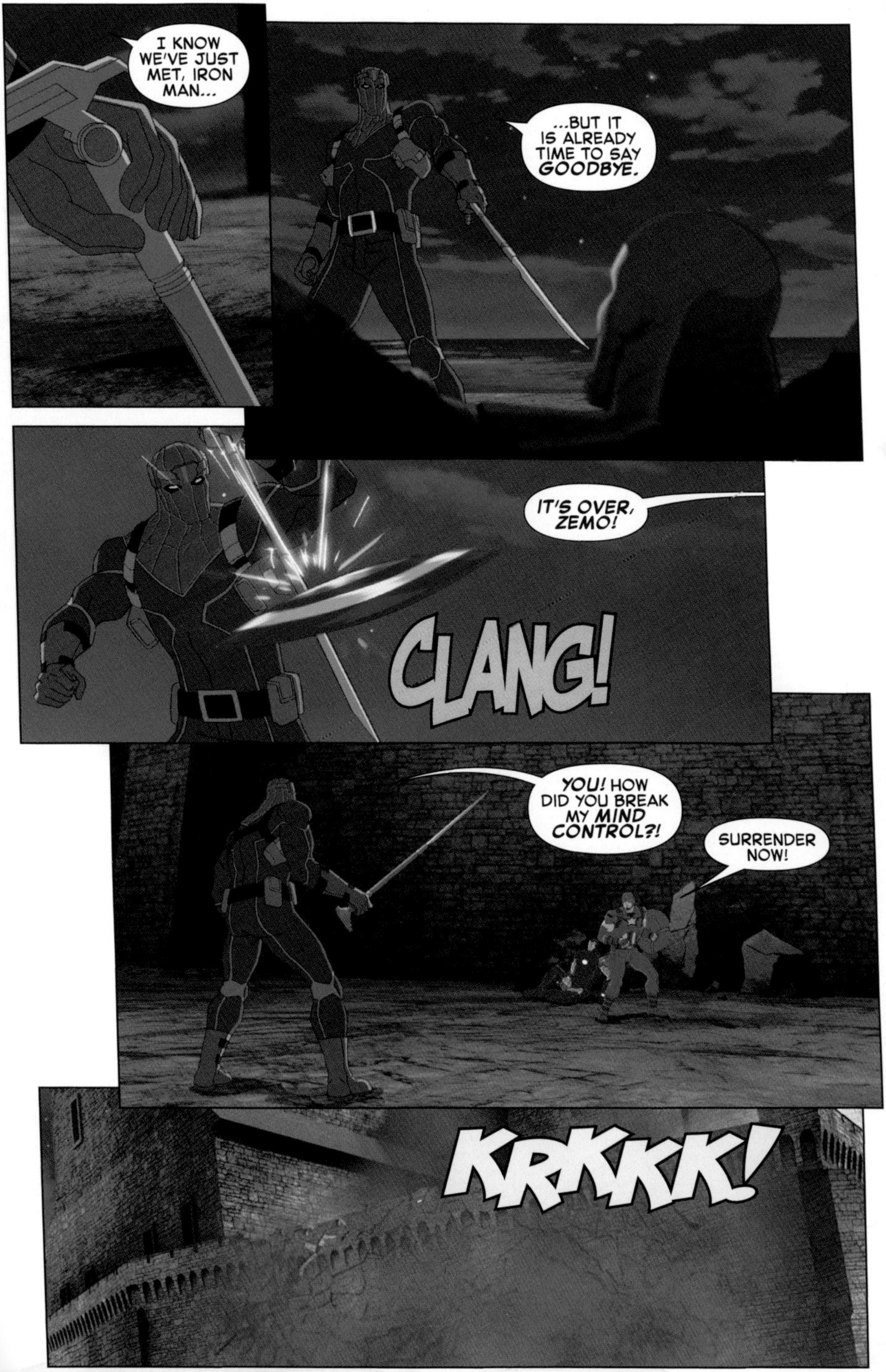
I KNOW WE'VE JUST MET, IRON MAN...
...BUT IT IS ALREADY TIME TO SAY GOODBYE.
IT'S OVER, ZEMO!
CLANG!
YOU! HOW DID YOU BREAK MY MIND CONTROL?!
SURRENDER NOW!
KRKKK!

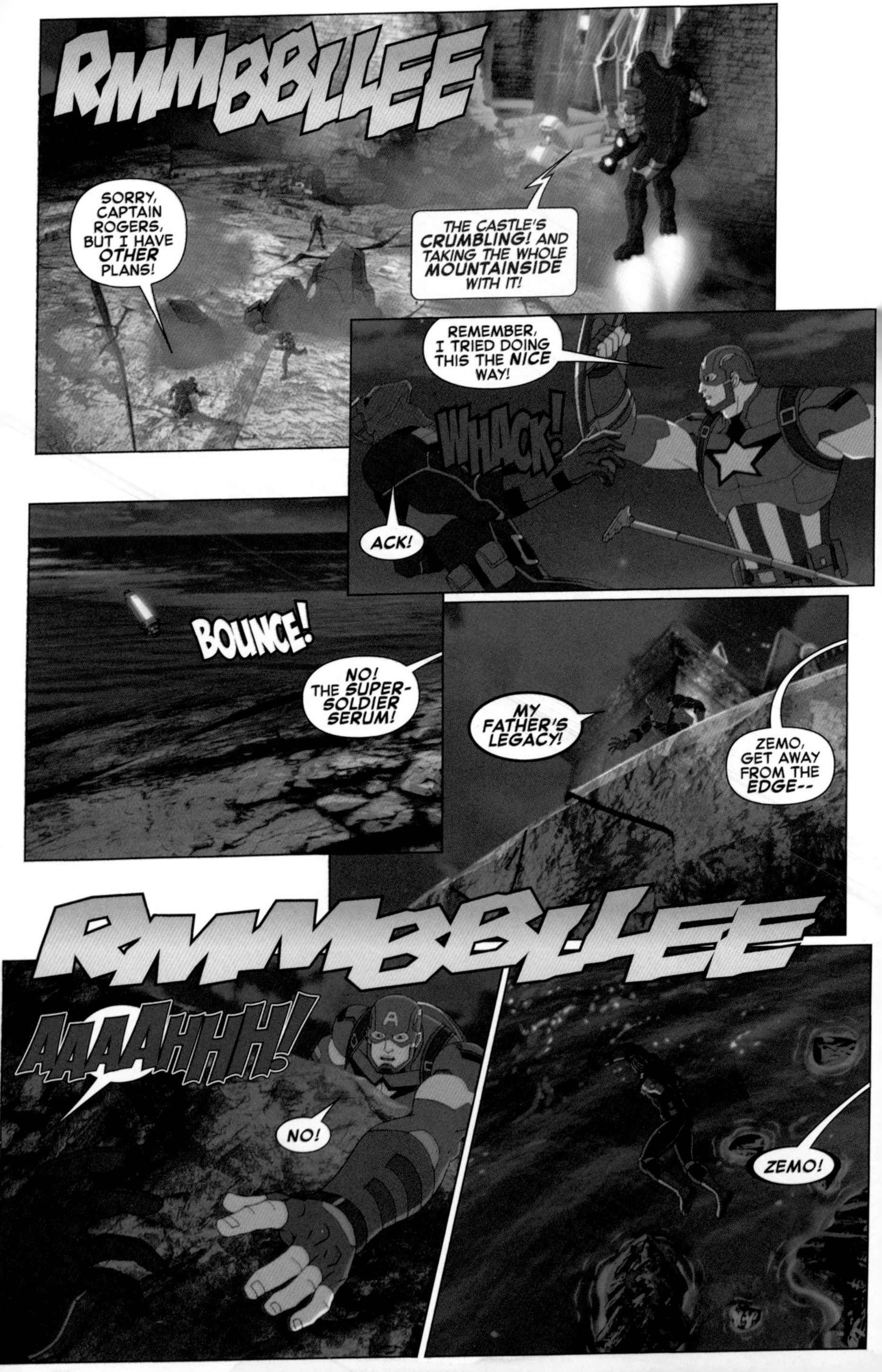
RMMBBLLEE
SORRY, CAPTAIN ROGERS, BUT I HAVE OTHER PLANS!
THE CASTLE'S CRUMBLING! AND TAKING THE WHOLE MOUNTAINSIDE WITH IT!
REMEMBER, I TRIED DOING THIS THE NICE WAY!
WHACK!
ACK!
BOUNCE!
NO! THE SUPER-SOLDIER SERUM!
MY FATHER'S LEGACY!
ZEMO, GET AWAY FROM THE EDGE--
RMMBBLLEE
AAAAHHH!
NO!
ZEMO!

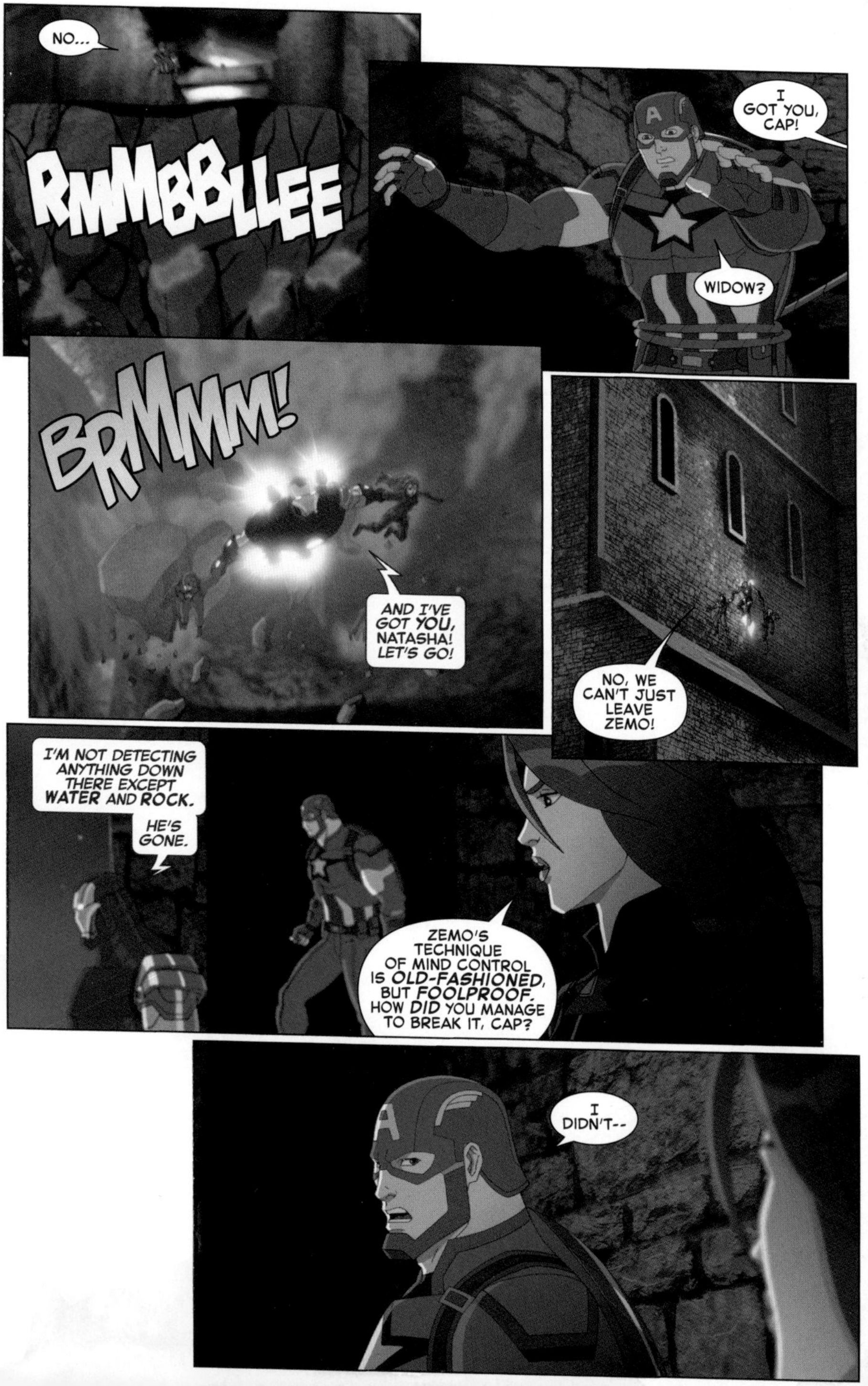

NO...
RMMBBLLEE
I GOT YOU, CAP!
WIDOW?
BRMMM!
AND I'VE GOT YOU, NATASHA! LET'S GO!
NO, WE CAN'T JUST LEAVE ZEMO!
I'M NOT DETECTING ANYTHING DOWN THERE EXCEPT WATER AND ROCK.
HE'S GONE.
ZEMO'S TECHNIQUE OF MIND CONTROL IS OLD-FASHIONED, BUT FOOLPROOF. HOW DID YOU MANAGE TO BREAK IT, CAP?
I DIDN'T--

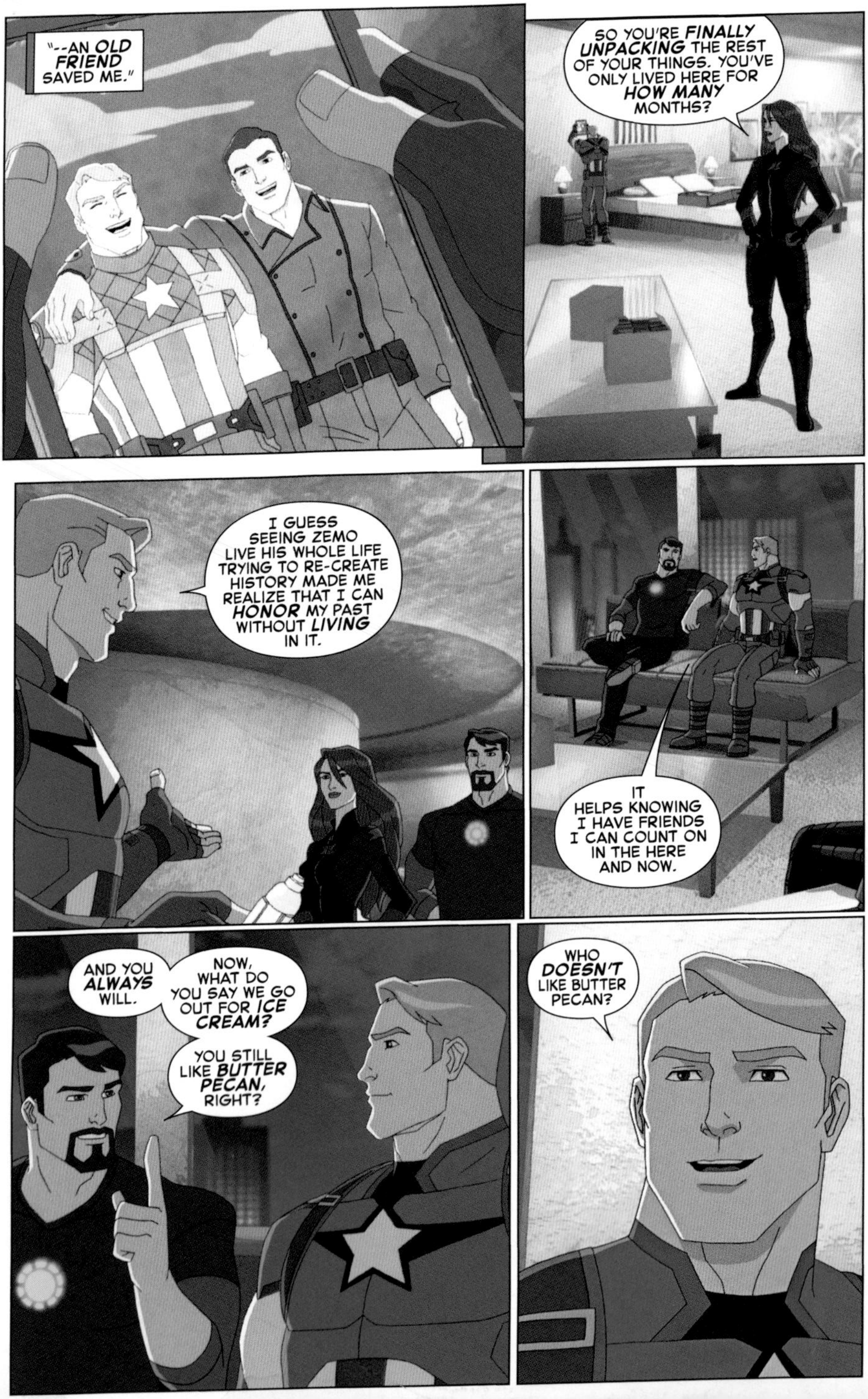
"--AN OLD FRIEND SAVED ME."
SO YOU'RE FINALLY UNPACKING THE REST OF YOUR THINGS. YOU'VE ONLY LIVED HERE FOR HOW MANY MONTHS?
I GUESS SEEING ZEMO LIVE HIS WHOLE LIFE TRYING TO RE-CREATE HISTORY MADE ME REALIZE THAT I CAN HONOR MY PAST WITHOUT LIVING IN IT.
IT HELPS KNOWING I HAVE FRIENDS I CAN COUNT ON IN THE HERE AND NOW.
AND YOU ALWAYS WILL.
NOW, WHAT DO YOU SAY WE GO OUT FOR ICE CREAM?
YOU STILL LIKE BUTTER PECAN, RIGHT?
WHO DOESN'T LIKE BUTTER PECAN?

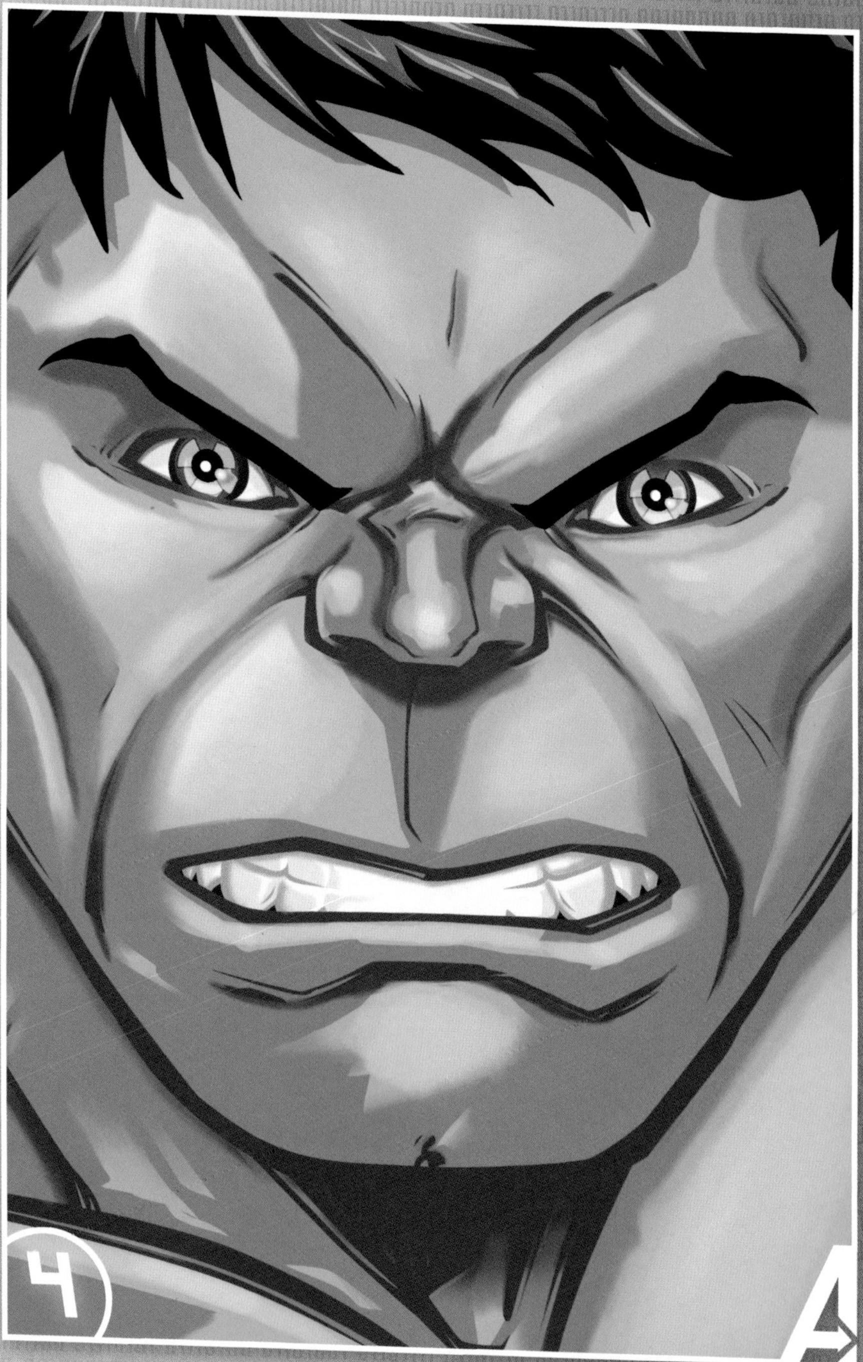
4

DEHULKED

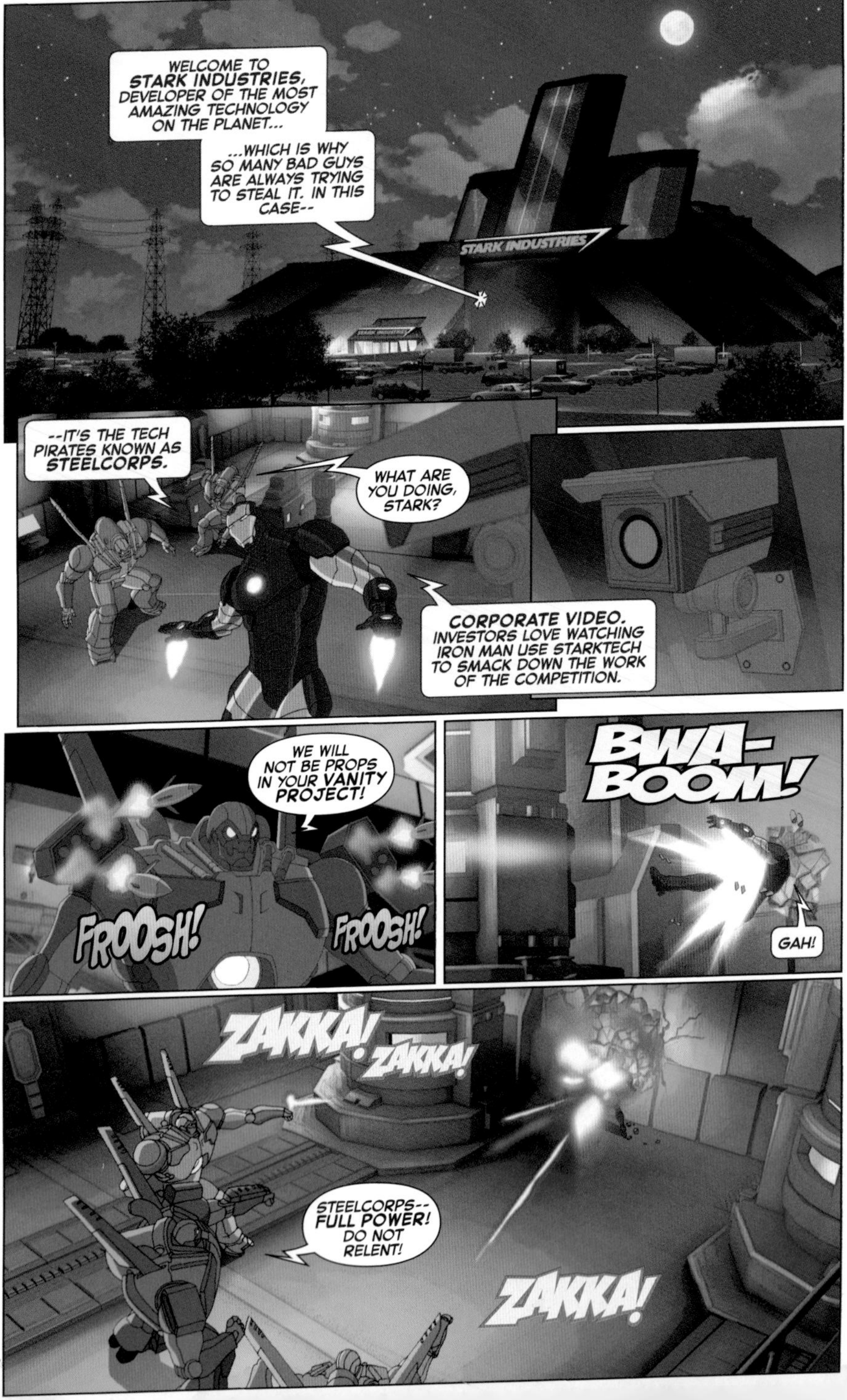
WELCOME TO STARK INDUSTRIES, DEVELOPER OF THE MOST AMAZING TECHNOLOGY ON THE PLANET...
...WHICH IS WHY SO MANY BAD GUYS ARE ALWAYS TRYING TO STEAL IT. IN THIS CASE--
STARK INDUSTRIES
--IT'S THE TECH PIRATES KNOWN AS STEELCORPS.
WHAT ARE YOU DOING, STARK?
CORPORATE VIDEO. INVESTORS LOVE WATCHING IRON MAN USE STARKTECH TO SMACK DOWN THE WORK OF THE COMPETITION.
WE WILL NOT BE PROPS IN YOUR VANITY PROJECT!
FROOSH!
FROOSH!
BWA-BOOM!
GAH!
ZAKKA! ZAKKA!
STEELCORPS-- FULL POWER! DO NOT RELENT!
ZAKKA!

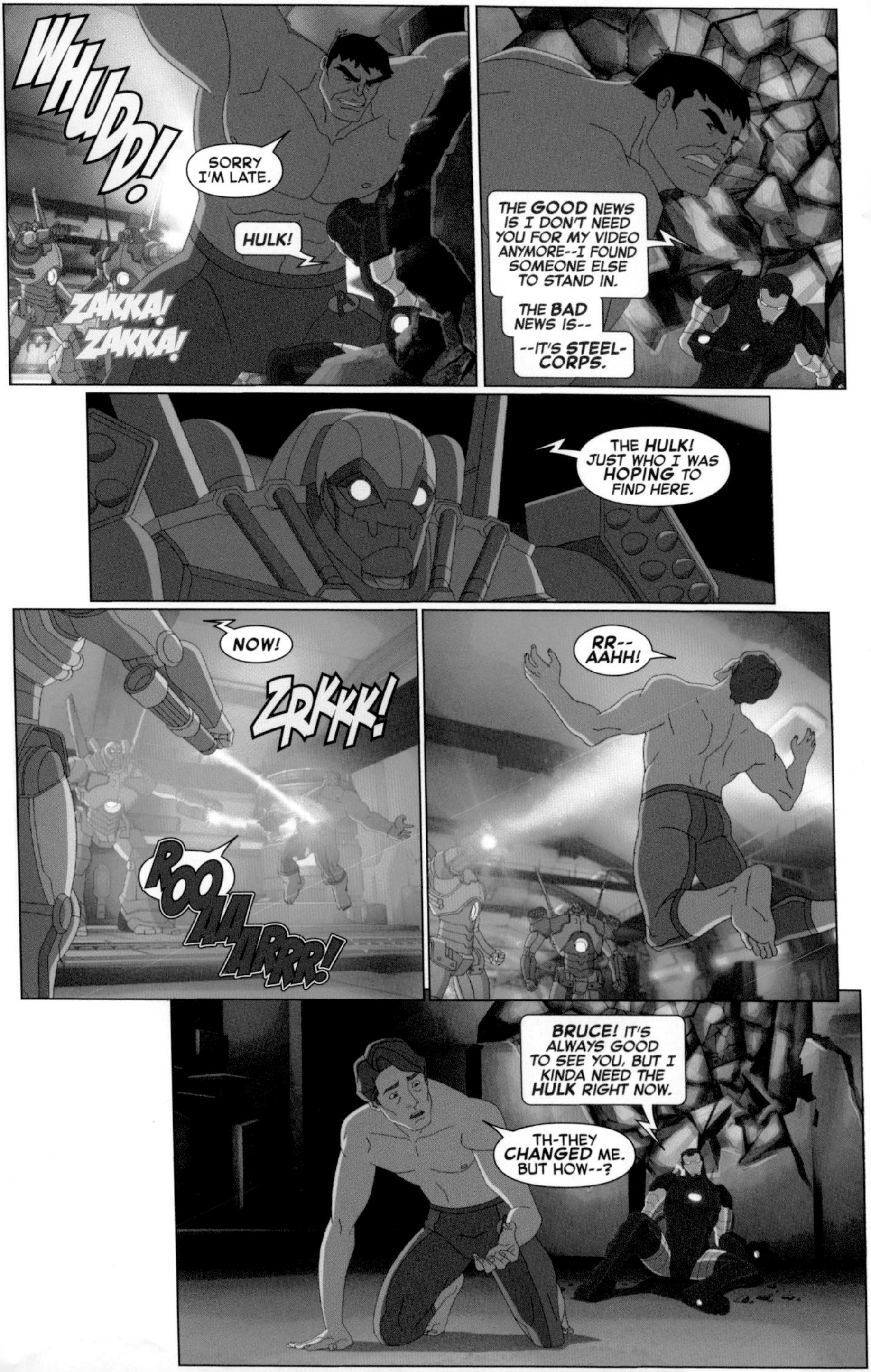
WHUDD!
SORRY I'M LATE.
HULK!
ZAKKA! ZAKKA!
THE GOOD NEWS IS I DON'T NEED YOU FOR MY VIDEO ANYMORE--I FOUND SOMEONE ELSE TO STAND IN.
THE BAD NEWS IS--
--IT'S STEEL-CORPS.
THE HULK! JUST WHO I WAS HOPING TO FIND HERE.
NOW!
ZRKKK!
ROOAAARRR!
RR--AAHH!
BRUCE! IT'S ALWAYS GOOD TO SEE YOU, BUT I KINDA NEED THE HULK RIGHT NOW.
TH-THEY CHANGED ME. BUT HOW--?

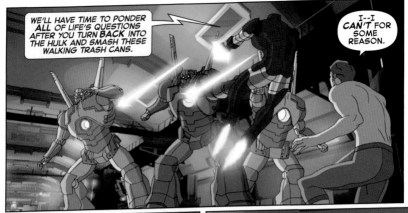

WE'LL HAVE TIME TO PONDER ALL OF LIFE'S QUESTIONS AFTER YOU TURN **BACK** INTO THE HULK AND SMASH THESE WALKING TRASH CANS.

I--I **CAN'T** FOR SOME REASON.

THEN I'LL HAVE TO GET YOU **AWAY** FROM HERE UNTIL YOU **CAN**.

WAIT! JUST 'CAUSE I'M NOT BIG AND GREEN--

ZAKKA! ZAKKA!

--DOESN'T MEAN I CAN'T STILL **HELP**!

NEGATIVE, BRUCE, ALL YOU CAN DO IN YOUR **CURRENT** STATE IS TO STAY--

ZAKKA! ZAKKA!

ZRASH!

AH!

HUH?

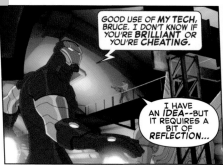

GOOD USE OF **MY TECH,** BRUCE. I DON'T KNOW IF YOU'RE **BRILLIANT** OR YOU'RE **CHEATING.**

I HAVE AN **IDEA**--BUT IT REQUIRES A BIT OF **REFLECTION...**

AH, I **GET IT!**

LET 'ER RIP!

ZRASH!

ZAKKA!

WE HAVE WHAT WE NEED. LET'S GO!

ZAKKA!

ZAKKA!

THEY'RE GETTING AWAY!

LET THEM. WE HAVE **BIGGER** PROBLEMS RIGHT NOW.

I LIKE HAVING MY SCIENCE BRO BACK, BUT WE NEED TO FIND OUT **HOW** AND **WHY** YOU'RE BANNER AGAIN.

THE **LEADER'S** VOICE-- IT SOUNDED **FAMILIAR.** HE SAID HE GOT WHAT HE CAME FOR. DID HE MEAN...

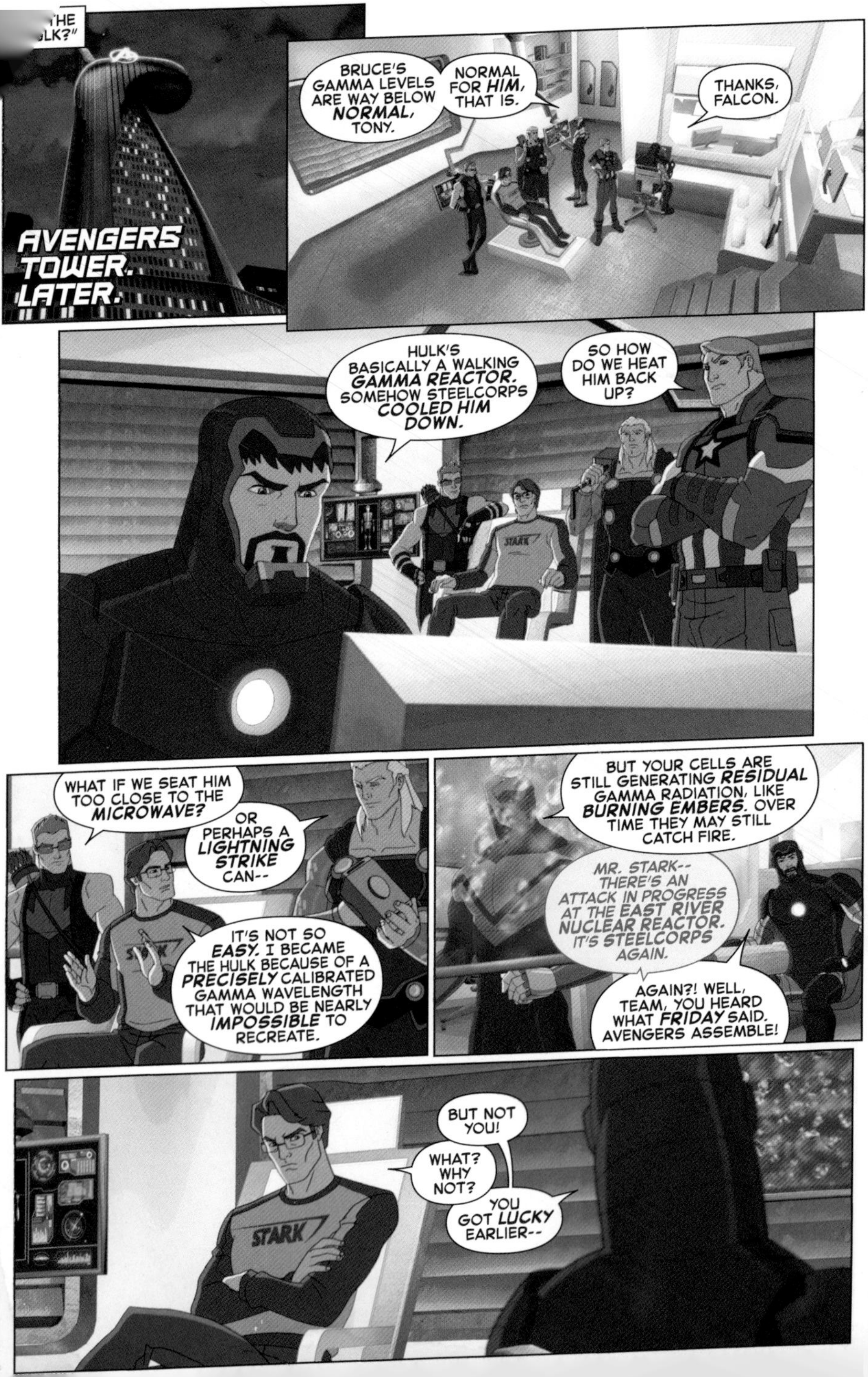
AVENGERS TOWER. LATER.
BRUCE'S GAMMA LEVELS ARE WAY BELOW NORMAL, TONY.
NORMAL FOR HIM, THAT IS.
THANKS, FALCON.
HULK'S BASICALLY A WALKING GAMMA REACTOR. SOMEHOW STEELCORPS COOLED HIM DOWN.
SO HOW DO WE HEAT HIM BACK UP?
WHAT IF WE SEAT HIM TOO CLOSE TO THE MICROWAVE?
OR PERHAPS A LIGHTNING STRIKE CAN--
IT'S NOT SO EASY. I BECAME THE HULK BECAUSE OF A PRECISELY CALIBRATED GAMMA WAVELENGTH THAT WOULD BE NEARLY IMPOSSIBLE TO RECREATE.
BUT YOUR CELLS ARE STILL GENERATING RESIDUAL GAMMA RADIATION, LIKE BURNING EMBERS. OVER TIME THEY MAY STILL CATCH FIRE.
MR. STARK-- THERE'S AN ATTACK IN PROGRESS AT THE EAST RIVER NUCLEAR REACTOR. IT'S STEELCORPS AGAIN.
AGAIN?! WELL, TEAM, YOU HEARD WHAT FRIDAY SAID. AVENGERS ASSEMBLE!
BUT NOT YOU!
WHAT? WHY NOT?
YOU GOT LUCKY EARLIER--

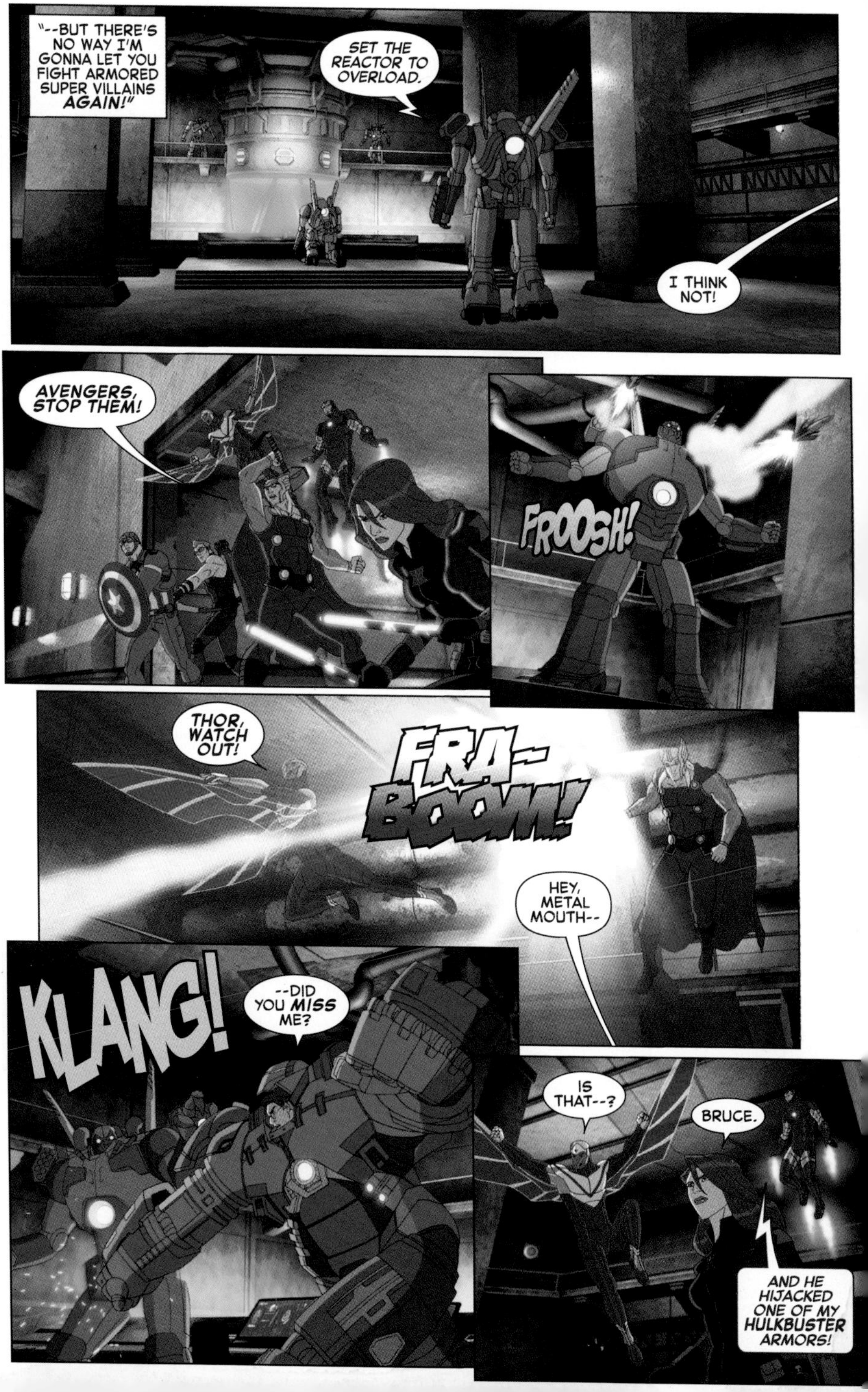
"--BUT THERE'S NO WAY I'M GONNA LET YOU FIGHT ARMORED SUPER VILLAINS **AGAIN!**"
SET THE REACTOR TO OVERLOAD.
I THINK NOT!
AVENGERS, STOP THEM!
FROOSH!
THOR, WATCH OUT!
FRA-BOOM!
HEY, METAL MOUTH--
KLANG!
--DID YOU **MISS** ME?
IS THAT--?
BRUCE.
AND HE HIJACKED ONE OF MY **HULKBUSTER** ARMORS!

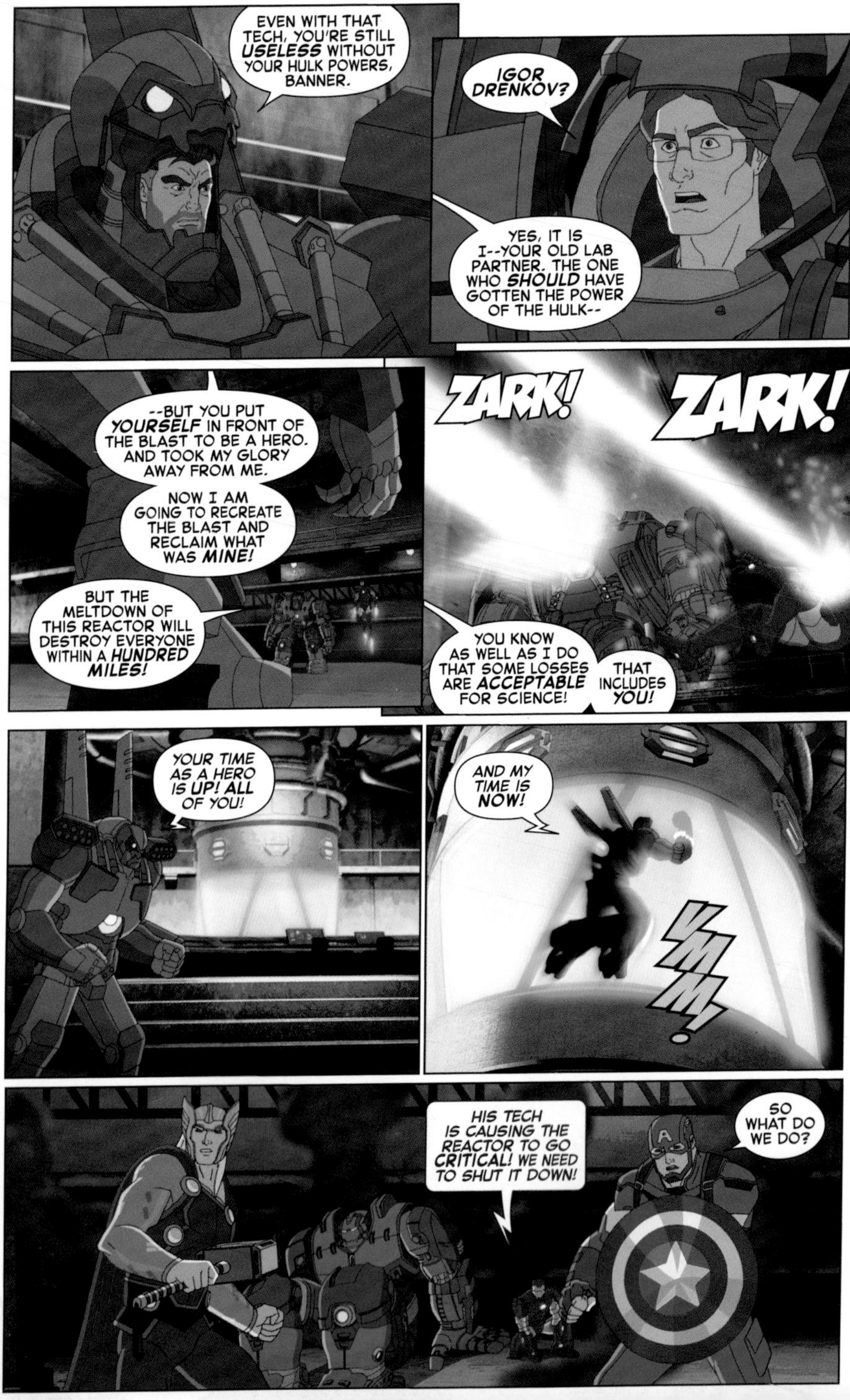
EVEN WITH THAT TECH, YOU'RE STILL USELESS WITHOUT YOUR HULK POWERS, BANNER.
IGOR DRENKOV?
YES, IT IS I--YOUR OLD LAB PARTNER. THE ONE WHO SHOULD HAVE GOTTEN THE POWER OF THE HULK--
--BUT YOU PUT YOURSELF IN FRONT OF THE BLAST TO BE A HERO. AND TOOK MY GLORY AWAY FROM ME.
NOW I AM GOING TO RECREATE THE BLAST AND RECLAIM WHAT WAS MINE!
BUT THE MELTDOWN OF THIS REACTOR WILL DESTROY EVERYONE WITHIN A HUNDRED MILES!
ZARK!
ZARK!
YOU KNOW AS WELL AS I DO THAT SOME LOSSES ARE ACCEPTABLE FOR SCIENCE!
THAT INCLUDES YOU!
YOUR TIME AS A HERO IS UP! ALL OF YOU!
AND MY TIME IS NOW!
VMMM!
HIS TECH IS CAUSING THE REACTOR TO GO CRITICAL! WE NEED TO SHUT IT DOWN!
SO WHAT DO WE DO?

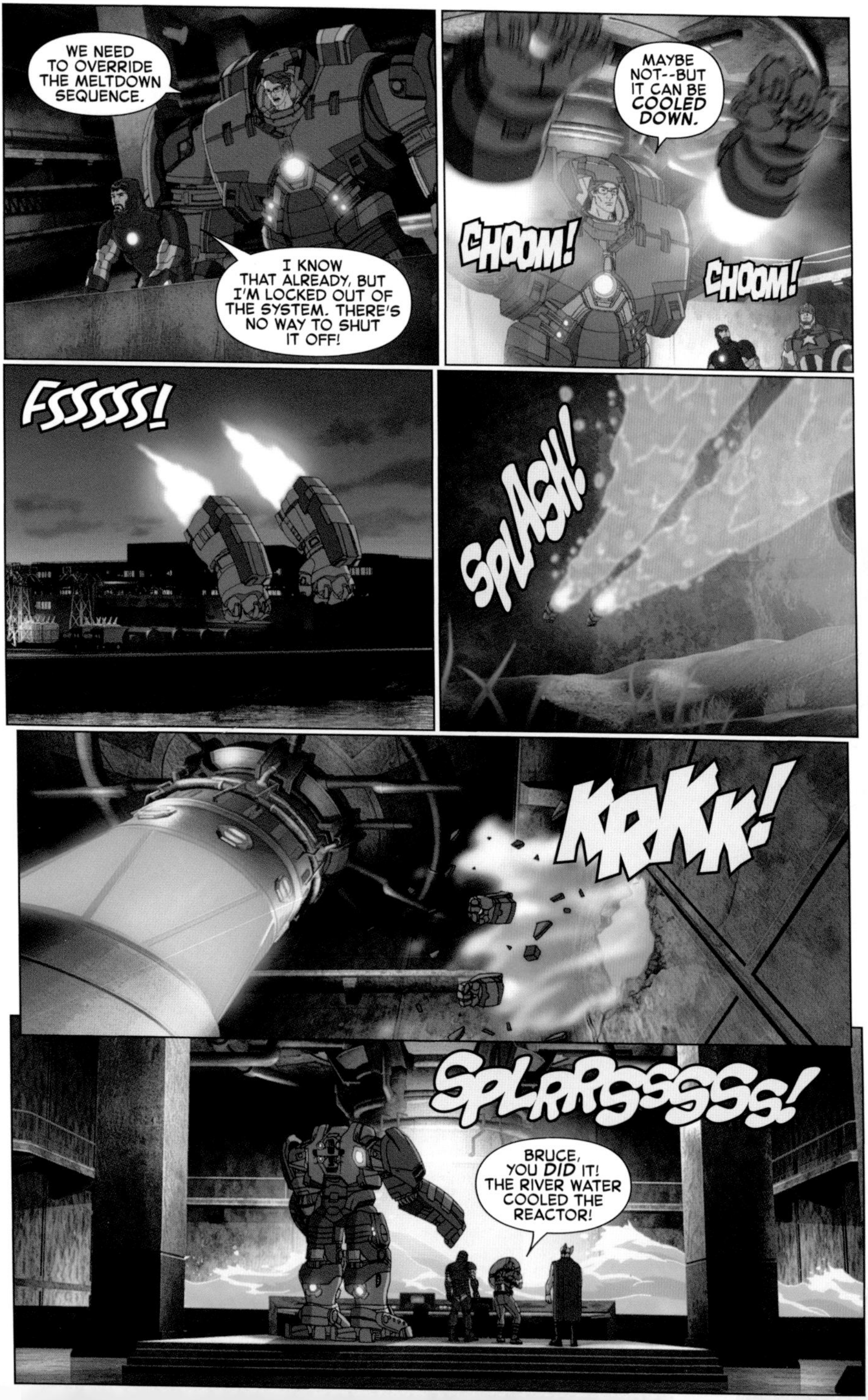
WE NEED TO OVERRIDE THE MELTDOWN SEQUENCE.
I KNOW THAT ALREADY, BUT I'M LOCKED OUT OF THE SYSTEM. THERE'S NO WAY TO SHUT IT OFF!
MAYBE NOT--BUT IT CAN BE COOLED DOWN.
CHOOM!
CHOOM!
FSSSSS!
SPLASH!
KRKK!
SPLRRSSSSS!
BRUCE, YOU DID IT! THE RIVER WATER COOLED THE REACTOR!

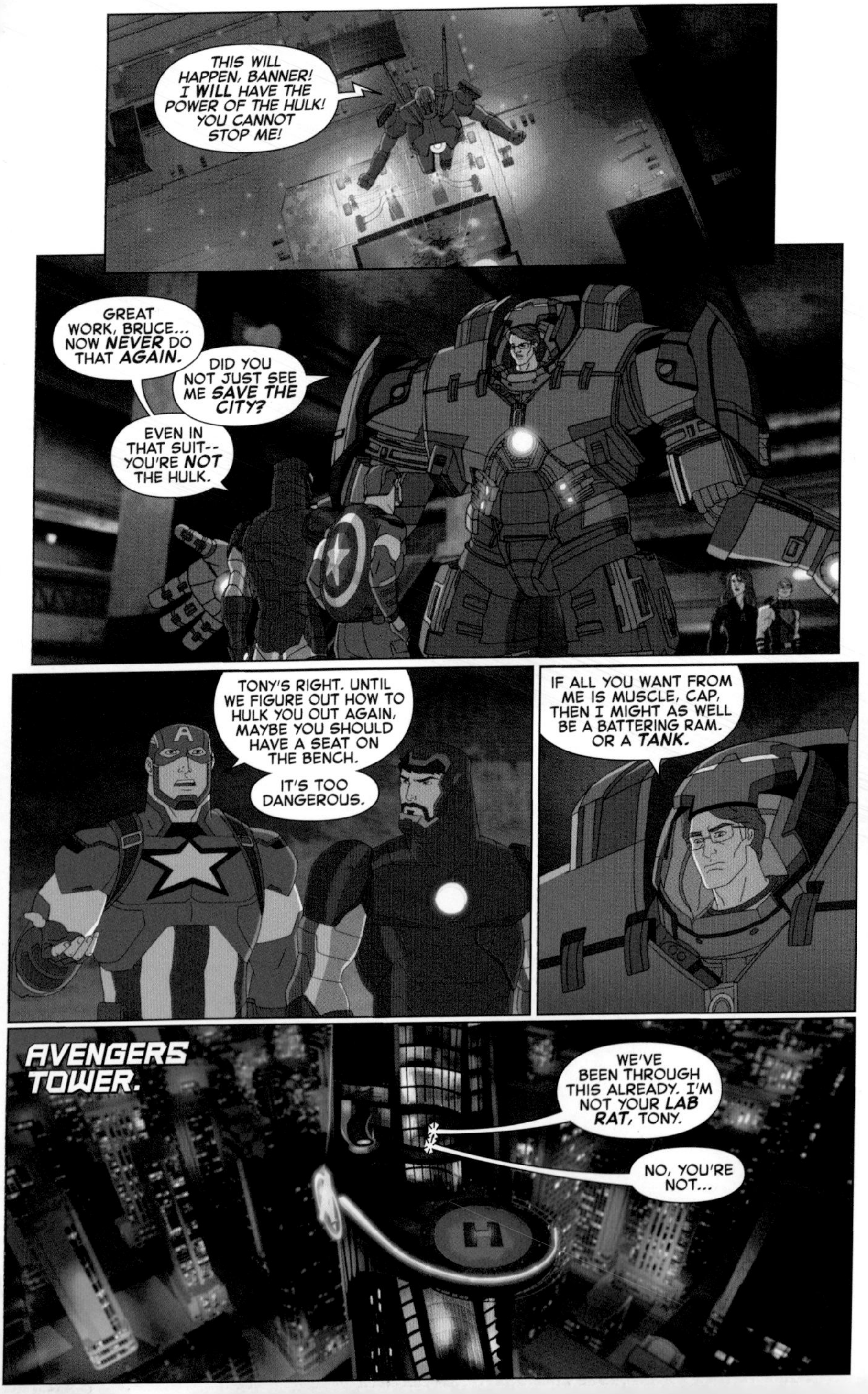
THIS WILL HAPPEN, BANNER! I WILL HAVE THE POWER OF THE HULK! YOU CANNOT STOP ME!
GREAT WORK, BRUCE... NOW NEVER DO THAT AGAIN.
DID YOU NOT JUST SEE ME SAVE THE CITY?
EVEN IN THAT SUIT-- YOU'RE NOT THE HULK.
TONY'S RIGHT. UNTIL WE FIGURE OUT HOW TO HULK YOU OUT AGAIN, MAYBE YOU SHOULD HAVE A SEAT ON THE BENCH.
IT'S TOO DANGEROUS.
IF ALL YOU WANT FROM ME IS MUSCLE, CAP, THEN I MIGHT AS WELL BE A BATTERING RAM. OR A TANK.
AVENGERS TOWER.
WE'VE BEEN THROUGH THIS ALREADY. I'M NOT YOUR LAB RAT, TONY.
NO, YOU'RE NOT...

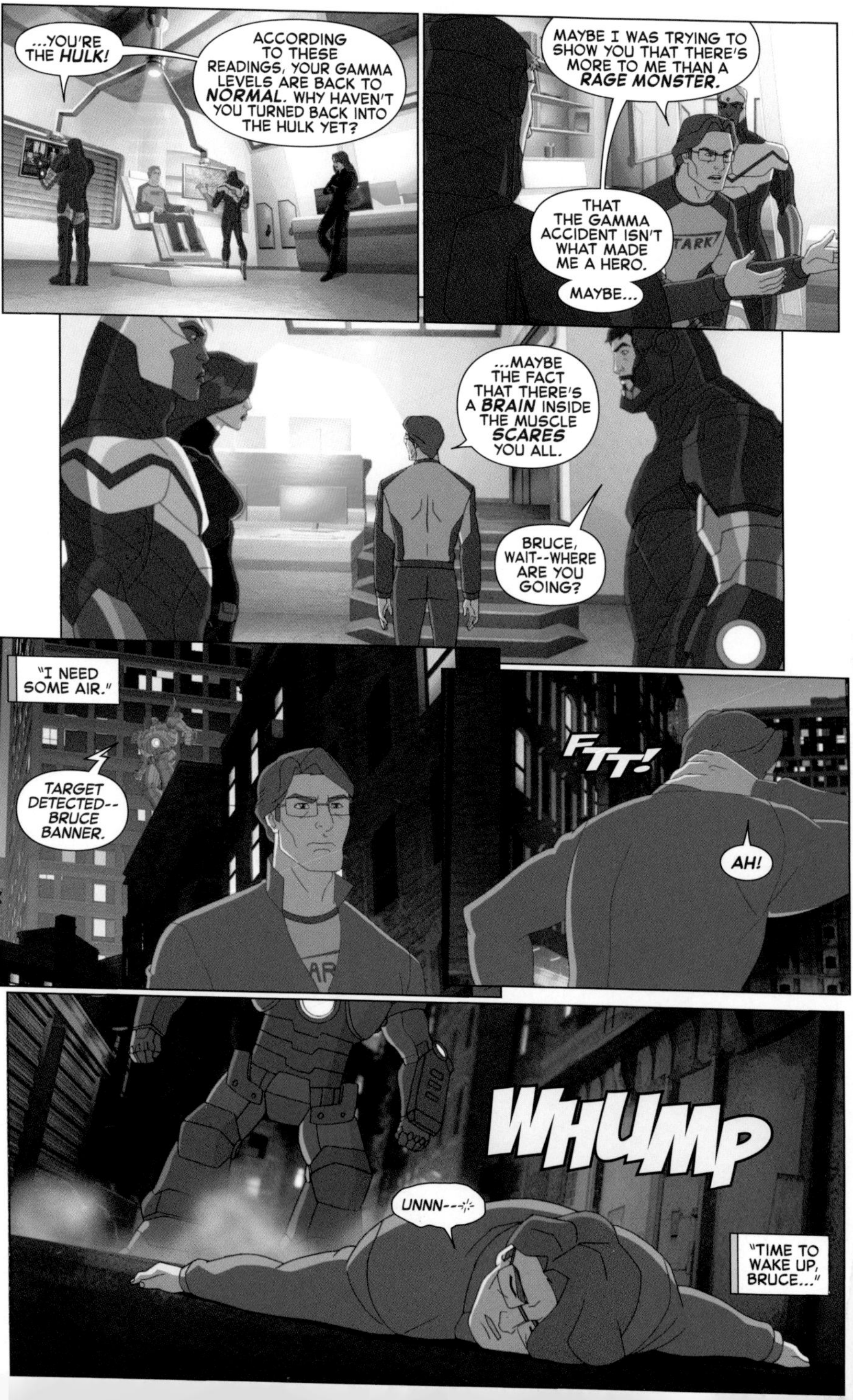
...YOU'RE THE HULK!
ACCORDING TO THESE READINGS, YOUR GAMMA LEVELS ARE BACK TO NORMAL. WHY HAVEN'T YOU TURNED BACK INTO THE HULK YET?
MAYBE I WAS TRYING TO SHOW YOU THAT THERE'S MORE TO ME THAN A RAGE MONSTER.
THAT THE GAMMA ACCIDENT ISN'T WHAT MADE ME A HERO.
MAYBE...
...MAYBE THE FACT THAT THERE'S A BRAIN INSIDE THE MUSCLE SCARES YOU ALL.
BRUCE, WAIT--WHERE ARE YOU GOING?
"I NEED SOME AIR."
TARGET DETECTED--BRUCE BANNER.
FTTT!
AH!
WHUMP
UNNN--
"TIME TO WAKE UP, BRUCE..."

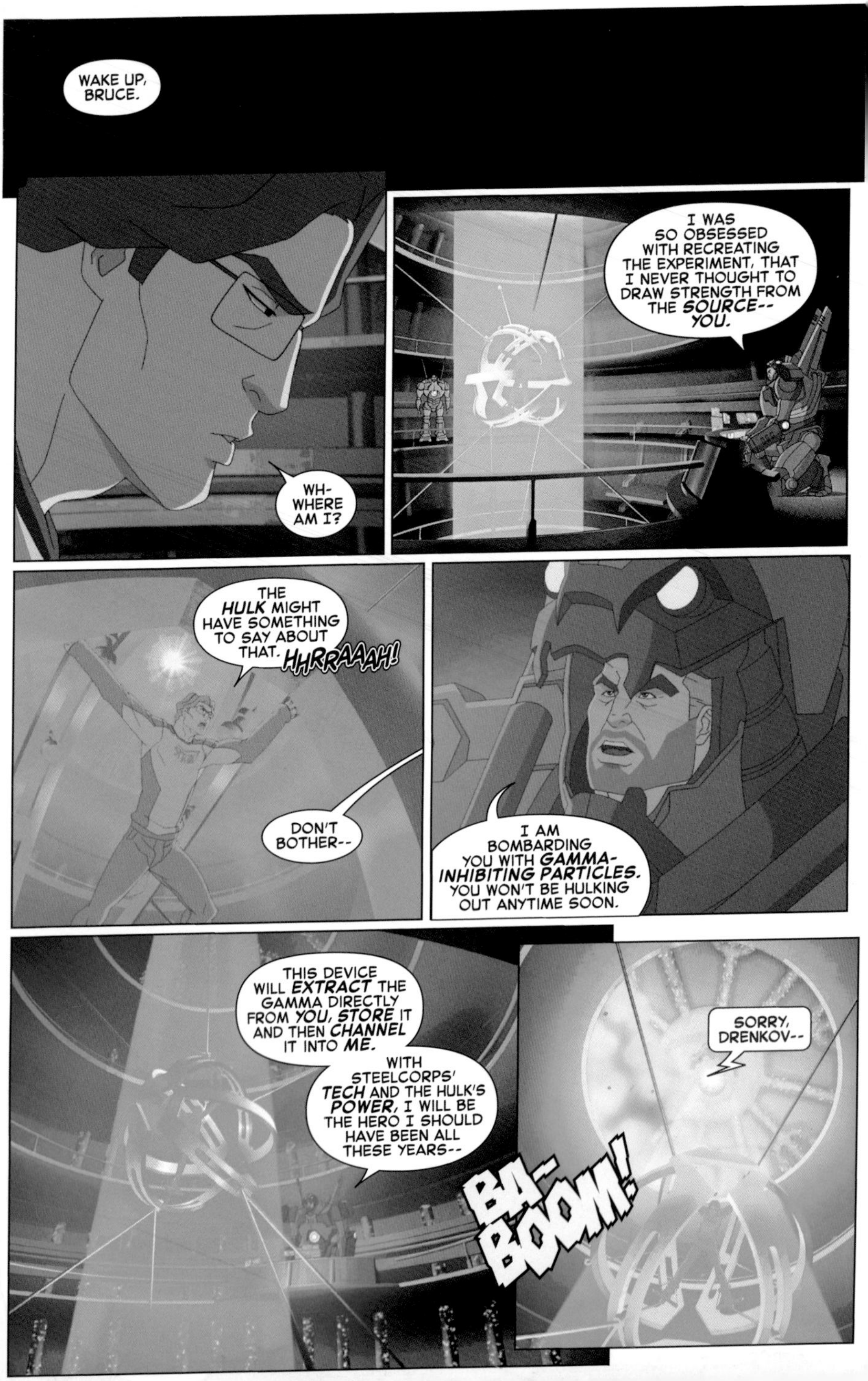
WAKE UP, BRUCE.
WH- WHERE AM I?
I WAS SO OBSESSED WITH RECREATING THE EXPERIMENT, THAT I NEVER THOUGHT TO DRAW STRENGTH FROM THE SOURCE-- YOU.
THE HULK MIGHT HAVE SOMETHING TO SAY ABOUT THAT.
HHRRAAAH!
DON'T BOTHER--
I AM BOMBARDING YOU WITH GAMMA-INHIBITING PARTICLES. YOU WON'T BE HULKING OUT ANYTIME SOON.
THIS DEVICE WILL EXTRACT THE GAMMA DIRECTLY FROM YOU, STORE IT AND THEN CHANNEL IT INTO ME.
WITH STEELCORPS' TECH AND THE HULK'S POWER, I WILL BE THE HERO I SHOULD HAVE BEEN ALL THESE YEARS--
SORRY, DRENKOV--
BA-BOOM!

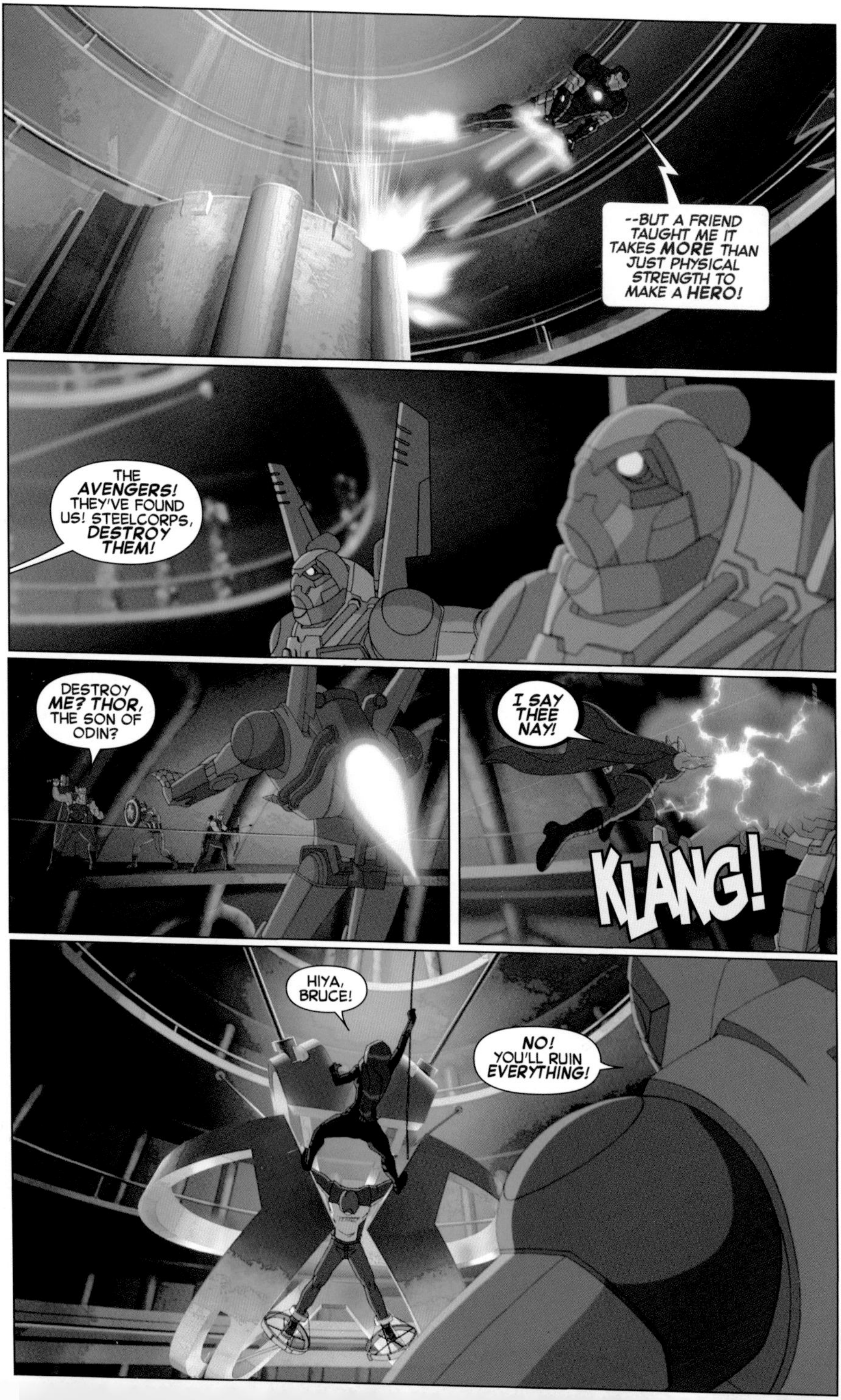
--BUT A FRIEND TAUGHT ME IT TAKES MORE THAN JUST PHYSICAL STRENGTH TO MAKE A HERO!
THE AVENGERS! THEY'VE FOUND US! STEELCORPS, DESTROY THEM!
DESTROY ME? THOR, THE SON OF ODIN?
I SAY THEE NAY!
KLANG!
HIYA, BRUCE!
NO! YOU'LL RUIN EVERYTHING!

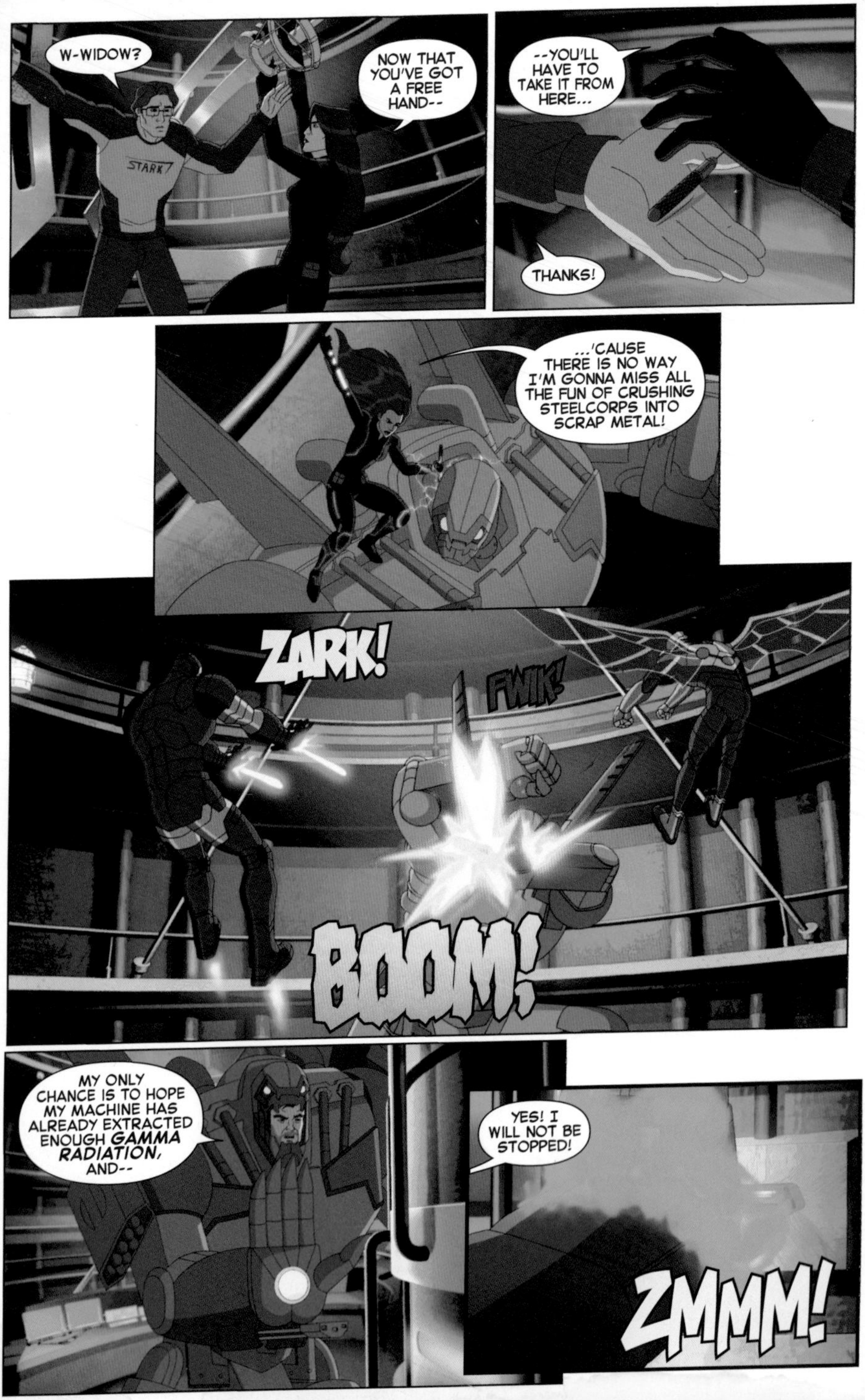
W-WIDOW?
NOW THAT YOU'VE GOT A FREE HAND--
--YOU'LL HAVE TO TAKE IT FROM HERE...
THANKS!
...'CAUSE THERE IS NO WAY I'M GONNA MISS ALL THE FUN OF CRUSHING STEELCORPS INTO SCRAP METAL!
ZARK!
FWIK!
BOOM!
MY ONLY CHANCE IS TO HOPE MY MACHINE HAS ALREADY EXTRACTED ENOUGH GAMMA RADIATION, AND--
YES! I WILL NOT BE STOPPED!
ZMMM!
STARK

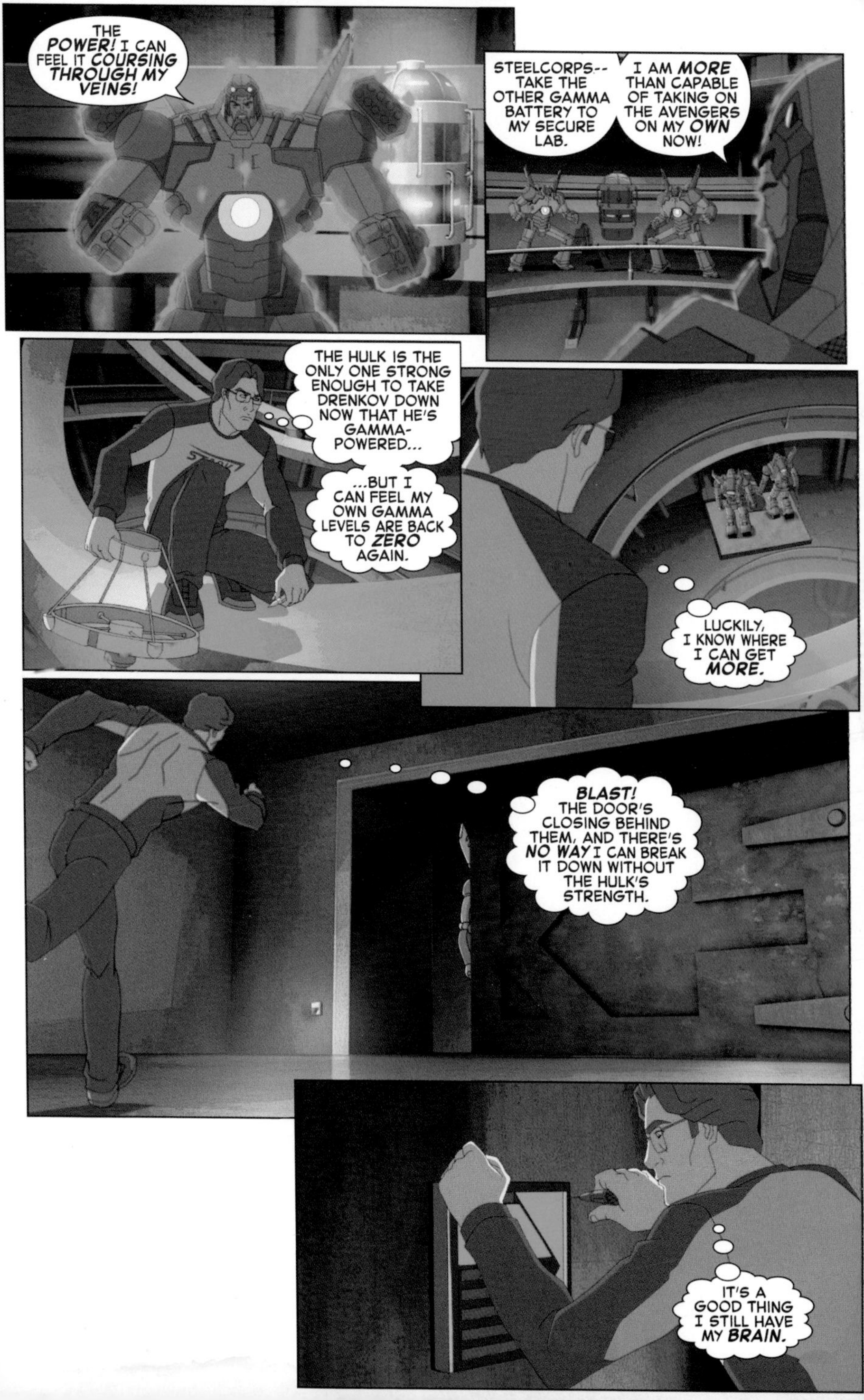

THE POWER! I CAN FEEL IT COURSING THROUGH MY VEINS!
STEELCORPS-- TAKE THE OTHER GAMMA BATTERY TO MY SECURE LAB.
I AM MORE THAN CAPABLE OF TAKING ON THE AVENGERS ON MY OWN NOW!
THE HULK IS THE ONLY ONE STRONG ENOUGH TO TAKE DRENKOV DOWN NOW THAT HE'S GAMMA-POWERED...
...BUT I CAN FEEL MY OWN GAMMA LEVELS ARE BACK TO ZERO AGAIN.
LUCKILY, I KNOW WHERE I CAN GET MORE.
BLAST! THE DOOR'S CLOSING BEHIND THEM, AND THERE'S NO WAY I CAN BREAK IT DOWN WITHOUT THE HULK'S STRENGTH.
IT'S A GOOD THING I STILL HAVE MY BRAIN.

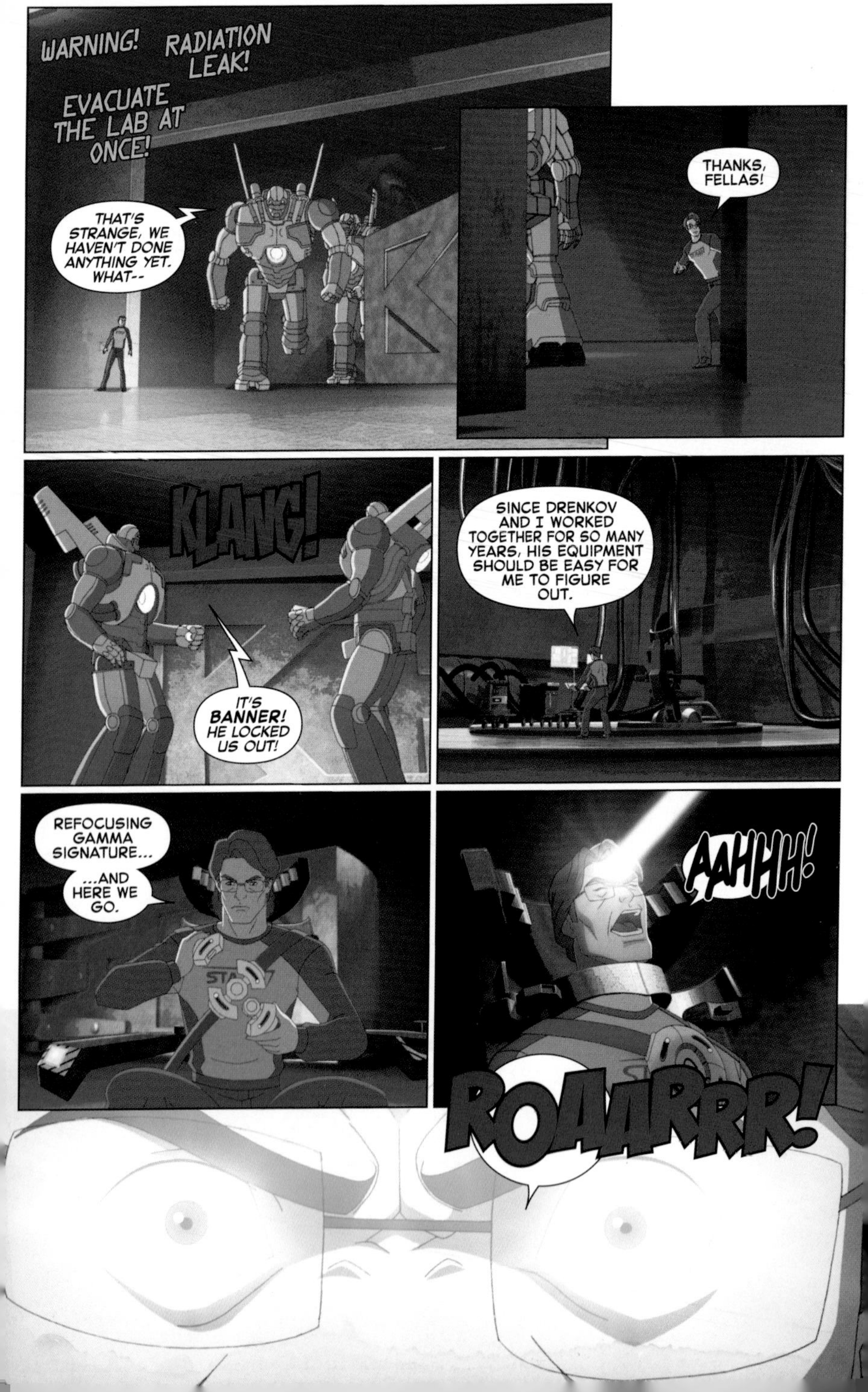
WARNING! RADIATION LEAK!
EVACUATE THE LAB AT ONCE!
THAT'S STRANGE, WE HAVEN'T DONE ANYTHING YET. WHAT--
THANKS, FELLAS!
KLANG!
IT'S BANNER! HE LOCKED US OUT!
SINCE DRENKOV AND I WORKED TOGETHER FOR SO MANY YEARS, HIS EQUIPMENT SHOULD BE EASY FOR ME TO FIGURE OUT.
REFOCUSING GAMMA SIGNATURE...
...AND HERE WE GO.
AAHHH!
ROAARRR!

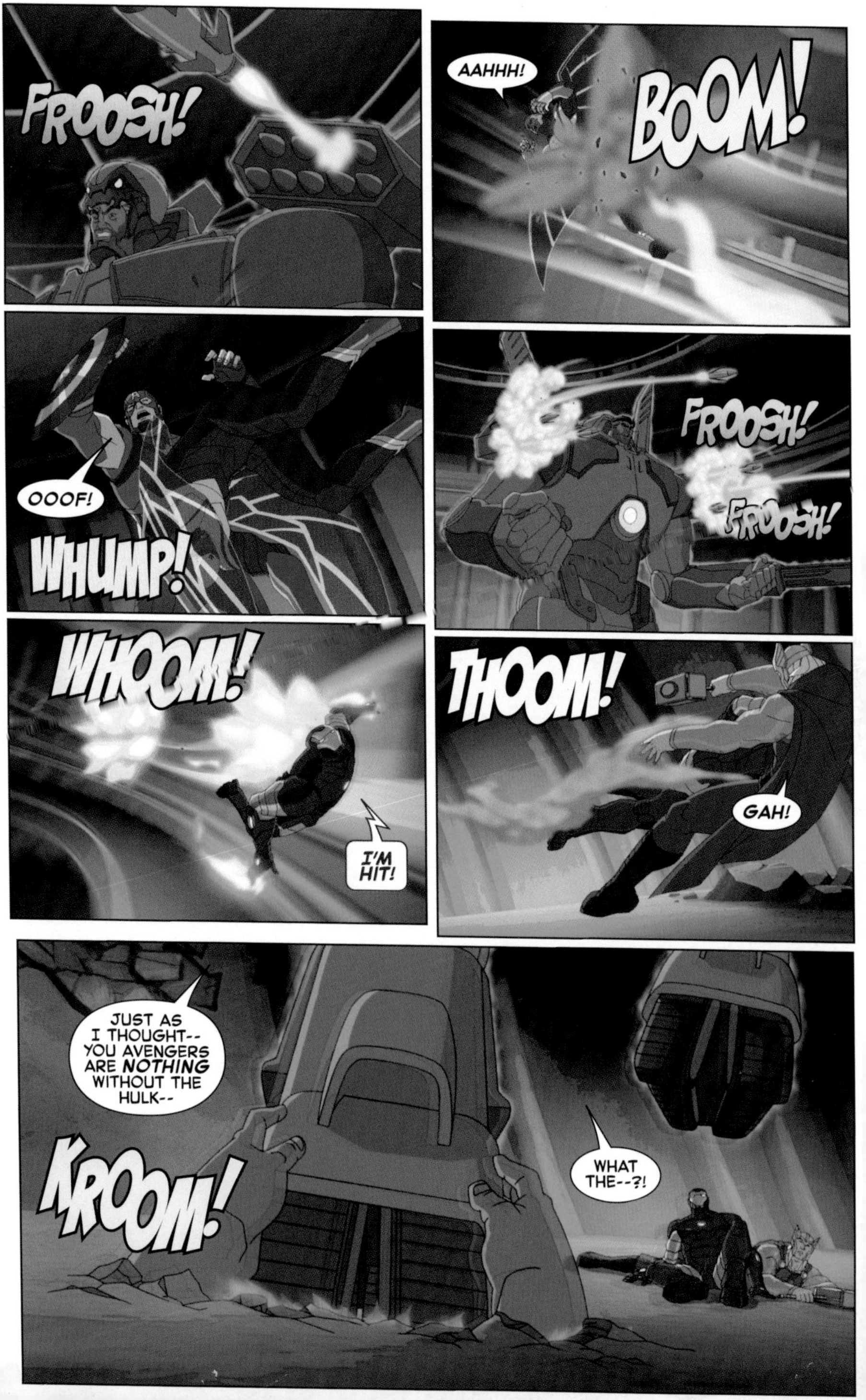
FROOSH!
AAHHH!
BOOM!
OOOF!
WHUMP!
FROOSH!
FROOSH!
WHOOM!
I'M HIT!
THOOM!
GAH!
JUST AS I THOUGHT-- YOU AVENGERS ARE *NOTHING* WITHOUT THE HULK--
KROOM!
WHAT THE--?!

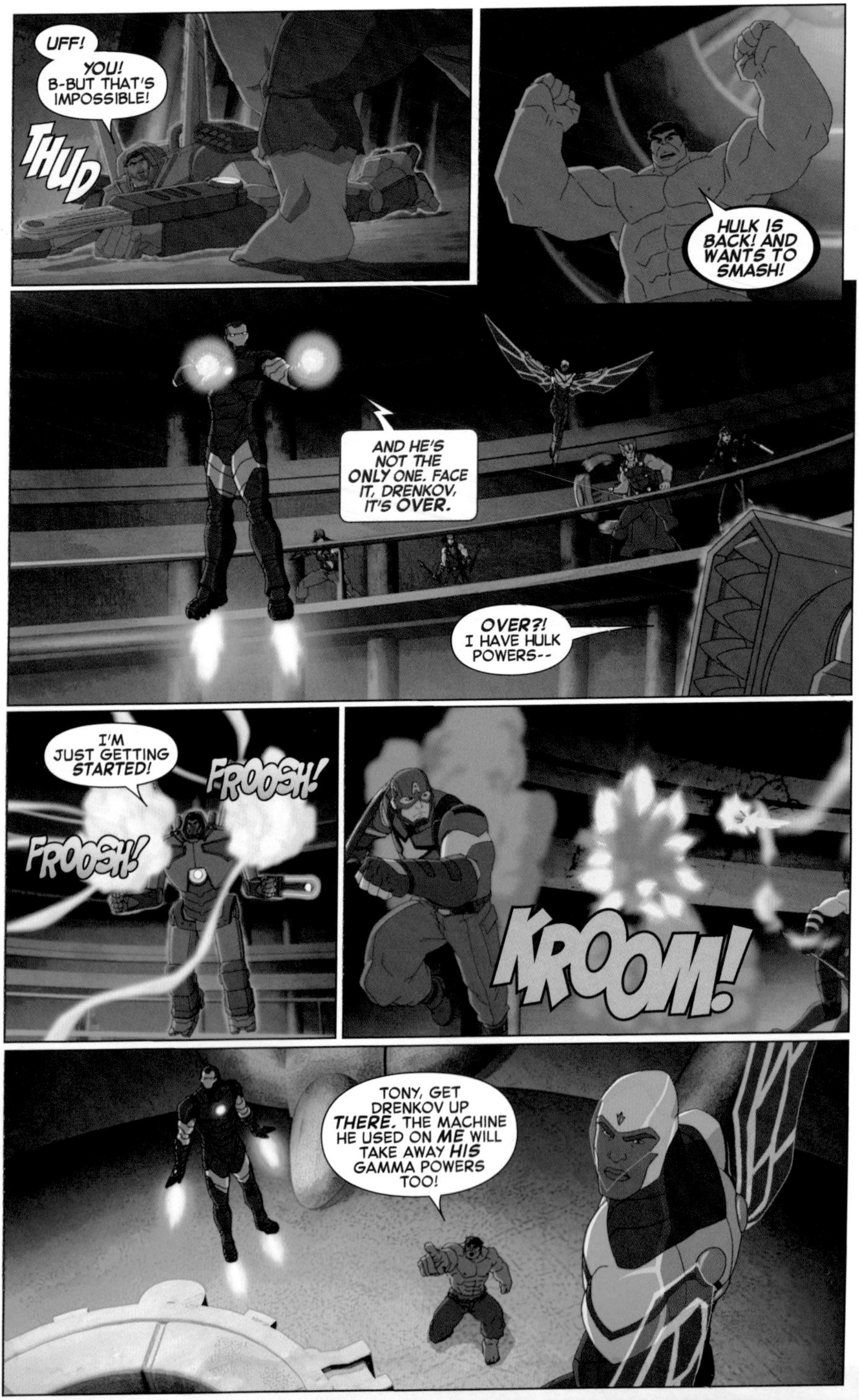
UFF!
YOU! B-BUT THAT'S IMPOSSIBLE!
THUD
HULK IS BACK! AND WANTS TO SMASH!
AND HE'S NOT THE ONLY ONE. FACE IT, DRENKOV, IT'S OVER.
OVER?! I HAVE HULK POWERS--
I'M JUST GETTING STARTED!
FROOSH!
FROOSH!
KROOOM!
TONY, GET DRENKOV UP THERE. THE MACHINE HE USED ON ME WILL TAKE AWAY HIS GAMMA POWERS TOO!

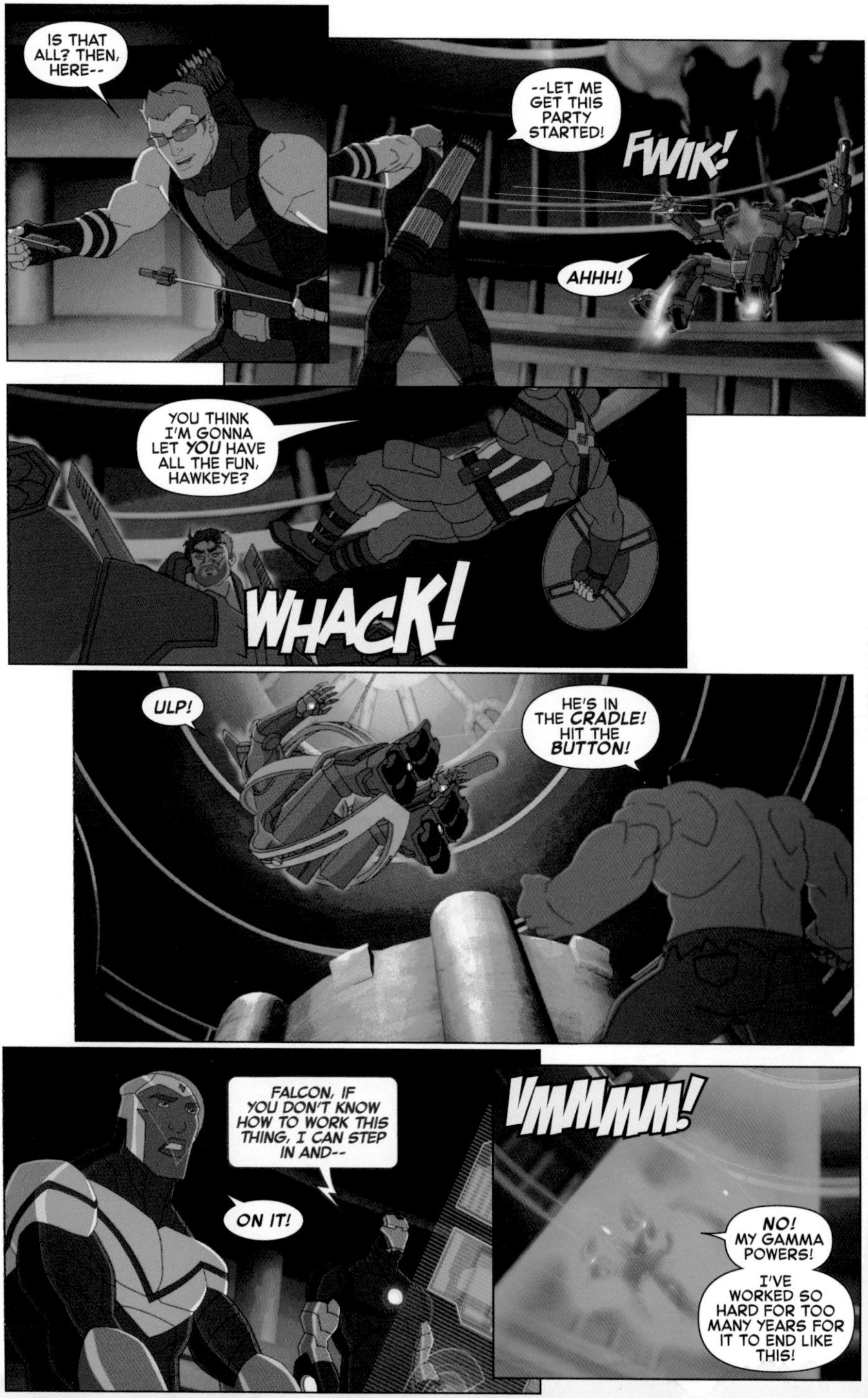
IS THAT ALL? THEN, HERE--
--LET ME GET THIS PARTY STARTED!
FWIK!
AHHH!
YOU THINK I'M GONNA LET *YOU* HAVE ALL THE FUN, HAWKEYE?
WHACK!
ULP!
HE'S IN THE *CRADLE!* HIT THE *BUTTON!*
FALCON, IF YOU DON'T KNOW HOW TO WORK THIS THING, I CAN STEP IN AND--
ON IT!
VMMMMM!
NO! MY GAMMA POWERS!
I'VE WORKED SO HARD FOR TOO MANY YEARS FOR IT TO END LIKE THIS!

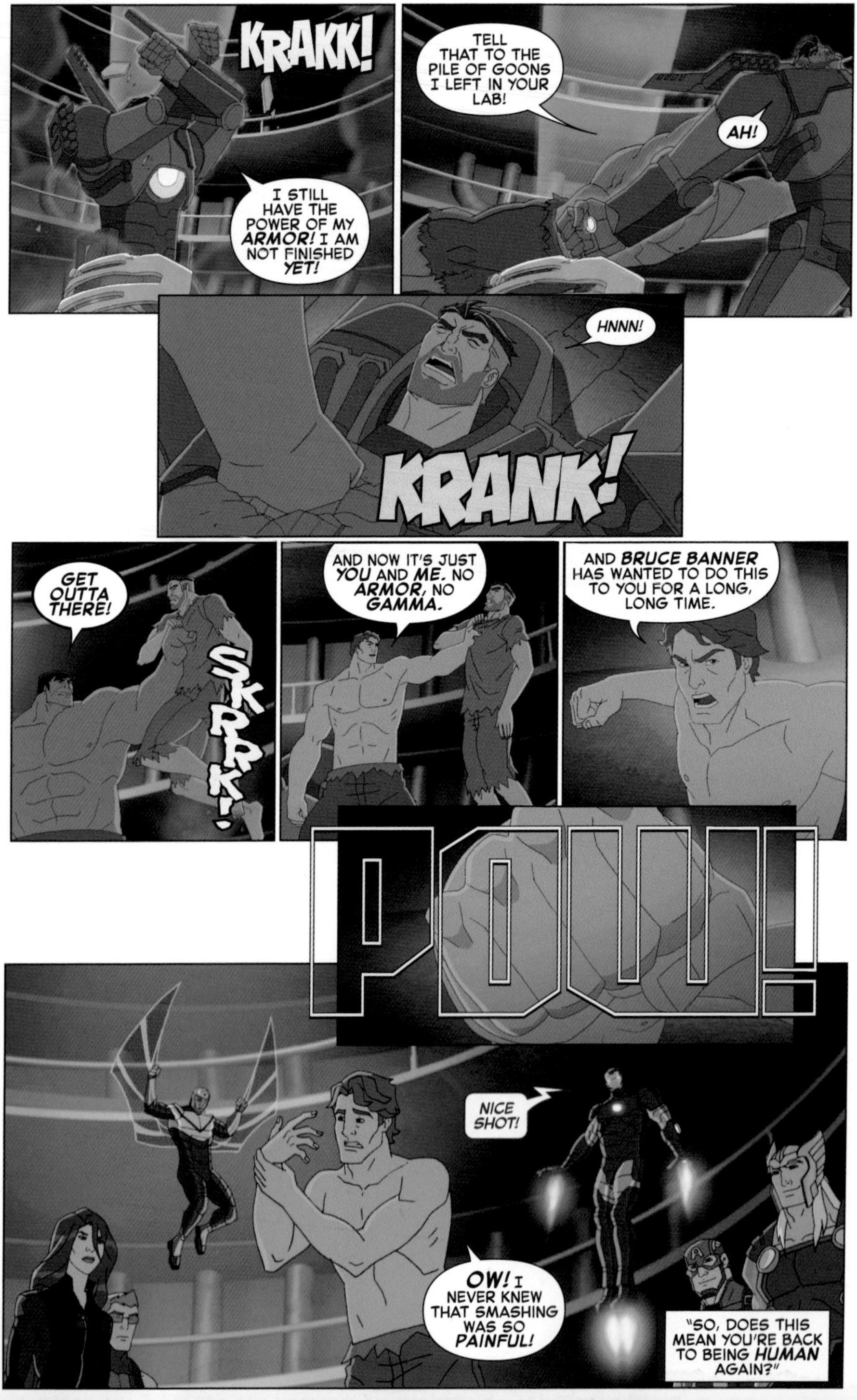
KRAKK!
I STILL HAVE THE POWER OF MY ARMOR! I AM NOT FINISHED YET!
TELL THAT TO THE PILE OF GOONS I LEFT IN YOUR LAB!
AH!
HNNN!
KRANK!
GET OUTTA THERE!
SKRRK!
AND NOW IT'S JUST YOU AND ME. NO ARMOR, NO GAMMA.
AND BRUCE BANNER HAS WANTED TO DO THIS TO YOU FOR A LONG, LONG TIME.
POW!
NICE SHOT!
OW! I NEVER KNEW THAT SMASHING WAS SO PAINFUL!
"SO, DOES THIS MEAN YOU'RE BACK TO BEING HUMAN AGAIN?"

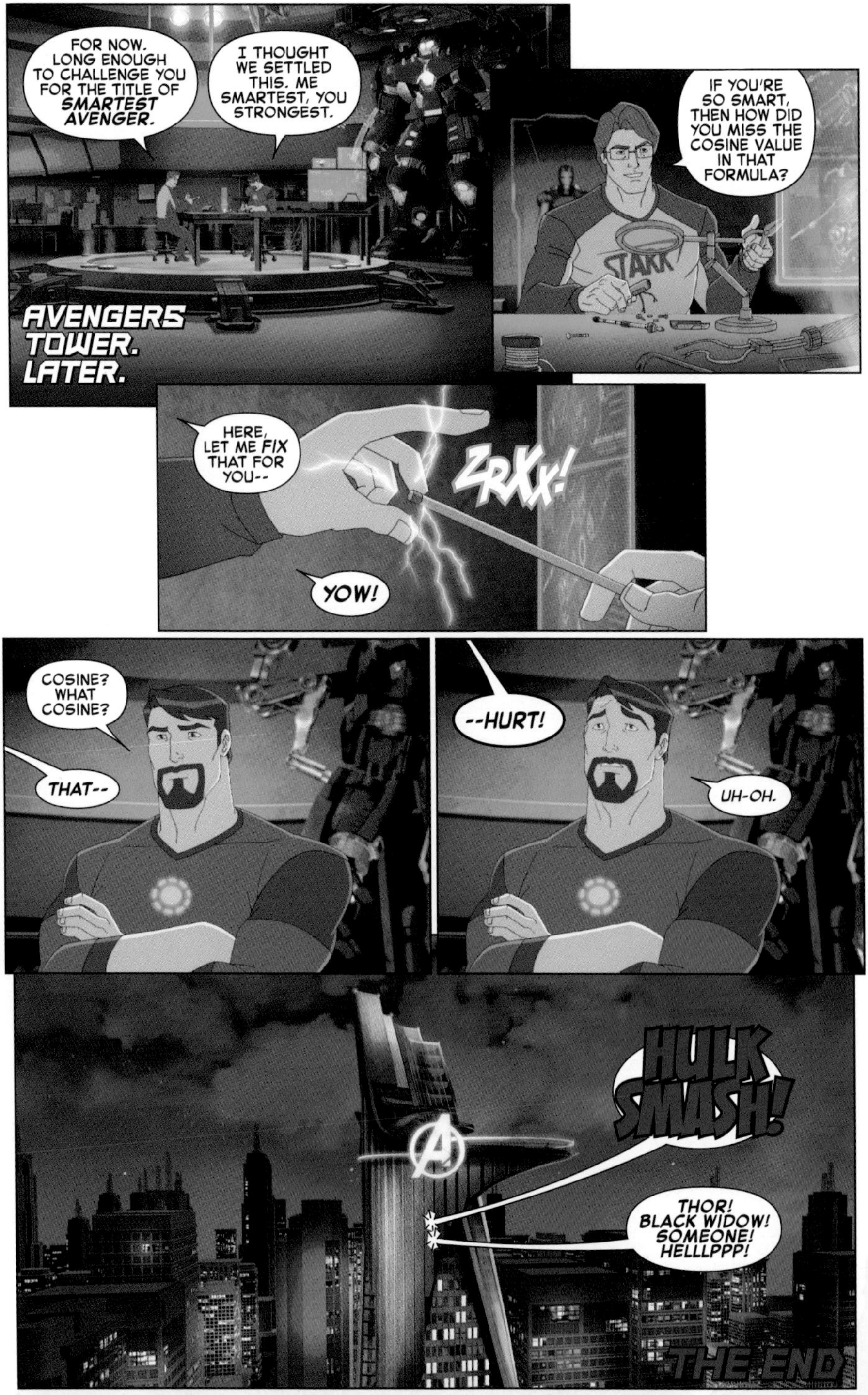
FOR NOW. LONG ENOUGH TO CHALLENGE YOU FOR THE TITLE OF SMARTEST AVENGER.
I THOUGHT WE SETTLED THIS. ME SMARTEST, YOU STRONGEST.
AVENGERS TOWER. LATER.
IF YOU'RE SO SMART, THEN HOW DID YOU MISS THE COSINE VALUE IN THAT FORMULA?
HERE, LET ME FIX THAT FOR YOU--
ZRXX!
YOW!
COSINE? WHAT COSINE?
THAT--
--HURT!
UH-OH.
HULK SMASH!
THOR! BLACK WIDOW! SOMEONE! HELLLPPP!
THE END

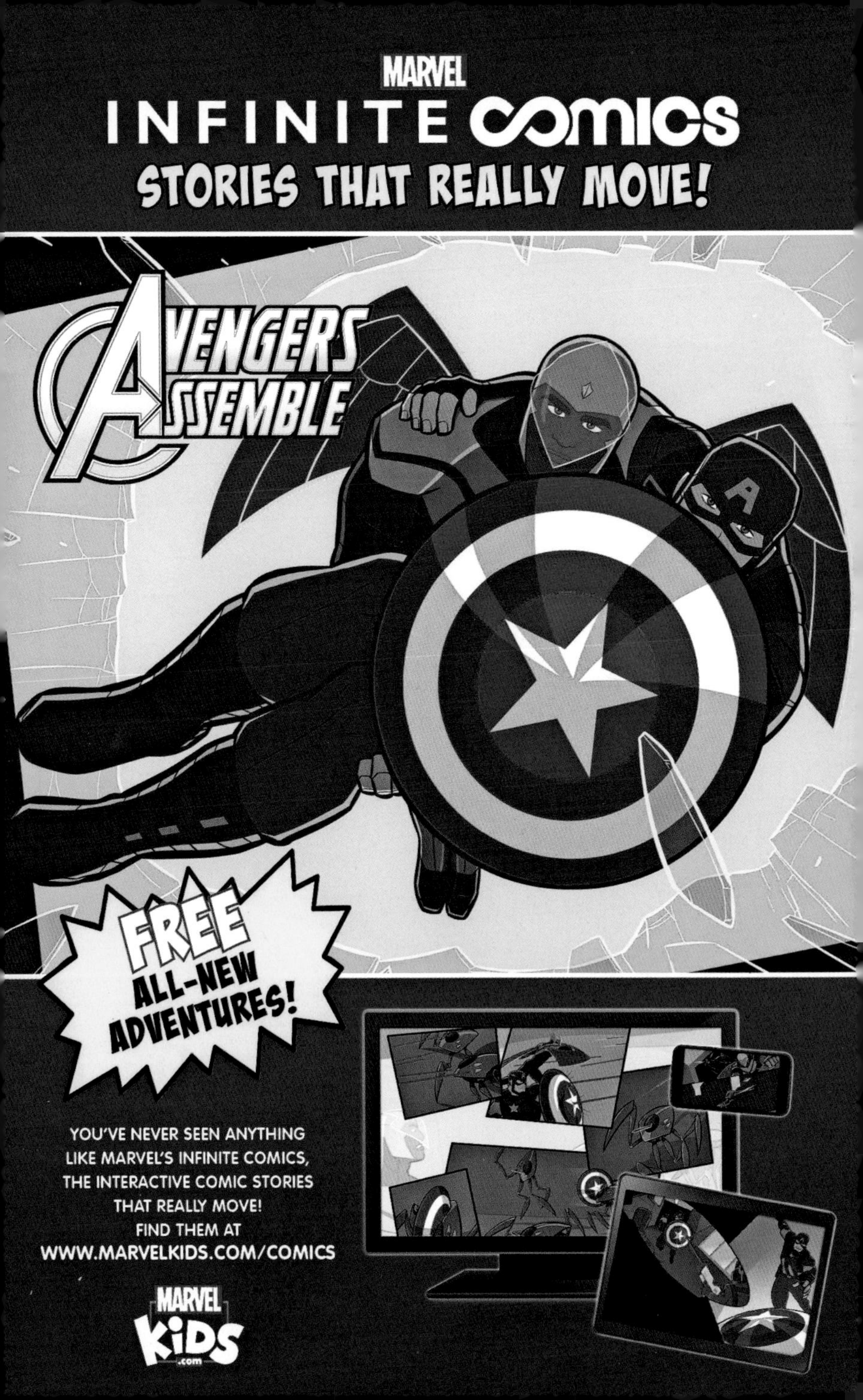
MARVEL
INFINITE COMICS
STORIES THAT REALLY MOVE!
AVENGERS ASSEMBLE
FREE ALL-NEW ADVENTURES!
YOU'VE NEVER SEEN ANYTHING LIKE MARVEL'S INFINITE COMICS, THE INTERACTIVE COMIC STORIES THAT REALLY MOVE! FIND THEM AT WWW.MARVELKIDS.COM/COMICS
MARVEL KIDS .com

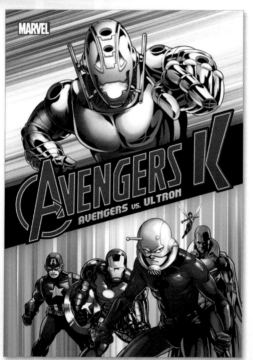